'Is it not strange that two men from the same family disappear and never come back to see their kids?'

'I grew up thinking it was normal.'

COPYRIGHT

First published 2015

All rights reserved
© Peter Bourne, 2015

ISBN 978-1-506-17329-0

AUTHOR'S NOTE
Into the Blue is a work of fiction.

All of the characters in this novel are fictional.
The story includes references to real historical events.

Many of the places are real, others fictional.

Visit the website:
www.intothebluenovel.com
intothebluenovel@gmail.com
@intotheblue2015

ARTWORK
The cover design and map of Birmingham were produced by
Mark Murphy, Surely
www.surely.uk.com

THE AUTHOR

Peter Bourne was born in Birmingham in 1979 and grew up in Selly Park. He currently lives in the Jura-Nord Vaudois area of Switzerland and works in sports management. He has also lived and worked in Turin and Paris. *Into the Blue* is his first novel.

MAP OF BIRMINGHAM

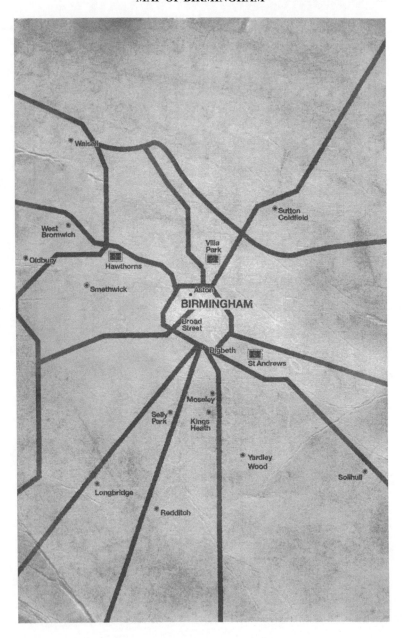

To Janina Pietralska

CHAPTER 1
WALSALL

(Early 2010)

Parka reeks of cat piss. Fyodor recently passed away after eighteen years, eighteen long years. Loyal cat, kept solid company during the long nights coding and hacking. Lady said the two new kittens would be housetrained in a month. *Bullshit*. Pissing and scratching everywhere.

Officers are barely out of their teens. *Cheeky cunts.* First time in almost twenty years Morgan has come face to face with the pigs. Waiting to hear the charges. Pirating, credit card manipulation, pension fund tampering. One if not all. Officers going through the hard drives. Morgan knew he'd not kept security as tight recently. Had got sloppy trying to finish everything on time. He fiddles with his Vietnam War Zippo. Searches for a stray jelly baby in his deep, musty pocket. Stays mute.

Something serious seems afoot. *Senior detective talking to the two cheeky cunts outside the interview room.* Silver-haired old fox, angular cheekbones, looks like an ex-army type who has become a weekend endurance runner. Carries a narrow leather clipboard under his arm. Slim navy suit, sharp powder-blue tie married to a silver tie pin. Has come across from Birmingham HQ. Enters with some frizzy-haired redhead who looks more like a lawyer than an officer. Redhead introduces herself as Tammy Wilcox, doesn't mention rank. Senior detective is called Bryson. No first name mentioned. They've found Morgan some second-rate lawyer. A sweaty element called Brian Harkins, condiment stains peppered over his red and white pinstriped shirt.

'Cooperation,' starts Bryson, 'Word you are aware of, I presume? It would be in your best interests to talk to us this morning. You see, we're not only interested in discussing the filth on your computer. Seems you may also be able to help us with something else as well.'

'Go on,' returns Morgan, economically.

'Does the name Dwight Nake mean anything to you?' offers the redhead. All too rehearsed for measure.

'No,' snaps Morgan.

'Well, let me refresh your memory. Dwight Nake's been behind bars for the last ten years, various things, nothing to concern you with. Only our friend Mr Nake has developed a taste for the communal wine, if you catch my drift. Become tight with the prison chaplain, let's say he's realised purgatory is not for him. Been talking about all sorts of escapades, bodies going missing, that kind of thing. Cooperation, Mr Morgan, I'd familiarise myself with it.'

Morgan smiles nervously, almost sarcastically.

'We've got Steven Baker in the room next door,' prods Bryson. 'You see, he's already cooperating.'

CHAPTER 2
MOSELEY

(Spring 2009)

Rachel's gazing out of the window. Twitching irritably. Br.
aggressively. Molesting her BlackBerry. Muting Editors' *Well Worn*
Rapidly sinking into an abysmal mood. The silence is end.
Uncongenial.

Carter despised these moments. They were becoming incessant. 1
gloomy disposition. The sullenness. The preposterous arguments. *Spendi*
too much money. Of her money. Not enough time together. Too much tir.
together. Not enough of this. Too much of that. Didn't pull his weight.
Never cleaned. Never cooked. Head down, hands on wheel, let it pass.

An End Has A Start runs into an oppressive silence long before the CD
player cuts out returning to the Sunday charts. *X Factor crap.* Carter's
increasingly irritated. Manufactured music on Radio 1 becomes Villa on
Five Live. *Winning. Fuck Off.* Volume muted. Hands gripped to the
steering wheel. Absorbing the frustration. Stressful day.

Chipping Norton. Half way there. Early evening drizzle. Mild headache.
Dehydration. The Barfoots had popped open the Bollinger. Carter probably
shouldn't be driving. Needs a fix. Stops for a coffee. Rachel huffs. First
words since leaving The Oracle.

'Can't we just go home? You've had three already today!'

'I'm falling asleep, need a buzz,' responds Carter, effects of caffeine
pounding irritability through his veins. 'I'm the one who's bloody driving.'

...impressed. Carter heads for his fix. Rachel
... Caresses BlackBerry. Desperately trawling
...ponse. Even Freeman Porter didn't work on

...espresso. Orders another. Picks up three items
...on the counter. Almond biscotti. A giant chocolate
...ow stick. Necks the second espresso. Burnt. Granules
...eat at the back of his throat. Throws in a Perrier. Trudges
...zing. Headache. Dehydrated. Annoyed.

...ing to be like this for the rest of the day?' snaps Carter,
...he car door behind.

...g as it takes!'

...es what?'

...or you to be less bloody selfish.'

Rachel never swore. Hardly ever. Whenever she said selfish it came out shellfish. Carter restrains from giggling. Rachel removes her BlackBerry from its faux Louis Vuitton pouch. *Is she Tweeting this shit?*

'How the hell have I been bloody selfish? I've driven us there and back. Laughed at your old man's crap jokes. Pretended to like Formula 1. Didn't scratch my nuts in front of them. Didn't start pouring drinks for myself. Fucking deserve a medal, I do.'

'Sometimes you just don't see it,' interjects Rachel, dismissively.

'Well then. Fucking enlighten me.'

Rachel tuts. Turns her head away again. Windows steam up. Carter's knackered mustard-coloured Renault Clio continues to absorb the tarmac.

'And put that fucking BlackBerry away. Who the hell is online on a Sunday?'

'Friends. Friends you never take an interest in.' Rachel's response as readymade as it is condescending.

'Since when?'

'Since always. You never make an effort. Everything is always on your terms. Your mates, your life, your bloody little world.'

'What the fuck has that got to do with today?'

'Everything. Everything.'

Rachel places the BlackBerry back in her handbag. Fearing for its life. Carter almost wished the Villa were back on the radio. Head down. Hands on wheel. Stratford-Upon-Avon. Closer to home. Not close enough. Silence draws on for another five minutes. Seems longer.

'What the fuck has it got to do with this weekend?' risks Carter.

Pause.

'Can you not hear me or do you just enjoy ignoring me?'

A more lingering pause.

'Perhaps it will make you understand how I feel most of the time.'

'I ignore you? Since fucking when?'

'You just don't take an interest, that's the problem.'

'You don't let me take an interest.'

'How?'

'You tell me everything anyway. All the time. It's all you. When do you take an interest in me?'

'You are a closed book, Dan. I can never talk to you. Unless you're drunk or it's about *your* music. Or films. Or football. For the rest you're useless. I need someone who can contribute, someone I can share my feelings with.'

Pause. Hands on steering wheel. Focus. Stratford-Upon-Avon has become Henley-In-Arden. *Nearly home. Head down. Get home. Go and see Mason. Have a few jars. Few laughs. See out the weekend.*

Rachel looks distinctly less attractive when angry. And she's becoming increasingly unhappy. Good-looking girl, Rachel. In a girl next-door kind of way. Her smile is the switch that illuminates her features. Angry, she resembles her ashen-faced, rigid, owl-eyed mother. *Rigid mother who thinks her daughter is better than Birmingham. Better than Carter. Better than living in a 'poky' flat.*

'You're always like this when we come back from yours. I made a real fucking effort with your parents this time. And your sister, who is a boring twat.'

'Dan!'

'Well, she is. All she fucking talks about is money. Fucking kids. Fucking money. Fucking job. She's a right pretentious twat.'

'That's my sister you are talking about. By the way.'

By The Way. In capital letters. Carter despised the condescending emphasis.

'Did your dear mother pull you to one side and tell you that you should be aiming higher than me?'

'She wouldn't say that.'

'She wouldn't say that? But she fucking thinks that. She should have the balls to say it.'

'Why are you so pent up?'

'Because it's true.'

'If you made more of an effort to talk to them then maybe they'd like you a bit more.'

'So they don't like me?'

'I give up.'

Carter is becoming increasingly cantankerous. Dolphin farts. Text message. Rachel puts hand in bag. Mum. *'Had a lovely weekend. Dan seemed troubled. Very quiet.'* Starts replying. Not in the mood. Not right now.

'You could just try harder sometimes,' offers Rachel. 'Make them feel a bit more involved. They ask you about your work, your plans and you clam up. Everything sounds wishy-washy, like you don't give a damn and I know you do. It's like you've got no ambition and no direction. My parents don't want to hear that kind of thing.'

'I don't give a shit.'

'Don't be a child.'

'And you never say thank you.'

'What do you mean?'

'Dad brought out his best bottle today, they got you a nice birthday present, paid for lunch yesterday, got your car fixed, and it pains you to say thank you.'

'I am not very good at that kind of thing.'

'Not everyone understands that. You seem ungrateful.'

Clio's crawling towards the city from the south. Cheswick Green. Shirley. Hall Green. Rain pissing down. Radio back on. United score twice. Villa drawing 2-2. Villa losing 3-2. Villa lose 3-2. *Good.*

***

Flat feels small and damp. Bottles everywhere from Thursday night. Scattered pizza boxes. Mason left some weed. Slipped down the side of the couch. Put his foot through a pint glass downhill skiing on the Wii. Garry and Deepak nearly came to blows during the boxing. Carter wants to do the same tonight. Rachel heads for a bath. He'd better clean this mess up. *You and your mates take the piss. Heard it all before.*

Bottles in bin bag. Weed in a used jiffy bag for Mace. Pizza boxes thrown out. *Fuck recycling. They throw it all in the same skip anyway. Slice of Hawaiian still looks good. Heat it up. Shit, shower, shave, head out soon.* Rachel returns from her soak. Fluffy, lilac-coloured dressing gown peels open. Cleavage shows, Carter can almost see her peaches. Quite horny. Carter fancies a fuck. *No chance tonight.*

'You going out?'

'Going to see Mace down the Prince of Wales. Might have another gig at the end of the month.'

'Thought we were going to have a night in?'

Storm. Brewing.

'Just think we need to talk,' pleads Rachel.

'Might be better to wait. Till you've calmed down.'

'I am calm. I want to talk now.'

Carter shrugs. Sits down on the shallow ivory-coloured leather sofa. Present from the Barfoots. Waits for Rachel to start. Rachel heads back to the bedroom. Precisely yet angrily dries hair with a towel. Slips on a slim fit tangerine-coloured t-shirt. No bra. Nipples resemble stiff acorns. Loose yet slim jogging bottoms. Carter still fancies a fuck. Rachel selects some lounge music. *Pan Asian crap.* Carter heads to fridge. One can of Krony left. Pulls off the ring. Beer fizzes. Overflows. Carter drinks from can. Tastes like tin.

'I just think we need to talk,' insists Rachel. *Again.*

'Fine,' replies Carter, stubbornly.

Rachel pours herself an almost transparent-looking glass of white wine. One of those chats. Need a drink. Proper drink.

'I want you to open up a bit more and make more of an effort, otherwise it's not going to work.'

'It's worked fine for three years, we're happy aren't we?'

'We've been happy. It was more fun before but I want things to move on. Find somewhere bigger. Do more as a couple. Move on. Like normal people do.'

'I can't afford somewhere bigger. Work is shite. What more do you want to do? We go to gigs, cinema, see friends.'

'*Your* friends, *your* gigs.'

'You don't like me seeing your friends. And your colleagues are boring and only talk shop. Not involving for me, is it?'

'They're not boring, you just have to get to know people, take an interest in them and then it is easier to talk about other things.'

'I've tried.'

'Not for a while.'

'And I am always the one suggesting things to do.'

'No, I am always the one agreeing to what you want to do whilst you ignore it when I hint at doing things.'

'You like doing what I do.'

'Not always. And maybe you should try to be involved in what interests me, like seeing a show, going cycling on a Sunday, going for a nice meal and not always with your mates and their hangers on.'

Carter rests his can. Naturally not on the Fairtrade Kenyan rhino coaster. It's been a soggy period. April always is. Work has dried up. Companies finding more internal means to produce artwork. Best mate is getting married. Becoming a doormat. Rachel bringing home three times as much. Ran out of cash in the third week of last month. Stuck in a rut. Carter picks up can. Finishes last drop. Heads to fridge. Starts on the plonk.

'You have a problem engaging with people outside of your safe crowd. It stems from your family,' continues Rachel. *Broken record.*

'What've they got to do with anything?'

'Everything.'

'No, nothing. Because I don't have much to do with them.'

'Maybe you should. And maybe I'd like to get to know your family.'

'They're a bunch of cunts.'

'Dan! There's no need for that.'

'Well they are. I've spent the last ten fucking years trying to get away from them. They're miserable, bitter people. I've got nothing in common with them.'

'Your sister's not.'

'She's alright. In spurts. The rest are, cun…, fools.'

Carter stands up. Switches off the lounge music. Fiddles with iPod speakers. On goes *Whole Lotta Love.* Zeppelin. Tempo raised. Wants to get out of flat. Necks wine. Heads back to fridge. Only a spot left.

'Is there any more wine?'

'You've had enough.'

'Need more, need to get a bit pissed. Got a shit day tomorrow.'

'Try the cupboard. It won't be cold.'

'Doesn't matter.'

Screw top. Shitty wine. *Someone brought it for dinner. Gail, no doubt. No taste, that girl. Villa fan.* Carter brings bottle into lounge. Picks up packet of crisps. Smokey bacon. Slumps back down.

'Why don't you invite your sister and Leon round at some point? They could bring Amber. It's been a while since we saw them. You always get on with Leon.'

'Maybe.' Carter stubbornly refuses to show any enthusiasm.

'Yeah, and maybe, we will be having the same discussion in about six months.'

'My sister could call me.'

'Doesn't always work like that. She's busy with her life.'

'What. Cutting hair and drinking alcopops?'

Carter knew the conversation would draw beyond Leanne. He looked out of the large bay windows onto School Road. Somewhere else would be good. Strumming. Creating music. Away from this. Tosses wine down. Barely hitting the sides. Grapes began to taste like a headache. Has to be in early tomorrow. Got an advert for a tractor trade fair to finish. Fucking

Gorman will be barking. *Do what the client wants. Save time. Usual bullshit.*

'I'll get in touch in the week then.'

'Do that and…will I ever get to meet the rest of your family?' continues Rachel. Barely placated.

'Hope not. One day you might have the pleasure.'

'When did you last see your mother?'

'Christmas. When you were home. It was shit. Like the year before.'

'Why don't you invite her around?'

'We've had this discussion before. You don't know what she's like.'

'I'd like to meet her.'

'I'd rather spare you from that.'

'I won't love you any less for meeting your mother. It might help me get to know you.'

'I've told you, she is not worth the effort.'

Rachel's losing the energy to delve into the one-way conversation further. Hit the same wall before. Carter clams up. Becomes defensive. Moves across sofa as if drawn closer to the front door. Rachel needs to try something new. Running on empty.

'What if I go and find her myself?'

'You wouldn't do that.'

'Maybe I would.'

'And what would you say? 'I'm Rachel, I'm dating the son you never really gave a shit about and want to meet the rest of your retard family'.'

'No, I am just curious to know what she is like.'

'A selfish bitch.'

'Dan!'

Carter picks up his battered leather jacket. Slams door. Heads out.

***

Gorman is in a prickly mood. After the drought, the glut. Three adverts today. Two for trade fairs, one for a DIY company. *And fucking Maisy is off. Again. Sick. Fucking had a skinful, more like it. Festival down in Brighton over the weekend. If not hungover, stoned. Not that Gorman knew. Selfish tart.* Gorman stands over the screen. Change the font. They said chestnut. Give them chestnut. Eleven point, not ten. Not fucking beige. Bring the picture in more. Crop that. Give it more light. Centre the address. *Why don't you just take the fucking mouse and do it yourself? Talentless fucking bully. Bald twat.*

Rachel's called. Left a message. Wants to meet for lunch. *Too late. Gotta deadline. Gotta finish. Crap prawn and avocado wrap at desk.* Carter's streaming some tunes. Elliott Smith. Back to the bench sale. Cans on. *Gorman can fuck off.*

Gorman's back. Client's not happy. Typo in email address. *Told you before to fucking concentrate. Not at the races.* Sorry, Phil. Don't want to hear sorry. Don't want the clients ringing. This is not your best work. Raise your game or you will start losing projects. Tamara's over. *Looking lovely. Bit of tanned thigh.* Carter wants a smoke. Can't. Bullied into quitting. Tamara and thighs head out. *Damn Rachel.*

Still two adverts to go. Garden centre people won't let go. Need the leaflets to go to print tonight. Mac's crashed. Printer on the phone. Barking. Not enough time to turn job around unless file arrives tonight. Gorman's back. Screaming. Spitting. *Bald twat.*

Head down. Listening to Wilco. *Ashes of American Flags*. Mind lost. Mind not here. Mac crashes again. *Piece of shit.* Call Deepak. Deepak says network is down. Files on network. Files lost. Starts work again. Gorman barking. *Gorman's a bald twat.* Work gets done.

'You nearly finished?' snaps Gorman.

'One to go,' replies Carter. Cans still firmly in place.

'Which one?'

'Garden lot.'

'I told you to do the other one first. They are waiting on us. Fucking big contract we have with them. Can't be late.'

'It's Maisy's client. Maybe you should be giving her the shit you are giving me.'

'Will come down hard on her fat, lazy arse tomorrow. Get it done.'

Carter's mind is drifting. Nearly home time. Rachel's going to be asking questions tonight. Prodding. Searching. Digging. Putting an emotional value on everything. Carter's got to see Leanne. Get it out the way. Get the token family thing done. Rachel wants better. Wants to move on. Carter's scared.

***

Deepak's proposed a post-work pint. At O'Neill's, Brindley Place. Happy hour. Guinness flowing. Coldplay seeping out of the speakers. Deepak's getting married. Needs a break. Looks worn out. Expensive business. Deepak orders a whisky chaser. Girlfriend's family high maintenance. Carter blabs on about Rachel. Deepak says he's fucked. Says he needs to buy her something. Take her mind away from it. Plan a holiday or something. Might be right. Rachel's not Virali. Deepak gets a call. Virali wants him home. Deepak's in a cab before *Spies* fades out.

***

Rachel's waiting impatiently. Skimming an IKEA catalogue at the kitchen table.

'You should have said that you were going to be late. Dinner's been ready for a while.'

'Had a busy day.'

'And I haven't?'

Carter moves towards Rachel, already changed and showered from work. Rachel turns away. *No kiss tonight.* Sporting a grey jumpsuit. *Hair tied back. Arse looks pert. Carter's got to raise his game.*

'You smell of booze. Really had a busy day?'

'Went for one with Deepak after work. He is a bit stressed about the wedding.'

'Can imagine, knowing Virali. It's still a few months away, isn't it?'

'She's intense.'

'Did you call your sister?'

'Not yet.'

'When are you going to?'

'Soon.'

Rachel's displeasure is crushing. Soon is not quick enough. Obviously. Rachel is making lasagne. Again. Accompanied by a big, tasteless, stale green salad. *She didn't get wine.* Finished that last night. Rachel's hiding something. Something more to say. Questions to pose.

'Not hungry? How's dinner?'

Carter doesn't let it out. Worst lasagne she's ever made. Too salty. Not enough pecorino. Pasta crunchy. Should have had the pub burger.

'It's good. Just been a long day. Gorman's putting me under pressure. Bald twat. Thinks what we do is easy and it can all be done in twenty minutes.'

'Have you told him that you want to take on more projects and manage your own clients?'

'Stop forcing it.'

'I am not forcing it, just wish you would show a bit more drive.'

'It's not that easy.'

'It's not that easy having to lend you my money at the end of each month.'

'Piss off.'

'Sorry. I went too far.'

Carter storms off. Rachel had this habit of making him feel small. Insignificant. Loser. Last few months he's brought home less than usual. Paid on number of projects finished. Fewer projects, less cash. Hadn't worked much from home either. Band practice taken time. Too much football on the box. Been drinking more. Been a sluggish time. Carter buries himself in a paperback. Likes the classics, the books at school he'd read when escaping from his mother. *The Dubliners. Roll of Thunder Hear My Cry. To Kill A Mockingbird. A Tale of Two Cities.*

Rachel shuffles sheepishly into the bedroom. Looks apologetic. Carter knows there are points to be won back. Plays the victim. Lets the moment pass.

'I am sorry about what I said. It was unfair.'

'Not wrong.'

'Can we pick up where we left last night?'

'Can't we just pick up from where we left last time we were happy?'

'We can't just sweep everything under the carpet. I just want the best for you and for you to be happy and for us to feel a bit more normal.'

'Maybe tomorrow night we can go for dinner in town?'

'Dan, I think it is going to take more than dinner.'

Rachel heads out. Comes back in. Heavy, tatty book under her arm. Torn plastic sleeve. Deep Bordeaux-tinted cover. *Should never have kept it.* Dusty memories. *Kept it out of curiosity.* Like a bad teenage tattoo. A permanent scar following surgery. One day Carter may want to know who these degenerates were. Photo slips out. Leanne as a kid. Know what's coming. Point of. No return.

'What the fuck are you doing with that?'

'Found it sorting through some stuff last night.'

'Sorting through my stuff?'

'If we're going to move, need to know how much worth keeping is in the boxes in the cupboard.'

'We're not moving.'

'I will be if this carries on.'

'This carries on?'

'What else did you find going through my stuff?'

'I wasn't looking through your stuff. It was the first thing in the box. You can hardly blame me for being curious!'

'I should never have kept that crap.'

Carter escapes to the lounge. Moving appeases his nerves. Rachel drops onto the sofa in a sympathetic manner. Puts her arm around Carter. Carter's angry. Yet numb. Opening the album would reopen all of the creases in his life. Nobody capable of ironing them straight. Carter's conflicted. *Argue this with Rachel. Throw the book out. Burn out. Reason. Listen. Go through it. Maybe it will help. Burn it.*

'I've not looked inside it yet. Well, not properly, wanted to wait for you. You were a cute kid.'

'Aren't all kids cute?'

'Well, you were really sweet.'

Rachel points to another photo that has fallen out. Young boy. Knee-length shorts. Parted blond hair. Slightly squashed nose. Small rocking toy in the shape of a horse.

'That's not me.'

'No?'

'It's my cousin Lee. Or Paul. They're twins. Aunt Heather's kids.'

'The ones whose dad went missing?'

'Them.'

'Well, you look alike! Can I find one of you?'

By now they'd gone too far. All the other seedy characters would resurface. Slugs of youth. Loveless turds. Bearers of bitterness. Toothy smiles and permanent frowns. The hate mob. Passionate summer nights which became misty January mornings. A neglected birthday cake left to melt in the sun. Rachel turns the first few pages. Book in no apparent order. Like it had been put together in the chronological spirit of Alejandro González Iñárritu.

'Is this you?'

'Believe it is.'

'Well you were still cute.'

'And who's this?'

'Must be Leanne and the dog we had at the time. Pop.'

'Pop.'

'Think it was the first word Leanne ever learnt.'

'She's not changed. What was the second one…alco?'

Carter and Rachel smile in unison for the first time in weeks. Carter didn't want to go any further. *Close the book with that smile. Go as far as Leanne. No questions, no games. There are no answers anyway. Have a drink. Talk about going on holiday. Fuck. Getting married would be better than this.* Rachel's glance is fixed on the picture of young Carter. Perhaps staring into the young boy's eyes would somehow open his mind. As the pages turned, the questions would get heavier.

'Is that your mum and dad?'

'Yep.'

'That's not how I imagined them.'

'What were you expecting, Pitt and friggin' Jolie?'

'No, well, don't know what I was expecting. Just not that. Your dad looks like he just came out of a trench. Or a pub fight.'

'He'd been in the Falklands the year before I was born. From what mom said, I remember he enjoyed serving his country.'

'Was he in the army?'

'In the navy for a while.'

'And then?'

'And then he fucked off.'

'When did he leave?'

'We've been through this.'

'We've never got past this point. What did he do after the navy?'

'He was a copper for a while, left home in '87. I was four. Never saw him again. Never.'

'What about your sister and mum?'

Carter twitches. Wish Rachel had got some plonk in. Wish he could still smoke. Wishes he was somewhere else. The questions began to make him feel sick. Push them to the back of the head. Don't carry on. Feel faint.

'Not sure. My sister remembers him more than me but don't think they ever saw each other again. She's thick-skinned, never really gave a fuck. Mom? He fucked off with another woman, so doubt it.'

'When did your mother meet your stepdad?'

'A few years after that. Do we have to carry on? I had a dad. He fucked off. Mum met another bloke. And everyone lived happily ever after.'

'Clearly not!'

'I am not sure what you are getting out of going through my old family memories.'

'Getting to know you. And helping you.'

'I don't need help.'

'You clearly do. Your family history is blocking you emotionally. There's more to it, and I have to know you if we are going to stay together.' *Rachel twisting the knife.*

Carter feels sick. Wanted to retreat into the spare room. Put on some cans. Listen to some beats. Even be at work. Retouch some photos. Anything. He knows Rachel is getting close. Getting close to what had been on his mind. Getting close to making him do something about it. The television had been all over it. Tributes. Commemorative issues. Twenty years on. *Another bleak day in the family tree. Another rotten branch.*

'Can we at least finish the album? Then I promise that we won't talk about it for the rest of the night.'

'Just the rest of the night?'

'Just be open with me and tell me what you know. What you feel.'

'Can we get a drink?'

'It won't fix everything.'

'It will help me.'

Carter heads out. Direction Moseley Village. The break would only delay the inevitable but would at least help him get his senses back together. Felt sick. Head throbbing. Rachel was good. A great girl. Great at knowing his weaknesses. Great at making him feel useless. Great at making him feel small. *She was only trying to help. Don't need help. Just need out.* Carter collects a couple of bottles of wine, two for ten pounds. Rachel doesn't drink red. Carter drinks white when there is nothing else. Wants to get some smokes as well. Doesn't. Crunchie. Wispa. Galaxy and a box of Pringles. *Mail* as well. Won't get to read it.

'You took your time.'

'Needed some air.'

'What did you get?'

'Too much chocolate. Too much wine. You still let me eat chocolate, don't you? Wanna glass?'

'If you're pouring.'

'Got some white for you. South African stuff.'

'That's fine, only want a bit, mind. It's Monday.'

Carter discovered the deep Marquis Vintage red wine glasses that Rachel's mother had got last Christmas. Expensive shit. Broken two already. Poured a large glass. Drank half. Poured more in. Felt better. Poured Rachel a glass of white. Large. Wine usually made her sleepy. Or less confrontational. Both would work.

'Can we carry on now you've had your drink?'

'Ready, boss.'

Rachel turns another stiff, fag-smelling page.

'Your mum was good-looking. Bet she had no problem meeting guys.'

'Not by all accounts.'

'What does that mean?'

'Nothing.'

'It meant something.'

'Don't know what she was like when she was younger. She's had a few men, even after my dad left and she met Carl. There was a while when Leanne and me got a ride in a new car every Sunday.'

'When did she meet Carl again?'

'1989 or '90. Something like that. I'd started school.'

'He's been around since?'

'Not one for going far, our Carl. Thinks you need a passport to leave the Midlands. Went to Spain once with Mom and took his own beans.'

'Egg and chips holiday type?'

'That's the one.'

Carter found the banter quite a relief. The wine was helping to numb his anger. Calm his nerves. He always enjoyed ribbing Carl. Something he'd not really done as he and Leanne had drifted into their own lives.

'Your sister takes after your mum. The similarity is less obvious with you.'

'Thank God.'

Rachel turns the page. Family photo from Heather's wedding. The clan in all their glory. 1980s Birmingham. Orgy of Noddy Holder or military haircuts. Peroxide. Thin moustaches. Birds in white stilettos. Blokes donning white socks and cheap brogues.

'My Aunt Heather's wedding.'

'What year was that? Never seen anything quite so horrendously early 1980s.'

'Not sure. Must have been '80, '81. Twins were born same year as me.'

'Heather's your mum's sister?'

'Yeah.'

'Where is she now?'

'Drifted off after my uncle disappeared. Living over in Selly Park at the time Uncle Alan went missing. Then couldn't live in that same house. Went over to Solihull. Started drinking a lot. Kids got out of control. That kind of thing.'

'Are you still in touch?'

'Few times, Grandad's funeral. Only when necessary. Her and Mum don't see eye to eye.'

'And your cousins?'

'No. Just our Paul. Lee has been in the slammer for a few years.'

'For what?'

'Thought I'd told you about this. Take your pick by all accounts, GBH, I think. He's a right nobhead.'

'What do you think happened to your uncle?'

Carter had always liked Uncle Alan. At least remembers him more clearly than his father. Big Blues fan, Uncle Alan. 15th April 1989. Carter had been playing in the park with Lee and Paul. Stayed the night over at Heather's. Probably been to the McDonald's drive-thru on the Bristol Road. Had probably shared the giant bed with his cousins. The next day Alan hadn't come back. He'd been away to watch the Blues. Mom had come. Taken Carter home. Told Heather everything was going to be fine.

Probably got pissed up there. Blues had been relegated. Probably drowning his sorrows. Too pissed to drive back. Gone up there with his mates. Maybe fucked a hooker. Sunday newspapers. Hillsborough tragedy. Over ninety dead. Alan had been in Barnsley, not Sheffield. Alan was coming home. Alan had drunk. Maybe fucked a hooker. Alan was coming home. Alan never came home.

'Not sure. He'd gone up north. Watched the Blues play and never came back. Maybe fucked off with another woman like my old man.'

'You don't seem convinced.'

'Mom says he liked a wager. Spent all the savings on gambling. He had some big debts and a couple of fellas had come round to the house earlier that week looking for money.'

'You think someone may have killed him?'

'Basically no evidence to confirm or deny it.'

'Is it not strange that two men in the same family disappear and never come back to see their kids?'

'I grew up thinking it was normal.'

Rachel seems concerned. Perplexed. But curiosity overtook her. Fully engaged in solving a human crossword. She pours a second glass of wine. Feels vindicated in opening Carter up. Feels like she is getting closer to understanding the man she loves. Had seen him show emotion for the first time in months.

'Have you never wanted to find out what happened?'

'Find out?'

'Find out the truth.'

'How am I supposed to find out the truth? And maybe I don't want to know that my dad fucked off with another woman and left his two kids behind and that my uncle did the same, or worse, was clipped for not paying off his debts.'

'Maybe it would make you feel better.'

'Maybe it would just expose wounds that have long healed.'

'I don't think the wounds have even begun to heal.'

'Listen, love. My aunt spent about ten years hiring private detectives trying to find out what happened. And fuckin' zilch. Conspiracy theories that drove the rest of the family mad. My mom nearly smashed her over the head with a friggin' bottle once. My aunt's gone. Lost in drink and who knows what else. I don't want to get involved. There has been too much hurt. Too much searching only to find there is no light at the end of the tunnel.'

'What about your dad?'

'What about him? I grew up without one! I don't need one. Just drop it. If he wanted to find me, he could have. We've not moved that far. Fuck him. Fuck his medals. Fuck his shit fucking grin. Fuck him..'

Carter wants to cry. Doesn't want to play this game anymore. Doesn't even want to drink anymore. Closes the book. Closes the memories and pain. Rachel had gone far enough. Rachel knew the stories, had seen the pictures. Rachel knew it was time to stop. Time to stop for tonight.

'Shall we go to bed, love?'

'Yep.'

'You are going to call your sister though, aren't you?'

CHAPTER 3
DIGBETH

(November 1977)

Arthur's babbling on about the strikes. Schizophrenically cursing and rambling. *Tory bastards. Spineless Callaghan. Miners. Power workers. Firemen. Hospitals. What about the railways? Run your own trains on those wages. Twenty-five years. Up and down the country. Across the Midlands. Never a sick day.* Never a shift Arthur's not showed up for. *Fuck the bastards.* Winter of discontent.

Gladys's not had a pay rise in five years. *Five fucking years.* There're always younger girls who'll work for that pay. That's what they say. Fed up Gladys. *Face as long as Livery Street.* She's been reminiscing. Thinking back to the days on the campsite. On the beach. Always sunny when she thinks back. Carefree. Before things turned. Before she met a squat, charmless train driver from Erdington. Twenty-two years later. Same job, same hours, same shite pay.

Gladys is preparing Welsh rarebit. Arthur's partial. Arthur's slumped in front of Mastermind. News with Richard Baker. Got up. Switched over to ATV. *Charlie's Angels* on. Arthur likes a bit of that. Likes the eye candy.

His own angel getting ready. Hev's heading out for a date. Arthur doesn't know it's a date. Arthur's favourite. Always been as good as gold. Not like her older sister. Nothing but trouble, that one. One blow job away from becoming a slut. Arthur thinks she's off to meet Pat. Hev's been through a few guys recently. On the quiet. Not as many as her sister used to disappear into the night with.

Arthur's not approved of Pat sleeping over at Tony's. Tony at his parents in Smethwick. Boxy, messy little house. Despises the Coles, does Arthur. Rough, dishonest folk. Would steal the laces from your shoes. Arthur's putting a deposit down for a place on Wilton Road. Keep them close to home. Away from the Coles. Tony's working as a mechanic over in Smethwick. Does the TA at weekends. Talking about joining the army for good. Even the navy. Using his engineering skills. Tony's good with his hands. And not just in the pub. Good money and adventure for a few years. No danger of too many wars right now. Arthur's not keen. Not a big Tony fan. He's told Pat. But Pat's happy. Gladys thinks everyone should be given a chance.

Hev's off out with a mechanic from Dudley. Guy met through Tony. Date's a bit rough. Bit dangerous. Hev likes that. To a point. Steven Baker's his name. Hev's hoping to be romanced. Not a word in Steven's repertoire.

***

Bob the tool setter and Lynette Cole are down the Legion. It's not often they're both out. Bob the tool setter doesn't like to go out with the wife. Prefers her out of the bleedin' way. Tonight's quiz night. *Other birds going to be there.* Bob the tool setter is a hard drinker. Born with a pint in his hand. And a chaser on the side. Can take it too. Lynette's asthmatic. But Bob the tool setter has never stopped smoking. Even in the house. Even in the bedroom. Even when the doctor's said stop. Lynette's happy to be out of the house. Bob the tool setter will have his nine pints. Couple of shots of Irish. Talk Baggies and Blues to Cyrille. Ignore his wife. Except when passing her a drink.

Tony's back in the midget bedroom he grew up in. Bed's been too small for about ten years. Even more of a struggle with Pat in there. Spend most of their time screwing and smoking. Wayne's in the smaller room next door. Quit school early and passed his driving test. Wants to be a bus driver. Wayne doesn't bring girls back. Wayne sits listening to Tony roger away. Or AC/DC. Black Sabbath. Judas Priest. Jethro Tull. Wayne dreams of being Ian Hill.

Pat's gassing on about her hairdressing apprenticeship. Necked a half with Tina at the Old Tavern In The Town on the way over. Tina stole some lip gloss. Tina's a wild one. Short. Jet-black bobbed hair. Huge rack. Takes no prisoners. Will do anything for a freebie. Barman always gives free drinks to easy-looking girls in the hope of a hand job. Tina's there three or four times a week. Flashing her cleavage.

Pat's armed with the coach tickets. Five pound special offer. Friday afternoon to Sunday night. Down in London. Girls' hen weekend. Boys' stag do. Same city. Same weekend. Different schedules and desires. Pat, Tina, Hev, Karen, Stacey and Angela. Tony, Steven, Gaz, Martin, Wayne, Lee and Lee's brother Tommo who's bringing a guy called Al. Going to be carnage.

Tony's lying back in bed. Pat's been pushed onto the floor as she always is after Tony's got his way. Pat is crouching naked, back pressed against a cardboard box containing Tony's dog-eared records. Tony's blowing smoke rings. Demands a cup of tea. Staring into his old Blues newspaper cuttings and James Dean poster. Rocking out to Black Sabbath's *Paranoid*. Results-scribbled 1977-78 Sports Argus Fixture calendar hangs off the wall. Pat's reached for a smoke of her own. Tony never shares his. Pat's put a thick black cardigan over her naked body. The Cole's house is freezing. Bob the tool setter and Lynette only put the heaters on when they're home. *Tight bastards.* And in the rooms they occupy. *Misers.* It's dark and wet outside. Told Tony and Wayne they're not contributing enough. Want them out next year. *1978, it's already too late.* Bob the tool setter's mantra. The house is rundown and tatty. Tony's bedroom is barely fit for a scrawny fourteen-year-old. Net curtains sponsored by Woodbine. Decaying mutt Rover shedding hairs everywhere. Furniture from the nineteen fifties. Pat can't wait to move into their own place.

'Does everyone know where we're meeting on Friday?' turns Pat.

'Don't know. Don't care,' cuts Tony bluntly. 'They should know by now. Told Lee to sort everyone out my side. It's your fucking deal if the birds don't show up. I'm more worried about there being enough booze on the bus.'

'Think there will be plenty of that going. Are you going to be alright down there without me for the weekend?' replies Pat, winking.

Tony's mind has already drifted to the opportunities afforded to him in London on his stag weekend. Boys will be putting a kitty together.

Tony simply nods and aggressively exhales. 'Going to miss watching the Blues beat the Wolves. That's the fucking sacrifice.' Pat smacks him with a pillow.

'West Midlands police set up super-squad to deal with villains'. *'Sunderland off to Arsenal for half a million'. World's gone mad.*

***

Steven collects Hev up from the end of the street. Nice new Cortina. Fresh MOT job from the garage. Owner doesn't need it back yet. Steven arrives with a can of Tuborg nestling between his sizeable thighs. Offers to share it with Hev. Hev accepts. Beer's flat. Hev's too nervous to say no. Steven says they're going over to the cinema in Perry Barr. Bit of Bond. *Spy Who Loved Me*. Steven parks right outside the Clifton. Pulls another couple of cans and box of fags from the gearbox. Steven knows a way into the cinema without paying, sliding through the fire exit. Steven and Hev catch the tail end of the previous running of the film. Steven's conversation is money, cars and booze. Hev finds him impressive. Hev finds him exciting. Hev's got nothing to say. Steven's got his arm around Hev. Roger Moore's Keeping The British End Up. Steven's liking the look of Barbara Bach.

Steven's had his tongue in Hev's ear, tried groping her, says he's going to finger her in the car on the way home. Hev's a tad scared. Tad excited. Hev's not going to put out. Not tonight. Steven's enjoyed the film. Hev's barely concentrated on the epic car chases and downhill skiing. Lying in fear of what will happen afterwards. Steven heads to the outdoors on the way home. *Get more for your money than the pub.* Collects a bottle of Diamond White and a few cans. Steven's rolling his own fags. Offers Hev a drag. Hev doesn't smoke. Steven's finding Hev a challenge. A bore. Doesn't want to lose face with the lads. Steven's pulled out every innuendo possible. Steven's touched Hev's tits. Hev's resisted. Giggled. Tried giving her a good fingering. Asked for a hand job. Hev's kissed and petted. Says Steven's going to have to be a good boy and wait. Steven's not a good boy. Never has been. Never will be. Steven's dropped her home. Says he'll be wanting more in London.

***

Pat's spending the next few days at home. Doesn't get a good night's sleep at Tony's. Tony's always up till late, flicking through his well-thumbed pornos, playing his old records: Elvis, Dean Martin, Sinatra, supping on cans, engaged in darts competitions with Wayne. Checking the dye is defeating those grey streaks. Pat and Hev have got their outfits ready for the weekend. *Privates on Parade* tickets, arranged for a bit of pampering, even teas at Fortnum & Mason. Hev says she finds Steven Baker too much. Says she hopes Tony's different. Pat tells Hev that Tony's got a soft side even if he doesn't show it. *Just a big teddy bear.* Pat insists Tony will become domesticated and responsible when he has his own place. *All men do.*

'Creeping Chaos: City threatened with black outs'. 'Power workers on strike'. 'Rail workers on strike'. 'Miners on strike'. Whole country coming to a meltdown. Arthur's swearing in front of the television. *Fucking government. Selfish bastards. Bloke Scargill protecting the miners up in Yorkshire. Who's looking after anyone in Birmingham? Fucking unions.* News is bleak all over. *'Policewoman attacked in Handsworth'. Horrid area. Let the darkies kick the shit out of each other. 'Truck spills emulsion all over Solihull bypass'. 'Areas of Birmingham to be threatened with blackouts'.* Arthur orders Gladys to get the candles in.

***

'Alf Ramsey in charge of the Blues'. 'New supremo, new era'. Tony's headed out with a few mates from the garage. Older chaps. Solid blokes. Working on the weekend. Not got the cash to come down to London. Procured tickets for the wrestling at Digbeth Civic Hall. Big Daddy. Amazing King Fu. Haystacks. Logan. Robarts. Night's a good crack. Boys had a few beers. Got the taste for it. Tony's heading down to London tomorrow. Not been since he was eleven. Bob the tool setter took him after the World Cup win. Birmingham's a mess. *'Aston Distressway'. 'Union bosses and electricity chiefs fail to agree'. 'More cuts ahead'. 'Aston Expressway at a standstill'.* Signals and lights out. Traffic chocker.

City centre's fine. Tony's got petrol in the motor. Boys want to go to the Sunset club. Hinckley Street. 'For Adults Who Like The Best'. Watch a porno. Tony's more for The Time, The Place. Some women of the night. Boys chip together to get Tony a dance. Tony's hungry for tits and fanny. Boys not put enough together. Tony gets smashed instead. Tony's back at four am. Collapsed alone in his tiny bed. Going to have to wait to London for company.

***

Pissing down in Digbeth. Violent rain blowing right into the bus shelter. Litter circling everywhere. Shady types frantically puffing on drenched rollups. Pat and Hev are there first. Armed with flimsy wheelie suitcases and carrier bags full of booze. Been down Lipton's: got a load of Diamond white, Mateus Rosé, Keelings Advocaat, some Mother's Pride, Dairylea and multipacks of TUCs. Tina's out of work early. Stacey, Angela and Karen all there before the fellas show up. Boys have met at The Anchor. Had a jar or two to pass away the late morning. Conversation is filth. Tony's boasting about the girls from last night. What he wants in London. Boys better deliver. Steven Baker's exaggerating his antics with Hev. Waffling on about seeing The Tubes next week. Good excuse for a scrap. With whoever is up for it. Lads betting on everything going. Who will have who. Who will be first. Who'll go without. Orgy of back-slapping and banter.

Lee's turned up with his younger brother Tommo. And his mate Al. Quiet fellas. Younger. Bit shy. Al's asking about the birds though. Says he's never been down to London. Tony's the court jester. Tells the lads to follow his lead. Won't go wrong. He'll be doing the same for them when they get wed.

45

Lads turn up at Digbeth with minutes to spare. Armed with forty-eight Newcastle Browns, twenty-four cans of McEwans, a couple of bottles of White Horse and Queen Anne. Enough booze to service a bar for a weekend. Girls are narky at having waited in the cold. Pat smacks Tony with her garish pink handbag. Steven Baker rests his hand on Hev's rear. Hev shuffles away. The lads populate the back seat of the bus, throwing off a few teenagers who had the cheek to sit there. Ring-pulls are drawn back every few seconds. Foam forms all over the floor of the bus. Loud and imposing. Girls are drinking rosé out of plastic glasses. Karen's a bit older. Didn't want to come. Pat's older cousin. Responsible one. Gladys talked her into it. Karen's preparing tiny, triangular cheese slice sandwiches and trying to restore calm. Lee tells Karen she's a bore. Pat tells Lee he's a twat. Steven Baker's already pulled a moony at a group queuing for the 14:20 to York.

'Win, lose, always on the booze!' 'Shit on the Villa,' rings out every five minutes.

Steven Baker's frenetically tongue-wrestling Hev. Got her on his lap on the corner back seat. All bravado. The girls find him odious. Tony Cole's in the middle of the back row. Ringleader. Directing operations and flowing beer cans. Gaz and Wayne are either side of him, scoffing sandwiches, throwing rolled up bits of tin foil down the bus. Martin's already made a beeline for Stacey, Gaz's got his eye on Angela. Tina's taking no prisoners, chain-smoking Silk Cuts next to Pat.

Tommo and Al sit a few rows in front. Subdued. Engaged in Blues chat. *'Francis going to gun down the Wolves'. 'Sbragia playing in defence'. Who the fuck's Sbragia? Sir Alf's going to make things great. Turning the corner.* Al gives some tips on Cradley Heath and Willenhall. Getting into his dogs. Tommo's talking about applying to be a metal spinner. Some good jobs going down Bromford's tube works. Gaz's working down

Leyland. Training as a paint technologist. Says it's easy work. Al's flicking through the classifieds in *The Mail*. Doing a plumbing apprenticeship, thinks about going to do something that pays more. *'Marooned'* says *The Mail*. Good weekend to be out of Birmingham.

Al's sucking on a pack of herbal tablets. Come down with a minor cold. Been out most nights this week. Nothing that's going to stop him going full pelt during the weekend. Al's glanced a few times at Hev trying to escape from Steven's aggressive prodding. Hev's thrown back a few 'rescue-me' glances. Hev wouldn't mind joining Al.

Tony Cole proposes some drinking games. Jokes about getting out a Ouija board.

'How about some truth or dare?' he bellows out, 'Could get the whole bus involved!'

Pat tells Tony to keep it down.

Tony's two finger-saluting motorists from the back window. Enormous cocks have been fingered into the steamed up windows. A veritable feast of loutishness prevails.

The remaining passengers are already shifting nervously in their seats. Retired couples at the front clutching flasks and Tupperware. On their way to see *King Lear* or *The Tempest* in the West End. Saved up for months. Just want a bit of peace and quiet and to finish their crosswords. Some young lovers wanting a peaceful escape. The odd travelling businessman. A few other hoodlums.

'I'll start,' says Tony Cole. 'For every pass, there's a fucking shot of scotch going round.'

Tony takes the first sip of White Horse and holds it aloft like the FA Cup.

'Ok, easy one, Wazza. When's the last time you got laid?'

Bellows of laughter.

Tony Cole knows his brother's not seen any fanny for a while. If ever. 'Fuck off,' snaps Wayne.

'You couldn't score in a brothel,' is chanted. Wayne turns bright red.

Tony says he will this weekend. Pat gives him a sharp look. Tony tells her to loosen up.

Wayne takes a swig of whisky. Tony says he will keep asking questions, until he gets an answer. Wayne punches him in the arm. Tony Cole smacks him back twice as hard.

'Fuck off skunk,' snaps Wayne. Lads don't know about Tony's Grecian 2000 habit. Subject needs to change.

'Alright, young lad over, there, Al, would you rather shag a darkie or a paki?,' offers Tony Cole.

'That's a fucking easy one,' moans Wayne.

'Let him fucking answer!' exclaims Tony Cole, 'he might be a queer for all we know.'

Cue chorus of sitcom-style giggles.

Al's a little hesitant, shifting in his seat. Pat gives him an encouraging smile, 'Yeah, it's an easy one,' she prods.

'Got to be a jungle monkey,' says Al.

Round of applause breaks out.

'Ever had one?' shouts Lee.

Al shakes his head.

'Your go then, son.'

Al looks around. Picks Tina. Sees it as a chance to win the support of the lads. Keep the banter going.

'Tina, take a gob of that whisky or flash your knockers at those cars going past.'

'I hate that shit anyway,' says Tina, fag spilling out of her big trap.

Tina's pulled up her top. Flapped her sizeable rack out of her navy blue bra and pressed them against the window, nearly giving a frail-looking elderly white van driver from Solihull a premature heart attack.

Round of applause breaks out.

'Get your tits out for the lads!' is sung in unison.

'That's my girl!,' shouts Tony Cole, as he shuffles down the aisle breaking into an foolish impression of Elvis's *A Little Less Conversation*, meekly escaping the tame coach stereo.

Tina looks at Pat.

'So Pat, how big's Mr T?' she says. 'And remember it's truth or dare.'

'She's got no need to lie, never had any complaints,' jokes Tony as he mimics getting his cock out of his faded Levis.

Pat moves her hands to resemble a ruler. She's exaggerating. Tony's proud. Strutting his stuff.

The game carries on. Gaz talks about his hookers. Caring little for how Angela might feel. Angela plays deaf. Karen, reluctantly, about losing her virginity. Tommo about his mum catching him wanking into a sock. Steven Baker says Bo Derek, Farrah Fawcett and Jane Fonda. All at the same time. Tina's got her tits out again. Wayne refused to answer any more questions. Lee's done the cracker challenge. Bottle barely survives a single round. Tony Cole launches into songs about Cockney bastards. About London being shite. About the power cuts. Shit on the Villa.

A few heads turn round from the front of the bus. *Eat your fucking sandwiches. Do your fucking knitting.* Steven Baker's lit a joint. Passes it round. Hev's moved away. Only Tina and some of the fellas partake. Al winks at Hev. Hev smiles back. Al's scared of Steven Baker. Carries a reputation. *Got arms like Popeye.* Al wants to make a move on Hev. Al thinks he might be able to have Tina as well.

Steven Baker's starting to get hyper. Tony tells him to calm it down. Steve's pissed in a plastic bottle. Steven's joking about getting someone to drink from it. Steve takes bets for throwing it down the bus. Nobody's gambling. Nobody wants him to do it. Steve launches it down the bus. Smacks a purple-haired lady, dressed in a spanking new cream suit, on the back of her head. Screams. Panic. Few chaps from the front of the bus move forward. Tell them to calm it down. Tony Cole and Steven Baker charge down. Fists thrown. People swaying sidewards onto seats. Steven Baker's landed some big punches. Hitting men twice his age. Driver swerves to stop. Service station somewhere near Watford. Calling the police. Tells everyone to get off. Locks the *Birmingham mob* at the back of the coach. Steven Baker threatens to smash it up.

Gang carry on drinking like nothing's happened. Only Hev and Karen appear concerned. Steven Baker says they can't prove anything. Karen tells Baker he's an idiot. Steven Baker calls her a slag. Hertfordshire police turn up. Four officers. Start interviewing driver and passengers lined up under a grim bus shelter. Lots of pointing towards the bus. Lady with the purple hair in floods of tears. Been inside the shitters to clean herself up. Steven Baker's swearing at them. Laughing. Gesticulating. Husband's upset. Steven Baker calls him a puff. Two blokes being seen to by emergency services. Police step onto bus, invite the women to get off. Under orders to make their own way to London. Tina's screaming. Says they've done nothing wrong. Calls the old lady a liar. Police say they will arrest Tina unless she calms down. Pat pulls her away. Girls collect their trolleys and plastic bags still weighed down with booze. Pouring down outside. Angry looks from other passengers. Female copper says they will need to get a taxi to Watford Junction if they want to make it to London. Pat says she's not going anywhere without the boys. Same copper says boys are being taken in for questioning. Another copper calls them a bunch of Brummie slags. *Worse than the Birmingham Six*. Tina won't shut her gob. Karen drags her away. Pat waves at Tony. See you down in London.

Pat's cursing Steven Baker. *Liability. Drunk. Causing nothing but trouble. Again.*

Sergeant Wilson invites the blokes to get off one at a time. Big Scottish bloke. Doesn't mince his words. Nor his threats. Powerful, bald chap. Small patches of red hair. Carries his truncheon like a man intending to use it. Gaz, Wayne, Martin, Tommo, Lee and Al put up no resistance. Cuffed and taken away by arriving vehicles. Steven Baker and Tony Cole refuse to concede any ground. Steven says he will knock anyone out who comes near him. Steven pisses on the floor. Tony's defending his honour. Says they're innocent. Tony knows he should get off. Doesn't want to lose face. Tony says the lady made it all up. Police get back on board. Charge onto bus. Steven Baker throws punches, smacks an officer. Officer smacks him back, giving him a black eye. Tony Cole's resistance has faded.

***

The girls make it down to London. Spend most of their time drunk. Karen drags them to the show. Weekend sponsored by Lambrusco, Silk Cut and broken TUC crackers. They never make it to Fortnum & Mason. Al, Gaz, Wayne, Tommo and Lee head down later that night. Carnage continues. Agree it's a better crack without Steven Baker. Pat tells Hev she's not to see him again. Boys meet up with girls. Al gets it on with Hev. Tells her she deserves better. Says he's going to take her out when he's back in Brum. Pat says Tony will square it with Steven Baker. Boys spend Tony Cole's stag do money on strip shows and the bookies. After checking in and dropping off their sports holders, the lads don't spend a single minute in the tiny and scummy King's Cross lodgings.

Tony Cole and Steven Baker are detained overnight. Tony Cole's given a warning. Told to clear off. Baker's got previous. Tony Cole can't locate the boys in London. No sign of them in the dive of a King's Cross hotel.

Never came back. Tony Cole drinks himself into oblivion in menacing Irish pubs next to menacing Irish sorts. Heads off back to Birmingham. Fuming and cursing the fellas.

Steven Baker's given a court hearing the following week. His third this year. Time for Steven Baker to do exactly that. Time.

'Firemen threaten to strike'. 'Blues beat Wolves'. 'Midlands doctor fined for keeping women waiting in their undies for twenty minutes'. Winter of discontent.

CHAPTER 4
ASTON UNIVERSITY

(Spring 2009)

Leanne's hungover. Dregs of last night's British reggae tribute night. Organised by Lethaniel, Leon's kid brother. Kwesi Johnson. Judge Dread. Rudy Grant. Harsh. Big crowd. Bigger noise. Lot of rum. Good night. Headache-inducing.

Mandy's booked in. All gob as usual. Heading on holiday. Dominican Republic. Off with her kid sister. And kid sister's repellent mate. Mandy's got a new tat. Teardrop behind her ear. Mandy's got a load of tats. Dolphins. Chinese lettering. Swallows. Large, meaningless stars. Mandy's on a mission to get laid. *Mandy's a slag.* Mandy's talkative. Mandy wants it done different from last time. Not as short. More ladylike. Blonder. *Mandy needs to shut her gob. Mandy's going to feel these scissors in the back of her neck.*

Mandy's colour is setting. Reading *Heat*. Cup of builder's brew. Leanne's still hungover. Can of Cherry Coke. Packet of cheese and onion. Gets a text. Personalised recording. *Mummy you gotta text message.* Dan. Out of the blue. *Who the fuck has died? Needs me to ask Mom something. Never simple with him. 'Alright sister slapper. Wanna meet on Sunday for lunch? D'.*

Leanne's free on Sunday. Leanne texts Leon. Leon's okay. Leon likes Dan. Sunday it is. See you there. Moseley Village. *Maybe he's getting married. Rachel. Nice enough. Bit stuck up. Bit better than the rest of us. She'll see through him eventually.* Mandy's ready for the trim. Mandy's still jabbering on.

Carter's not slept. Tossed and turned. Turned the pages of that album. *Those awful fucking faces. Cowards and drunks.* People who named him. Never really raised him. *Just a book playing tricks.* Carter's not done this for a while. *Not going to do it again. Waste of time. Got work to do.* Gorman's got some new clients. Gorman's intense. *Impress Rachel. Take more on.* Carter's not going online. *Not going to do it. Just a couple of minutes. See what's new. See what's changed.*

Just one name. One for today. See what's there. No harm done. Facebook. Paul Jeavons. Paul's on it. Seen him before. Not a friend. Not yet. Paul's not clued up on the security settings. Paul's got his life on display. Paul's been to Pamplona. Week in Rhodes. Paul spends a lot of time on Mafia Wars. Paul's engaged to Carmen. Irish family. Nice smile. Deep blue eyes. *Met her once at Nan's. Nice lass.* Paul's grown his hair out. Crew cut gone. Paul's got his own business. Small double-glazing company. Paul's doing well. Paul likes *Lord of the Rings* and *Blade Runner*. Paul's in a *Black Eyed Peas* group. *Paul's a fucking Villa fan. Turncoat.* Ashley Young for England. O'Neill is God. Small Heath 0 Villa 1. *Fuck Off.* Paul's mates with Lee. Lee Jeavons. In the slammer. *Not seen Lee in a decade.* Went off the rails. Stopped going to school. Worked as a labourer. Hod carrier. Aggressive stare. Fists always clenched. Dealt drugs. Took more. Taxed cars. Robbed from pensioners coming out the post office. Arson. Assault. The works. Down in Stafford. In prison. Mates hidden. Can't see Lee's profile. Just his photo. Scary fucker. Homemade tats on his neck. Those eyes. Piercing. Intense in their misplaced hate.

Carter's scanning through Paul's mates. Looking for a connection. Nothing going. No Jeavonses. No Coles. Few Carters here and there. Distant family dregs. Carter needs to see Gorman. Take on those jobs. Maisy's back. Maisy's had Gorman's winkle pickers up her arse. Maisy's always taking on the fun jobs. *Just one more hit. One more look. Shouldn't do this. Google. Alan. Alan Jeavons. Ford car dealer. Cat dentist. Cellist. Sweet fuck all.*

'Alan Jeavons, missing, Birmingham'. Always the same hits. *Gazzette* archive. 1989. By Bob Rowntree. 'Father of two goes missing'. 'Blues fanatic fails to return from away game'. Day team were relegated. Day of Hillsborough. Seventeen miles from Sheffield, Midlands man goes missing. Loving father. Selly Park. Painter and decorator.

Second hit. 27th April 1989. Police desperate in attempts to locate Midlands father. Alan Jeavons. Thirty-one years old. Loving father of twins. Still missing. Family no contact. Wife distraught. No motive for disappearance. Family appeal for any information. Birmingham City fans invited to call helpline.

Third hit. 4th May 1989. Missing Midlands Man had gambling debts. Alan Jeavons. Father of twins. Missing since 15th April. In Barnsley. Up to a thousand pounds in unpaid gambling debts. Possibly connected with his disappearance. No foul play suspected at this point. Anyone with further information invited to contact West Midlands police.

Then the void. Nothing. Nothing more. Three stories. Then gone. Drug wars. Riots. Kids on railway lines. Teacher strikes. Pub raids. IRA. Too many sex shops. City MPs declare war on Birmingham Grand Prix. Alan's gone. Paper gives up. Police not got the resources. Police give in. Irish stop knocking on the door. Irish not involved. Heather goes frantic. Heather begins a mission to track down Al. Heather hires a private agent. Nothing. Nil. The great void. Gorman's coming. Too late.

'You wanna speak to your mates, then you might have all the time in the world soon.'

'Was just researching.'

'Researching what? Your mates' fucking holiday snaps. My office. Now.'

Carter's not in the mood. Not in the mood for another bollocking. Last chance. Already handed a yellow card. As Gorman likes to call it. Persistent offending. Usual clichéd football manager talk. Carter's feeling under-dressed. A-team t-shirt. Holes in his jeans. Not showered. Smells of booze. Going to get a bollocking.

'I need you to head to McDonald's,' directs Gorman. 'We've got an interesting deal with them on. Good money. They want us to do all the street flyers for the summer season in the area. Bit of signage. Decent cash, man. I'm putting you in charge, and giving you *the* dreaded vote of confidence. Get yourself across town. I need you to meet this bird I just had on the phone. She's got a funny name. Hungarian or something like that. Here it is, take this piece of paper, it's got a number as well. That's her surname, Klob. There it is. Zanky. Zanky Klob. You can head in now. If you do that right, you can do the folk festival stuff as well.'

Carter was charged. Rachel would be happy. Off his back about the family crap. Out of the office. Maisy's pissed. New Scottish lad's jealous. Maisy's real pissed. *Shouldn't have got smashed in Brighton.* Carter heads home first. Change of clothes. Diesel jeans. Fresh, white Ralph Lauren shirt. Rachel's choice from Selfridges. Splash of Paul Smith. Carter's feeling good. Carter's getting the 35 back into town. Heading to Stephenson Street.

McDonald's is packed. *You'd think there was nowhere else to fucking eat.* Aggressive mothers and screaming kids. Place is a mess. Carter heads to the counter. Finds Mustafa. Looking for Miss Lob. Try again. Miss Klob.

Your manager. Try again. Mustafa's playing dumb. Mustafa asks his colleague. Miss Lob. Who's Miss Klob? Might have got the wrong McDonald's mate. Boss here is Mr Groves. Mr Groves breezes down the stairs. Ginger chap. Early twenties. Big I am. Open-button shirt. Big gold chain. Mr Manager.

'Been sent here to speak to a Miss or Mrs Klob about doing some flyers.'

'Sorry, fella, never heard of her. Who said come here?'

'My boss. Maybe she's a rep or something?'

'All you got's the name? Got a number, mate?'

'Yeah, he gave me a number. Should try it.'

Carter punches in the digits. Leant on an overflowing bin full of condiment wrappers and lettuce-ridden boxes. Feeling strange. Maybe he wasn't listening. McDonald's in town. Twelve o'clock. Carter's feeling odd. Phone answers. Strange echo. Speaker phone. Ms Klob? Fits and laughs. Hysterics. *Fucking Gorman. 'Come back, you knob. Fucking lazy knob.'*

Carter's annoyed. Carter's not going back to work. *Fuck Gorman. Bald twat. Taking the piss.* Carter's gone shopping. Got *The Wire Series 4*. New jacket. *Fuck Gorman. Bald twat.* Heads for a coffee. Develops into a pint. Tap & Spile. Reading the newspaper. Libyan student tucked in the bar. Having a few jars. Group of lads come in. Having a laugh.

'What you doing in Birmingham, mate?' asks the ringleader. Name probably Steve. Or Rob.

'Studying,' mumbles the Libyan.

'Where you studying?'

'Aston University.'

'Alright, Aston.'

'Doing a degree in Virtual Engineering.'

'Virtual Engineering……? '

Long pause.

'……you mean you pretend to study?'

The Libyan didn't follow. The group were in stitches. Carter cheered up. Nice pint. Brummie humour. *Fuck Gorman. Geordie git. Bald twat. Taking the piss. His best fucking designer. Not going back. Fuck him. Fuck his projects.* Carter's phone's ringing. Nino Rota. *Il Padrino. Fucking Gorman.*

'Where the heck are ya?'

'Still looking for Ms Klob. You twat.'

'Get back here, and don't answer me like that. Got some proper work to be doing. Few things have come in. I need you back.'

Carter can't be bothered. Hangs up. *Fuck Gorman.* Gorman leaves voice message. Call back or don't bother coming back in. Carter doesn't call back. Carter has another drink. Gets lost in *The Mail*. Off to see the Blues tonight. *Fuck Gorman. Bald twat.*

***

Carter's sunk nine pints. Wrecked. Slept in. Rachel's narked. Disappeared to work without saying goodbye. Carter's thrown up. Taken a shit. Not flushed the toilet. Got to head to work. *Pay the bills.* Face Gorman. *Bald twat.*

***

Gorman drags Carter straight into his Ikea showroom-esque office.

'Didn't come back in because I didn't think it was acceptable that you all took the piss out of me and wasted my time,' stutters Carter.

'You've been wasting my time for the last six months, lad. Surfing the net, sleeping on projects, getting stuff in late. Your work's dog-eared. Not sure what's happened to you. You used to be better than this.'

Gorman was right. For once. Carter had been depressed. Been in the doldrums. Not sure why. Just couldn't connect. Not been right since Christmas. Argument with his mother. *Mom playing the guilty card. Mom's got no more love to give. Mom can't answer your questions. Mom's hiding stuff.* Wanted to get away. Bored with life. Bored with the flat. Bored with being told what to do. Bored by being stuck in a rut. Not being able to move on. Bored of not having a real family.

'It's just a phase,' pleads Carter, 'getting through it. Just give me some work so I can crack on. I just need something to get my teeth into.'

'This is your last chance. I mean it. No going off and doing your own thing. Do what the bloomin' client wants. You like music, then do this music festival stuff. And in your downtime you can work on the free ads as well.'

Carter hated the classifieds. Shovelling shit. Precise, monotonous work. Detail not his strong point. Liked to be free. Free to create. Others can do the checking. The tidying up. Carter leaves Gorman's office. Gorman's playing Keane. *Somewhere Only We Know.* Gorman's got the biggest screen. Most powerful Mac. *For answering emails.* Carter's phone rings. It's Rachel. Got to answer.

'Where are we going with your sister at the weekend? Shall we get some food in?' she begins, without the merest of greetings.

'I said to meet in the village. About two o'clock. We can head for a walk, or go to the pub. Have a few drinks at ours. She's bringing the nipper.'

'As long as you don't get as drunk as you did last night. You better clean up what you did in the bathroom when you get home.'

Carter's back to work. Head down. Head hurting. Illustrator. Paths. Layers. Lines.

***

Leanne's early. In the Yellow Beetle. *Always colourful, Leanne.* Skunk-style streaks blended into her bright blonde hair. *Looks like a porcupine. Put on weight. Looks less like Mom.* Got on a yellow top and purple bra. Big mermaid tattoo on her shoulder. In full view. Low cut jeans. Pink stilettos. *Always colourful, Leanne.* Leon's driving. *Means Leanne's getting pissed. Going to be a long afternoon. Rachel. Leanne. Nothing in common. Nothing to talk about. Play Wii with Leon. Head down. Have a few drinks. Get through it.*

Leanne's waffling on about X Factor. On her first Bacardi and Coke. Leon's looking after Amber. *Good lad, Leon.* Leanne wants a second kid. Having some problems. Leanne's open about them. Leon's embarrassed. Keep on trying. Been seeing doctors. Leon doesn't want to talk about it. *Shut up, Leanne.*

Idiot Rachel. Not put the book away. Left it out. Underneath the coffee table. Poking out. Carter wants to give it a kick. *Nobody will see it. Distract them. Nobody will see it. Leanne knows that book. Been looking for it. Mentioned it a few years ago. Never seen it. Not sure what happened to it. Leanne can't see the book. Just need to distract her. Poke it under the table. Under the sofa.* Leanne's full of questions. Always nervous in front of Rachel. Tries to be a bit less herself.

'You seen our mom recently?' launches Leanne.

'Not since Christmas. Did me head in.'

'Maybe you should go over and make peace. You know how stubborn she is, always playing the bleedin' victim.'

'My life's a hell of a lot easier when I am not dealing with her. Let Carl take the heat. What about you?'

'Went over a few weeks ago. Had her looking after Amber. Went to the Kingfisher, got a mate who works down there. Mom's alright. Said she was going to get in touch. Meet you in town or something.'

Rachel's smiling. Trying to get involved. Rachel doesn't know much about the argument at Christmas.

'I saw some photos. Your Mum was good-looking when she was younger,' launches Rachel.

'She scrubbed up alright.'

Carter's twitching. Rachel shouldn't have seen the picture. Rachel's not met Mom. Leanne's curious. Leanne's going to be curious.

'Has she aged well?'

'She's still alright. Always smoked too much. Got old skin, too much sun. Like a fucking camel she is. She still does alright though. Spends all her cash on clothes, trying to look like a friggin' nineteen-year-old or something.'

'Do you take after your mother?' continues Rachel, fully aware of Carter's irritation.

'Basically we're both stubborn bitches, like. So no doubt,' starts Leanne, supping her Bacardi and Coke. 'Mom's always been more secretive than me and way more insecure. Don't know who I take after really.'

'Do you remember much about your father?'

Carter's edgy. Conversation has already got onto the family. Leon's distracted setting up the Wii. Amber's licking a gingerbread man.

'Maybe Leanne doesn't want to go over this, Rach?'

'No, it's alright. Got nothing to hide me, it's the others that don't want to talk about it. I was about eight when Dad left, Dan, you were about four. He fucked off in the summer just before my birthday. Remember being really upset when he wasn't there. Him and Mom had a big argument one Saturday. Uncle Wayne came round, I think. Dad was mad, got quite violent. Smashing things up like a lunatic. He put through the big glass bookshelf.'

Leanne gulps the rest of her drink. She's very matter of fact about it. Carter had never had this conversation with his sister. Never had the chance. Never had the inclination. Carter-style. Sweep it under the carpet. Pretend it never happened. Leon's locked on the Wii.

'Not sure what happened. Dad got me a present for my birthday. Some My Little Pony stuff. Uncle Wayne came round a few times, think with money from Dad for me. Not sure I ever saw it. Then Uncle Wayne stopped coming as well.'

'Did your dad ever come back? Ever see you again?'

'No, not a word. Maybe he called Mom. Maybe Mom wouldn't let him see me. They got divorced a year later. Know Dad had met someone else. Mom was already with Carl.'

'Do you even know if your dad is still alive?'

'Rach! What you trying to suggest? Stop prodding,' barks Carter.

'It's alright. We tried having this chat at Christmas. Mom wouldn't open up. Dan, you got pissed off and angry. You said a few things to Mom that were probably out of turn.'

'Just sick of Mom never telling us anything. I gave up after that. Gave up trying to find out, trying to speak to her, get any sense out of her. She's a fucking emotionless bitch.'

Rachel's finding it easier to open Carter up in front of his sister. Harder to close up when you've got more witnesses. Harder to close up when you need to express an opinion. When your opinion is being challenged. Rachel's made snacks. Quiche. Hummus. Nibbles. Leon's sabotaged the pizza.

'Anyway, where were we?' contemplates Leanne, 'Think Dad fucked off to Coventry or somewhere. Know he stayed with the police for a while. Managed to find him when I was about sixteen as I'd been curious. Mom had been doing me head in, was feeling rebellious like.'

'You've never told me this,' replies Carter, angrily.

'Never wanted to upset you.'

'You could have FUCKING mentioned it.'

'It was fifteen years ago. You were about twelve. What was the point!'

'Calm down, Dan,' placates Rachel, 'Let your sister talk. How did you find him? What happened when you saw him?'

'Ran into Martin Collins in Corporation Street, remember him, Dan? He was a mate of one of Wayne's kids. He let out that Dad was running this pub in Coventry. I went over there but he'd moved out. The lady who'd taken over there gave me this new address.'

Carter's twitchy. Carter's curious. Carter wishes they'd had this conversation before. Why hadn't Leanne raised her voice at Christmas?

'So Uncle Wayne was still in touch with him?' quizzes Carter.

'Not sure. For a while definitely, but don't think they have contact. Asked him once, said he didn't know how to find him. That I should let it go. That I'd only be upset.'

'Then what happened?'

'He was down in Warwick at the time. Living with this lady who ran a pub down there. Not sure if he was still a copper. I went down on the train and managed to find the pub he was supposed to be at but lost my nerve so went into this bleedin' tea shop opposite. Stayed there hours, I did. The lady was even closing up. Then I saw him come out of the pub. He looked a lot older, hair all grey and he had put on some weight.'

'Did you talk to him?'

'No. I felt like crying, just took the train and went home and think I got pissed with my fella.'

'That Eddie fella! Geez, forgotten all about him. Skinny Eddie!'

'You've had some rough slappers in your time as well!'

Rachel shoots an edgy look.

Carter's fetches himself another beer. Banks's best. *Real ale.* Gone to pour one for Leon as well. Leon's lost in a ski jump challenge. Not finished his first beer. Carter's standing up. Needs something to do. Scratching his nuts through his pockets. Feeling nervous.

'Did you go back and see your father?' breaks Rachel, making sure the topic is not lost in Carter's quest for a drink.

'About a month later, I went back. Went back with my boyfriend for a bit of support.'

'So fucking skinny Eddie has seen my dad and I haven't!'

'Let it go, Dan,' snaps Leanne.

'Fucking unbelievable!'

'Then what happened?' continues Rachel, expertly steering the conversation on course.

Rachel was curious. Pulling that long, earnest and concerned face again. Leanne was evidently finding this bit more difficult. She had an attack of verbal constipation; hurried, high pitch statements were replaced by a calmer, reflective tone as she searched for words.

'I went into the pub. Ordered a couple of drinks. Eddie was a bit older so got them in. I used to get ID'd all the time. Think the lady Dad was seeing was serving the drinks.'

'Dad came out from behind. He had one of those big Umbro football manager coats on and was going out. He didn't notice me. He was walking out and then I got his attention.'

'What did the old twat say?' replies Carter.

'He recognised me straight away. Had the look of evil in his eyes. Like he'd seen a ghost. He just told me I shouldn't be there and to fuck off home and don't come back. Basically.'

'That was it?'

'Basically yes. He said a few other things which weren't that nice. About Mom and about what he'd do if I came back. He walked out and the landlady said it was best I left. So we fucked off, got the train and that was it.'

'Charming fella,' adds Leon, who'd deceptively been following the conversation. Leon's like that. Feigning lack of interest.

'I don't think I've ever felt so bleedin' crushed, so much hatred, so frigging scared.'

Leanne was upset but not going to cry. Wasn't going to let him beat her. Wasn't going to open up scars which she'd self-healed slowly and painfully. Healed enough to get on. Carter didn't like seeing his sister like this. Was angry with Rachel for bringing it up. Happy with Rachel for bringing it up.

Rachel insisted on carrying on.

'Did you ever go back?'

'Not intentionally. A few years later I was in Warwick. Lisa's hen night. Girls wanted to go in the same pub. I just waited outside. Was too friggin' scared. We had a drink and moved on but there was a new name over the door. Someone said it had been taken over. Presumed the old fart had moved on. Probably fucked off as soon as he saw me. That was his style.'

Silence prevailed. Carter felt annoyed that he hadn't had this conversation before. Annoyed with himself. Annoyed with Leanne. Rachel went quiet. Like this was now a family affair. None of her business. Hit raw nerves.

'Is that the last time either of you has been in touch?'

'I gave up after that and cut my losses. Never mentioned it to Mom, or anyone else.'

'Do you think your dad has contact with anyone in the family?'

'Not sure. Don't see much of that side of the family anymore. All live over in Smethwick. Don't get over that side of town. Not seen my gran and grandad in about twenty years. Don't even know if they are still alive. Think Mom maybe took us over after Dad had left but that was it. Never again. Dad must have said he didn't want them to see us again.'

'Does it not seem strange that side of your family disappeared completely?'

'Does now, not when you are younger. You don't think about that sort of crap. Probably a bit disappointed in them really. They could have made an effort, even without Dad. We moved around a lot, maybe didn't get our address. Mom might have kept it from them. It's in the past.'

'Aren't you curious to know whether your grandparents are still alive?' offers Rachel.

The atmosphere is serious. Like a wake. Everyone has stopped drinking. Leon's gone out for a second. Making a call. Brother's got some computer problems. Carter's caught in two minds. Doesn't know whether to carry on just this one time or let it all go.

Leanne keeps babbling on.

'It's kind of like they didn't exist. Mom got remarried. Carl's parents always got us presents. They're not like our grandparents or anything, but we've never missed out. Us kids can't be the ones expected to make the effort.'

Leanne looks down. Waiting for someone else to talk. Maybe waiting for the subject to change. Leanne notices the book. *The fucking book. Rachel should have put it away.* Leanne's leapt on it like it's a suitcase full of cash.

'So you've been hiding this all this time?'

'Not really. Rach found it the other day. Didn't know I had it, must have been in some old box when I moved in.'

'Liar,' snaps Leanne.

'Honest.'

'Seeing as we're here, may as well take a goosy gander.'

Leanne scans the album. Curious enough to look at the pictures. Too horrified to focus on them. Carter's avoiding eye contact. Rachel's got her eye over Leanne's shoulder. Mom's wedding. Dad's pre-war shot. Baby Leanne. Baby Carter. Carter's first birthday. Carter with the twins. *Look like triplets.* Dad and Uncle Al. *Dad's a fucking scary nut.* Dad with the kids. On a beach. Benidorm. Heather's wedding. Lots of shots. *Some scary fuckers there.* Big fellas round a table. Trophy girlfriends. Heather looks a lot better. Heather looks happy. *Handsome guy, Uncle Al.*

Rachel's involved again.

'And has anyone ever mentioned what might have happened to your uncle?'

Leon pitches in. Leon's back from his phone call. Leon wants to put on Sky Sports. Spurs versus Newcastle. 1-0. Leon tries getting involved. Token effort.

'Weird story, that one. Remember when we saw your cousin that time in town? Says your aunt blew her rocket or something.'

'Always been a bit of a taboo in our family,' pitches Leanne, 'no-one ever brings it up. Used to see a lot of my aunt. But think her and Mom pissed each other off. Mom got tired helping out. Or so she says, and just gave up. See her occasionally now but she's a bit of a mess. Lives near us like. Been done for drink driving a few times, driving without a licence, that sort of crap. She used to be a bit of a lady. Shame really, if you think about it.'

'What does your aunt think happened?'

'Not sure. Like I said, she got this detective bloke in for a while. Know this from Mom. He found nothing. Think my uncle liked a wager, maybe got involved in some other stuff but don't think the police could ever put any evidence on anybody. There was this Irish mob involved that were a bit dodgy at the time but the Old Bill couldn't chase any leads. Probably couldn't be bothered.'

'Do you think it's conceivable that he just disappeared out of choice?' persists Rachel.

'No-one seems to believe it. Maybe he had another woman on the go for all we know. Not sure our aunt ever wants to think that. Would probably find it easier knowing he was dead. Wouldn't you?'

'Do you think his twins are curious?'

'Not sure, maybe, probably. Least we know our dad went because he was sniffing after another woman. Least we know the reason, even if we have to accept he's a bastard. And that he rejected us. They've probably grown up never knowing. They can't hate like we can'.

Leanne had actually put it quite well. Carter was impressed. His sister was not the most articulate. But far more willing to reason than she used to be. Used to be a right hothead. Probably Leon. Leon doesn't argue. Got too used to arguing with herself that she gave up. Carter suggests they go for a walk. Get out. Get one at the pub. Change the subject. Have a go on the machines. Carter knew all the answers in the Millionaire game in The Bull's Head. *Easy money. Distraction.*

'It was nice to spend time with your sister. She's actually quite sweet when you get talking to her,' reflects Rachel on the lazy stroll back down the hill.

'She gets nervous in front of you, thinks you're all posh or something.'

'That's just a complex you Birmingham people have.'

'Maybe. Think she is just a bit in awe of you.'

'In awe? Bit extreme.'

'You're good-looking, got a good job, nice company car on the way, money, nice clothes, speak proper, she's a bit intimidated.'

Rachel's beaming. Been a while since Carter had flattered her. It was easy for Carter to do. He felt much the same way as his sister. Second class. Not good enough. Lower down the food chain. B-grade.

Carter's still sober. Drinks had no effect in the pub. Conversation weighing on his mind. Leanne had seen their dad. Even Skinny Eddie had seen their dad. Gran and Grandad. That old, shabby house in Smethwick. Grandad, the original Blue Nose. Uncle Wayne. The Baggies turncoat who liked his metal. With his huge drum kit. Carter doesn't really remember much else about Uncle Wayne. Flashbacks. Faces from the photos haunting him like horror film stills. Colours faded like the passing of autumn. Dead October. The frozen smiles. The cackling laughs. The unexplained.

***

Carter's back on the computer. Back searching. Back typing. Thinks about friending Paul Jeavons. Get in touch. Go for a pint. See what he knows. Reseed the family tree. Go and visit Lee. *Always wanted to see a slammer. Maybe he needs help.* Aunt Heather. Alone and wallowing in clear and toxic Russian liquid. An attractive young woman. Had a career. Happiest day of her life. A fucking drunk and a bum. His own mother. Spoilt kids rotten. But never a hug. Never a kiss. Never a chat. *Have your bleedin' present and go play with it.* Out of the way. *Married a man with no balls. No fucking drive. Mr mediocre.*

Back on *The Mail and The Gazzette* archives. Bob Rowntree. *Know that name. Know that name. Glanced at these articles too many times.* Midlands man goes missing. No traces of Selly Park decorator. South Yorkshire police have no leads. Gone in the night. Fish and chip paper. Forgotten. The great void.

Rachel's drying the washing. In her work routine. New shirt, new day. Got a big week. Trademark dispute. Litigation. On the side of the underdog. Not the side she wants to be on. *Bright girl, Rachel. Going places. Got to cut the slack.* Carter needs to buck up his ideas. Become an adult. Take more on.

'What you up to?'

'Just checking the football results.'

'Thought there was only one game today.'

'Yesterdays. For the coupon.'

Carter had always done the pools. Carl's a poolsman. His legacy. X.1.2. Get the ten draws. Those ten X's. *Carl's a fucking pro.*

'Didn't realise you could get the football results on Facebook?'

'Can do more than one thing at a time.'

Carter's printed the old *Mail* articles. Going to go through them. Look for something that he's missed. Go and see Paul. Dad and Al leaving two years apart. Coincidence? Carter wanted to see his dad. Look him in the eye. See what a coward and a deserter looks like. See who brought him into this world and fucked off. Find out why, what, how. Carter was on a mission. Motivated. Mission to find out the truth. Find out why he wasn't good enough. Why his mom was emotionally useless and drained from the life she showed in those pictures. Why Aunt Heather is clinging on to a bloke who disappeared twenty years ago. What happened to a family tree that rotted overnight. *Got to face up to it.* Leanne saw Dad. Carter needs to do the same.

'What's that you've printed?' enquires Rachel, rather too rhetorically.

'Just some old articles.'

'Let me see,' says Rachel, managing to grab a few print-outs hidden under a tatty plastic folder.

'Nothing to do with you.'

Rachel's too fast. Rachel's scans the articles. Rachel says she has seen them before. Done her own search. Wasted her own work time.

'Just think it's time to find out for myself what happened.'

'I'm glad. And you know I am here for you.'

'Just hope it doesn't lead to more questions. Soon as it gets messy or complicated, I'm pulling out. Just want to know why there is so much hate and secrecy in my family.'

'You telling anyone you're doing this?'

'Well, it's going to be fairly obvious soon enough. I've got to start talking to the buggers.'

Carter's switched off the computer. Disconnected his brain. Can't believe he's doing all of this. *Getting involved. Going to regret it.*

CHAPTER 5

SELLY PARK

(February—April 1982)

Saunders gone. Heading to Blues. *'Barton new Villa boss'*. Al's cursing. *Being paid peanuts. Need head read signing up for this.* Heather's insisted. Keep Pat happy. Got a lot on her mind. New kitchen would be nice. *Home fit for a hero. All of that bullshit. Fuckin' Tony's got it easy. Sitting on his fucking boat. Polishing his boots. Playing cards.*

***

Al's got a spare twenty quid. Has got a good feeling. 14.10. Doncaster. Red Rose. 8/1. Sure-fire. Al can feel it. Been a good weekend. Al's won at cards. Four hundred sheets. Baker's face a picture. *Love taking money off that cunt. Greedy cunt.* Al throws down twenty quid. Perches confidentially on a stool, grimacing at the tiny screen nestled under the ceiling. *Should head to the opticians.* Al's horse is a winner. Red Rose. *Going to get Heather a box of chocolates. Keep it quiet though. Money not going in the tin.*

Al picks up some Silk Cuts. *Quid for a box of fags. Fucking Tories.* Al's feeling flush. Five hundred and sixty quid. In the pocket. *Just as well. Two hundred quid for this fucking kitchen. Free fucking labour. Working like a fucking Stani. Doing it for the family. Keep Pat happy. Fuckin' Tony's gone. Gone to be a hero. Got it easy, Tony. Got it easy.*

***

Pat's having a fag at the front door. *Looking good, Pat. Better looking than her sister. Had her hair done. Looks good.* Pat's off to see the O'Connells.

Micks, the lot of them. Early Paddy's night. Off to get pissed in Digbeth. Al's got a kitchen to finish.

'It's kind of you to be doing this, Al,' says Pat, pouting forcefully. As she does.

Not fucking wrong. Could be watching The Blues. Could be having a cheeky bet. Nice pint. Polishing the car. Getting some fanny.

'No worries, Pat. You know Tone wanted me to have it sorted. Keep you happy. Have something nice to come home to. Couldn't let Tone down now, could I?'

Lying through his gambling teeth.

'There's some cans in the fridge if you get thirsty later. Some bacon and beans and a couple of cobs. Few snags as well. Help yourself, bab. Leanne's at her nan's so make yourself at home.'

'Thanks, bab, I'll be here a little while by the looks of things.'

'Hope Heather's okay with that,' returns Pat.

'Hev's out with mates tonight. With the girls over in Harborne.'

'Make sure you get a good Sunday then,' says Pat. Still pouting.

Kitchen's a fucking mess. Needs tiling. New sink. New cupboards. Lick of paint. Mould everywhere. Pat's not done the washing up. Kids' crap all over the place. Al wants a beer. *Or a wank. In a cup. Place is a shit sty.* Al doesn't want to work. Al wants to watch Piggott. 16.20 Doncaster. Puts on the wireless. Blues. At home to Stoke. 2-1. Relegation still looms. Al's missing it. Again. *Fuckin Blues*. Ed Doolan. Blues playing with fire. Blues going down if don't buck up. *Six friggin' weekends this is going to take. Got to head to Sankey's and get the parts. Pat's not going to do that. Lazy tart. Boozing it up. When's Tony going to cough up? Fuckin' hero. Got it easy. Playing on his fucking ship.*

***

Al's there the next weekend. And the following one. Tony's down in Portsmouth, waiting to leave. *'No invasion yet, MPs are told' 'Britain accused in Falklands row'. Kitchen's still a mess. Fucking German Shepherd wagging its tail. In the bleedin' way.* Al heads out. Too often. Doncaster. Chester. Epsom. Ten quid here, ten quid there. Boredom. Al's started losing. Al's not happy. Pat's not paying for the kitchen, Pat's not getting the parts. Leanne's crying. Mom's chain-smoking. Mom smacks Leanne. Kid cries again. Kid could wake the dead.

Pat's reading *The Mail* and listening to KTC. Pat's not letting up. Pat's gassing. Worried about Tony. Tony's still in Portsmouth. Tony's not left yet. Pat's making chicken kievs. *Chips with fucking salad cream.* Al's still grafting. Pissed up the day at the bookies. Pat's watching Parkinson, Jim Davidson rattling on. Then Dallas. Tiling getting done. Navy and off-white squares. *Tony's going to pay for this. Floor still needs doing, electrics rewiring. Place is a fucking mess. No wonder they got it cheap.*

'You not going out tonight, Pat?' launches Al from the kitchen.

'Got no-one to look after our Lea.'

'Could have asked Hev, she's in tonight. Probably watching Dallas as well. Loves that crap. Not my cup of tea, I can tell you that much.'

'That's a shame,' responds Pat, voice croakier than usual from chain-smoking her way through the afternoon.

'She would have liked that. Would like to see more of ya.'

'You nearly done? You'd better get home.'

'On my way.'

Al wasn't going home. Al's heading out with Tommo. Have a soak at his place. Washed his donnies. Change of clothes. *Few jars in town.* Broad Street. *Few more jars. Have a crack. Lark around. Head to Bradford Street. £2.95 to see some tits. Time The Place. Pick something up. Get pissed. Always a good laugh. Fuckin' bored of staying at home.*

***

Tall, gormless-looking stranger gallops over, empty glass in hand.

'Alright, handsome. Looking to have a good time?' Quick and to the point.

'If you'll show me one,' replies Al.

'Think I can give you more than a good time.'

'What you charging? Your fucking mate conned me last time.'

'Let's say for a fiver you can do whatever you want to me.'

'And how much for you to do to me whatever I want?'

'We're going to have fun,' winks the slapper.

Al takes her to the Metro City. Runs it round the corner to a sheltered spot. Wishes he had brought out the Cortina. Lent it to Hev. *Never should have.* Tony's had this one before. Al's sure. Tony's had his cock in her mouth. Joyce unzips his jeans. Joyce plants Al's cock in her mouth. Al's had a long fucking day. Al cums in her gob. Pats her on the head. She's swallowed. *Good girl. That's all for tonight. Going home. Passing out.*

***

Hev looks beaten up. Deep rings under her eyes. Al makes a joke about her not paying the Avon lady.

'What time did you roll in last night?' snaps Hev.

'Late.'

'I know it was fucking late!'

'Well fuck off then,' volleys back Al.

Al's avoiding eye contact.

'I'm going over to Pat's. Spending the day over there. Going to see what you've done to the kitchen.'

'Do that.'

'Are you working over there today?'

'Need to get some paint and other crap. Will go over one night in the week. Whenever I get a break from work.'

Al's hungover, worried about the car. Left tissues. *Needs a clean. Hev better take the Cortina.* Al's still got some cash. Al wants to go and play cards. Al's got a long week ahead. Heather's served up breakfast. Full English. The works. Cup of tea. Heap of sugar.

Al's king again. Al feels better. Al lights up. Heather complains. Not in the house. Heather's heading out. To see Pat. *Hev's put on weight. Letting herself go. Wants to have kids. On the case. Kids cost. Kids going to be expensive. Another fucking reason to stay at home. Handcuffs.*

'Maybe we can go down Stirchley and get a curry tonight, Al? Have a proper Sunday evening,' pleads Hev.

Al didn't want to go out. Al wanted to fix the car. Have a wager. Lift some weights. But keep the peace.

'Sounds good. Need to take our own cans, though. Don't have a licence, those Stani bastards.'

'Get me a bottle of white then.'

'Will pick it up on my way to Wades.'

Taj Mahal. Heather's attacking poppadoms and a Korma. Al's gone spicy, Vindaloo. Sweat out the weekend. Man's curry. Few tins. Hev's made an effort, new silky top. Sky blue. Shiny, showing a bit of cleavage. Black leggings. High heels. Al's not made an effort. Loose t-shirt, old jeans, slip-ons. *Al looks good though. Always does.*

'Would be nice if we could do this more often,' starts Hev, devouring her naan.

'I've been working me nats off.'

'I know you've been graftin' but you've been away a lot of evenings as well.'

'Need to blow the cobwebs off. Got three kitchens on the burner. For a change it's bringing in the dosh. Paying the bills. You got a bleedin' cob on tonight.'

'I'm not complaining, bab. Just getting bored on my own. My mates have all got kids, me sister's got one as well. Would like us to start our own.'

'We've been trying. It's gonna happen soon. Just need to save a bit more up. Be able to take care of it properly like.'

'Can we have a go tonight?'

Al didn't want a shag. Tired. Al couldn't raise his game. Heather keeps going on about kids. Al isn't ready yet. Al wants to put it off. Could keep her busy though. Get her off his back. Heather stinks of curry. Al reeks of beer. And fags. Heather's gyrating on top. Bouncing away. *Those huge fuckin' tits. Tiny nipples. Hairy fucking pussy. Needs a trim.* Al's cum. Heather's barely started. Al rolls over. Al falls asleep. Al's passed out. Got the Gordons' front bedroom to redecorate tomorrow.

***

Fuckin' Argies have invaded. Shoot the lot, say *The Mail* readers. Tony's poised to leave. *Serving his country.*

***

Tony's heading out this week. Pat's panicked. '*Pym's called an emergency session. Diplomacy Failing'. Fuckin' Tories. Fuckin' Argies. Fuckin' war.* Pat's sobbing on the phone, hands it over to Al. Kitchen going fine, mate. Tony in good spirits. Tony ready to stick it up them. Tony's going to be a hero.

Mizzly day. Hev's gone out with Katie. *Whoever she is.* Warren Beatty at the ABC. Film called *Reds. Good-looking, bloke Beatty. Right charmer. Al's better looking though. Al's never had a problem with the birds.* Pat's alone. Been on the phone to anyone and everyone. Eighty marines already gone. *Tony's leaving soon. Tony's going to come back.*

'Says on the news that the invasion is about to get messy. Tony's on his way,' blathers Pat.

'He's going to be fine, bab. Will be over in no time. These Argies don't know what they're dealing with. Bomb them out of the fucking sea. He'll be home in no time. Right proud of him.'

'Hope you're right.'

Pat's watching the news, Points of View, Midlands Today. Man bludgeoned to death in Northfield. *Messy stuff. Knives. Coward crimes.* Pat wants a video recorder. *Pat's demanding. Five hundred fucking quid. Tony's got it easy. Tony's coming home.* Pat's gone to get some Silk Cuts. Leanne's crying again. Sink fitted. Al's off.

***

Al slept well. Like a baby. Pat's on the blower. Again. Decided on the colour. Lilac. Al heads down to Wades to pick it up. *Like a fucking slave.* Pat wants to go for a few drinks with Hev, Al's got to keep an eye on Leanne. *Fucking kitchen. Fucking screaming kid. Tony's got it easy.*

'*We'll free islands—Thatcher*'. Villa against Anderlecht. Semi-finals of the big cup. *Fucking nightmare. 'Ozzie still in Argentina'.* Tony's leaving. *Off to be a hero. Good luck, mate. Blow them up. 'I must tell the house that the Falkland Islands and their dependences are British territory. No invasion or aggression can alter that single fact.'* The Iron Lady's pissed. Prince Andrew's sailed out. Foot says government should go.

Al's finishing the kitchen. Needs a final lick of paint and shelving unit fitted. Tony's asked him to do the bedroom as well. Extra fifty quid. For old time's sake. Won't take long. Maybe the landing as well. *Tony's a cheeky cunt. Tony's got it easy.* Al takes the cash. Al does the job. Another month's work. Al's off to Handsworth. Off to play cards.

***

Spence is there. Tommo too. *The fucking Mick crowd.* Big stakes. Late session. Winner takes all. Al's not got the money. Al's been on a losing streak. *Got it coming in, though. Just a phase.* Didn't put it in the tin. Takes a loan. Lose it, pay the interest. *Declan's a big Irish cunt. Big fucking drinker. Bigger temper. Hands like shovels. Fuckin' terrorist.* Whisky's on the table. Declan's got his own bottle. With his name scribbled on it. Micks are puffing cigars. Smoke everywhere. *Can't fuckin' breathe.* Suffocating. Room's dark. *Like a fuckin' dungeon.* Smells of fresh paint. Slappers serving drinks. Declan likes them dark. Just not on a Sunday. Mother would turn in her grave. *Fuckin' poker.* Al prefers Black Jack. *Fuckin' Mick mafia.* Al's on a losing streak. Al starts badly. Al continues badly. The Irish are pros. Al plays his hand too early. Connor takes the piss. Maybe should go home now. Bring your missus next time. She can hold your hand. Don't want to lose those good looks. Al stays to the end, takes another loan. *Luck is going to change. Luck has to change.* Declan sends him home. Al's got to find two hundred quid. *Kitchen's not going to pay for that. Tony's not going to cover that. Tony's got it easy. Fucking hero. On his fucking ship.*

***

Argies capture eighty Marines, sent them to Uruguay. Heading home. Tony's alright. Tony's not arrived yet. Pat's worried, Pat's watching Dallas. Jock's dead. Jock wasn't a saint. Pat's having a cup of tea. Wedge of black forest gateau. Leanne's chasing Pop. Dog hairs everywhere. Stinks of piss. Al wants to shoot the twat. Al's finishing the kitchen. Al's done a great job. *Tony better come back. Come back alive.* Al's not doing all of this for free.

'You've been a rock, Al,' purrs Pat, 'been good having your company. Know our Tony would be right happy.'

'Like to keep me word, bab. We're a family, aren't we?'

Pat's looking less stressed. Pat's had her hair done. Gets it done free at the salon. Pat's wearing a short skirt. Al can see the inside of her thighs. Al wishes Heather had Pat's legs. *Not those friggin' chubby thighs.* Pat's got a gold chain round her ankle. Al liked that. Al liked the smell of Pat. Al had to concentrate on the kitchen.

'40 War Ships in Royal Navy Task Force'. No half measures. *'It is All Action as Britain Arms The Fleet'.* Invincible. Hermes. Fearless. Glamorgan. Glasgow. Coventry. Antrim. Defending a nation. Protecting what's ours. Kicking the invader out. Going to be over in a few weeks. Al's off to get a new oven. Creda. *Fucking half oven.* Pat's fallen for the adverts. Pat's demanding. *Nice legs, Pat.*

***

Al's done the Gordons' conservatory. Three hundred quid. Pays off Declan. Declan wants interest. Al says fuck off. Declan wants his ten percent. Declan knows where he lives. No ten percent, no more games. Al says one week. Declan says one week, fifteen percent. Al's in trouble. Al's on a losing streak. Al heads to the bookies. Twenty quid. 5/2. York. Sure-fire. Golden nugget. Horse stumbles. Doesn't finish. *Fit for the butchers.* Al's on a losing streak. Eighty quid left from a big job. Heather's going to be pissed. Exhaust needs replacing. Another friggin' thirty quid. Al's in trouble. Al borrows cash from Tommo. Heather doesn't know. Next month will be luckier.

'Carrington Resigns'. Fucking coward. Blithering idiot. Fucking Tory. Tony's nearly arrived. No contact. Pat's worried. Tony's not going to write. Tony's going to come home, though. Al's in the newsagents. Fags. Double Decker. *Evening Mail.* Twelve pence short. Will pay it back tomorrow. *'Britons want war—Ready for armed action'.*

Al's finishing the kitchen. Asks Pat for an advance on the bedroom. Needs to get paint. Again. Wallpaper. Some new tools. Needs to have a wage. Pat pays half upfront. Tony's left money in envelopes. Can't open them all yet. Get the rest in a few weeks. Pat's offered a few tins. Al sips up. Need some cash. Al sees a tenner on the side. *Nothing ventured, nothing gained. Fucking working as a charity.* Heather's had a good month, got a bonus. Not putting money in the tin. Al's got to make ends meet.

Pat's needs a drink. Wants to go The King's Arms for a vodka tonic. Leanne's in bed. *Leave her there.* She'll sleep, says Pat. *Only need an hour. Can't do that.* Al wants a drink. Al offers to go to the Outdoors. High Street. Bottle of Smirnoff. Four Tuborgs. Bottle of tonic. Twenty smokes. Al heads back. Addison Road. Door still needs painting. Needs new hinges. *Bound to be next job. Fucking charity work.*

'Take a load off, Al, have a few drinks. Invite Hev over if you wanna.'

'Just gonna finish the shelving. Won't be long. Hev's busy tonight.'

'Armada set to go'. Pat's concerned. Questions all the time. Colleagues. Customers. No escape. *He'll be fine. Over in weeks.* Pat has no news. Tony's fine. Fighting's not started. Over in a few weeks. Al's listening to BRMB.

'You seen what a fuck-up the police have made on the motorway?' offers Al. 'Torn up Spaghetti Junction, the tools.'

'Where did you hear that?'

'On the wireless. Tried this new traffic scheme, ended up causing six fucking accidents. Six! Plebs.'

'They're always trying to change things those pigs. Clueless tossers, they are. Come join me when you're ready, Al.'

Pat's in the lounge. On the armchair. Having a smoke. Sipping vodka tonic with big ice cubes. Pat's changed again. Black leggings. Red and white polka dot top. Shoulders revealing slender black bra straps. Pat's got her hair tied back. Pat's watching the nine o'clock headlines. Pat can't get away from the news.

'Been looking forward to this all day.'

'You've earned it. Kitchen's looking great. Tony will be made up.'

'Ta.'

'What else you got on?'

'Got a job on for a young couple end of our road. Living room and bedroom. Easy fuckin' money. Three or four days and job done.'

'Hope my sister appreciates how hard you are working.'

'All she's got on her plate is thinking about kids.'

'It's normal. She's broody.'

'It's a fuckin' nightmare.'

'You don't want some little nippers?'

'Yeah. Just not right now. It would do me head in.'

Pat's poured a second glass. Playing with her hair. Smiling. Curled up in the armchair like a giant moggy.

'What about you and Tony, any plans for number two?'

'Talked about it. Tony wants a boy. Another little Blue Nose. Think he was a bit disappointed having a girl first.'

'You been trying?'

'Not really. Something to look forward to when he comes back.'

'Turns out like Tony, he will be a little scrapper.'

'Let's hope not.'

'You're probably right.'

'Off to town tomorrow, Al, getting Lea some stuff from Adams. Let me know if you need owt for the kitchen.'

'Think we're sound.'

Al's had a few drinks. *Attracted to Pat. Shouldn't be. Can't be. Big Tone's missus. Not worth the hassle.* Al hasn't had a boner like this in front of Heather for months. Al's thinking about leaving. Pat offers more vodka. Rude to turn it down.

'Always glad my sister married you, Al. And not that bell-end Steven Baker or some of the others she knocked about with.'

'Not sure there was ever any danger of that.'

'They were dating for a while, remember.'

'Not sure Bakes has ever lived it down.'

'Not sure he has any feelings anyway.'

'Maybe not, but got pride.'

'It's funny. Hev's always been into the guys I've liked. Even when we first started boozing, would always try and compete with me. Or go for their brothers. Sure she liked our Tony at first.'

'You ever liked the blokes she was into?' poses Al.

'Sometimes. Stole one off her once. We've always been like cats and dogs over that sort of thing.'

Pat's wandered off to the toilet. Pat's come back. Moved alongside Al on the couch. Better view of TV. Dallas on. Again. Al wanted to take the conversation further. See if she had liked him. *Have a crack. Couldn't do it. Not Tony's missus. Debts to pay. Drink your drink. Get out.*

'Was a bit surprised when she parked up with you, though.'

'Yeah.'

'She'd always gone for bruisers. Bouncer types, big lads, you know.'

'Saying I'm a wimp?'

'Na, just good-looking.'

'I'll blush.'

Pat found the comment endearing. Al blushed. Pat rubs Al on the arm. Al's got a boner. Pat's being a fox. Sniffing around when her husband's away. Innocent fun. Bit of a male company. Pat's tipsy. Likes having him round. Likes the attention. Al's thinking about moving closer. Blame it on the drink. Al's keen. Phone rings. Game over. Al sees himself out.

***

Al heads to the Den. Pays off Declan. Back in the game. Al's feeling lucky. Al's feeling frustrated. Al's still got a lingering boner. Tommo's there, Chalky's in, couple of new timers, some guys from Sandwell. Connor says take it easy. Don't want to be chasing up debts again. Chalky's taken a beating a few weeks ago. Chalky's back in the game. Al's luck is changing. Al wins first game. Three of a kind. *Fuck that, you Mick twat.* Fifty notes in the bag. Declan's not there. *Probably getting sucked off.*

Al's won the second game. Sixty sheets. *Should go home. Quit when you're winning. Last shot of Irish. Last pint.* Al's glancing at his Timex. Brendan Murphy wants to play snooker. Double or quits. Al's good at snooker. Al always wins. Al breaks. Al screws up on the third red. Al doesn't get back on the table. Murphy take his money. Al's pissed. Al's cursing. Al needs a drink. Al's playing poker again. Al loses two hundred. Al has to borrow. Al's in trouble.

***

'War Threat to World Cup'. Home nations might not go to tournament. War might still be on. *'P&O cruise ship sent to war, holidays of hundreds cancelled'.* Al's doing the Jones's bedroom. University lecturers. New in town. Easy money. Two up, two down. Al takes a break. Tea and a fag. Needs to get the money back. Needs some cash. Al's thinking about Pat. Al needs a wager. Al needs to get back in the game.

***

'Villa in Final Mood'. European Cup Semi-Final. Anderlecht. Al wants to skip it. *Scum.* Some scraps in town. Glasses thrown. Pub brawls. Al calls Tommo. Back to Bradford Street. Quiet night. Not happening. Wednesday night. *Must be slappers' night off.* Head down to Balsall Heath. Cheddar Road, *little Amsterdam.* Ladies of the night. One for Tommo, one for Al. Back to Tommo's place. No room in car. Tommo's in the bedroom seeing to a big blonde. Tommo grunts when he's getting laid. *Not sure how his missus puts up with him. Huge fucking ass, Tommo's bird.* Al's being sucked off by a redhead. Thinking of Pat. *Can't. Tony's missus.*

***

Heather's at Pat's. Hev's bought Leanne Hungry Hippos. Heather's agitated. Barely fitting into her frocks. Longer hours at work. Not just a receptionist anymore. Reports to file. Copying to be done. All a bit too much. Wants things simple. Need the money.

'Al's just in a funny mood at the moment. Always out. Working. Or out with his mates. Pissing me off that he's never home,' whinges Heather.

'Don't be too hard on him. He's working hard. Round here all the time. Making things nice, making an effort for Tony.'

'Doesn't mean he needs to be out on the razzle every night, spending up our money.'

'You two been at it?'

'Not much. Never seems interested.'

'Maybe you need to spice it up a bit. Bit of romance. Give him a reason to stop home.'

'Don't see why it should be me who needs to spice things up.'

'Probably just need something to grab his attention. Blokes are all the same. They need grounding. Least yours is around.'

'Sorry.'

Al's thinking of selling the City. *Two grand for that. Don't need two cars. Heather can take the bus. Two grand. Comfort zone. Can pay off Declan and get back in the game. Get back on a winning streak. Back lucky again.* Al's bumped into Connor at the top of Kitchener Road. Not a coincidence. The Paddy's not happy. Says Declan wants his money. Murphy's hassling Declan for the snooker winnings. Wants it all back.

'He said a week. He'll get it back by the end of the week,' swears Al.

'My boss is not a happy man. You know the frickin' rules,' barks Connor. 'Fifteen percent by Saturday otherwise we'll come and take the fifteen percent for ourselves. And it won't be pretty.'

'I'll be there with the dosh.'

'If you know what's good for you. You remember what happened to Tommo's mate. Saw to him with knuckledusters, now living at the fucking dentist's! And Chalky. Almost became a white man after we'd visited him.'

Two hundred. Plus fifteen percent. Two hundred and thirty quid by tomorrow. Heather's not going to let him hit the savings. Been there before. Heather's got it tied up. *Clever girl.* Al's got eighty quid. Needs cash fast. *Could sell the car. Can't sell the car.* Heather wants the money from the Joneses. Not seen dosh for weeks. *Got to raise cash. Got to raise it fast.* Al calls Tommo. Again. Tommo's pissed. Hard work with his hands. Fixing the M6. Tommo's got a hundred and fifty quid. Wants ten percent back in a week. Al can pay the Micks. Al's off the hook. Tommo's fuming.

***

Final touches to the kitchen. Pat's demanding. Bedroom's next. Pat's going to have to sleep in the spare room. Pat's mentioned getting the living room done. Another hundred quid. Another weekend. Pat's got her half oven. Baking a pound cake. Al's sawing, dusting, screwing, measuring, hammering. Hard work. Al's had five cups of tea. Villa won 1-0. *'Belgians a bore – says Barton'*. Villa close to the final. The Holy Grail of European football. Tony won't be happy. Ship best place for him.

Al's finishing the job. *'We're freedom fighters'*. *'Threat of sea war growing'*. Pat's glued to Top of the Pops. She's been in town. Hit Lewis's. Big bags, spending spree. New skirts, news shoes, bag full of tapes. Chaz and Dave, Bucks Fizz. *Load of shit.*

'I'll come back on Saturday and start the bedroom,' says Al, almost whiningly. 'Kitchen's done. Just needs a clean whenever you got a mo.'

'Thanks, Al, you've done a great job. Looks dead posh.'

Hundred fucking quid. Three weeks work. Charity. And Pat's busy filling her wardrobe.

'You're alright, bab,' assures Al. 'If you can clear the bedroom for Saturday will be sound as a pound. Going to the motor show in the morning, be round in the afternoon. Should take the weekend tops, maybe few nights next week. Got a new job on Cartland Road.'

'Alright, Al, can get some food in Saturday if you want.'

'Just keep making those cakes, grand they were.'

'Argies could have nuclear bomb'. Heather's watching Parkinson. Best Of: Ali. Astaire. Midler. She's had her hair done at her sister's. *Scrubs up half decent.* Made an effort. Dinner's in the oven. Wine glasses on the table. Best napkins are out. *Heather's after something.* Al's flicking through *The Mail.* '*Relegation Blues'.* Broadhurst says we're down. *Fucking Broadhurst. Captain cunt.*

'What's with the special effort?'

'Thought you needed cheering up. Not going out, are ya?'

'Not tonight.'

'Got those chicken things you like. And some roasties. It will be ready in half an hour. Have a scrub if you want.'

Al heads for a bath. Trims his chest. Dirty secret. Didn't like those curling hairs. Al's applying fake tanning cream. Al's got more products than his missus. Brut. Conditioner. Gels. Deodorants. Al's little secret. Al's washed. Al feels relaxed. Andy Peebles on the radio. Steven Wright. Bit of music. Bit of Floyd. *Comfortably Numb.* Feels good. Al has a tin in the bath.

Al's out of the bath. Slips into dressing gown. Smells like a film star. Looks better. *Handsome guy.* Al's heading to bedroom to get changed. Heather's there. *Dressed like a fuckin' nurse.* Got the whole costume. Stethoscope and all.

'Surprised?'

'Not half. Where the fuck did you get this? Did you mug the friggin' girl down the surgery?'

'Thought you might like it.'

'Suits yer down to the ground.'

'Don't be fucking shy, you Jessie!'

Al's got the bit between his teeth. Heather's like a new woman. Got no knickers on. Al glides in. Hands against headboard. Heather's screaming. *Fuck me. Fucking harder.* Al's fucking. Al's obliging. *Al's the man.* Heather lets him take her from behind. Al's pumping harder. Looking in the mirror. Looking toned. Heather's cum. Al's thinking about Pat. About that touch. About Saturday.

***

'*It's deadlock*'. US seeking peace. Trying to end the war. '*Birmingham filthy city*'. Needs cleaning up. Litter fines threatened. *Dogs can't shit in parks. Gypsies can shit in parks. Dogs can't. Fucking council.* '*It's No Deal*'. War inevitable. Iron Lady wants to keep talking. Haig says war greatest of all tragedies. *Send in the lads. Blow 'em up.* Come home. Villa fans riot in Europe. Could be thrown out of cup. *Fucking justice. Scum. Tony would be happy.*

Al's in the bedroom. Plastering. House needs blowing up. *Fucking shit hole. Paid eighteen grand. That's only going to buy you a shit hole these days.* Al's drinking tea. Listening to radio. '*Storm delays British attack*'. Two of our warships moving into South Georgia ready to attack. Al turns over. Blues playing Swansea. Relegation points. Al should be there. In the

Railway Stand. Keep right on to the end of the road. Hartford's fucking won it. Big Mick. 2-1. Blues staying up. Villa threatened with cup replay. *Great day.*

Pat's back from shopping. Spending more money. *Opening those envelopes. Could pay for the friggin' bedroom.* Leanne's at her nan's. Been a brat. Pat couldn't cope. End of her tether.

'It's coming on a treat, the bedroom. Reckon I'll have it done by Monday. You going to be alright sleeping in another room? Got space over at ours if you wanna come. Could drop you over, spend the night with Heather.'

'It's kind of you, Al, going to be fine here. Spare room's comfy enough. How long you stopping over?'

'Not much longer. Out with the lads tonight. Down the Hibernian. Celebrate the Blues win. Too fucking rare these days.'

'Want your tea first, keep me company? Seen that they're heading to war, in a storm right now.'

'Yeah, looks like they are moving in. Not fucking around anymore. Say the Falklands will be next after they get this Georgia place or whatever it's called.'

Pat's made cottage pie. Got the plonk out. Says she feels lonely. Worried about Tony. Pat lights up. Pat's crying. Mascara running. Smudged all over her eyes. Al says it will be alright. Al puts his arm round her. Tony will be home. Pat wants to get pissed. Forget about the world. Al's obliging. Finds the vodka. Necks the vodka. Pat says Al's done a great job. Been a rock. Pat wants Al to stay. Pat grabs his cock. Caresses it. *Shouldn't be doing this. Worry about that in the morning.* Al doesn't go out with his mates. Not tonight.

CHAPTER 6
SOLIHULL

(Spring 2009)

Bread's old, week old. Possibly more. Twenty-nine pence corner shop thin sliced white. *Doesn't matter.* Hev's ripping off the mould from the crust. Shakily spreading a heap of strawberry jam polluted with crumbs and curling butter. Milky tea overflowing from an archaic 'I love BRMB' mug. Got the shakes. GP's not prescribing any more valium. Prozac's not working. Been on a cocktail of anti-depressants. *For too fucking long.* Drank half a bottle of Sapphire yesterday afternoon. Neat. Two o'clock late enough in the day to enjoy a quick drink. Nothing better going on. Five o'clock passed out. Hev's cheeks are flushed. Not washed for a few days. Pits pongy and hairy. Dandruff nestles on her shoulders like summer snow on the Matterhorn. Not been outside the house for a week. Stopped counting. Not collected the bills stacked on the porch door. Not spoken to a soul in days.

***

Carter's decided to cycle to work. Lighter mornings, borrowed Rachel's tri-bike, only used once for an event she never finished in Windsor. Hits the canal in Selly Oak. Up through the university, Five Ways, passed ambling Korean students, leaving almost pedestrian barges in their wake, swerving into runners lost in their trance playlists. Carter's enjoying the breeze, even happy to go to work, ignore the plan of attack for a few hours longer, which one of the clan to approach first. Drawing some tiny comfort from having the power to control putting off the inevitable.

Maisy's slumped outside Costa having a café latte and fingering cigarette paper. Carter doesn't like Maisy. *Bad attitude, big mouth.* Carter's feeling open-minded though. Stops for a chat. Small talk. Weekend. Summer music festivals. Projects ahead. Gorman's a twat. Usual stuff. Carter pays, nine stamps on his loyalty card. Free coffee tomorrow.

Carter's engrossed in the music festival flyers. Gorman's off his back. Escaped to Dubai for the week. Rounds of golf and hotel dinners. Treat the missus. Scorching heat on his bald walnut-shaped head. Gives Carter time for extended lunch breaks. Plate of gorgonzola gnocchi, few glasses of Valpolicella. Three weeks before Deepak is hitched. Three weeks in Rajasthan and Goa afterwards. Meeting the extended family. *Hardly a honeymoon.*

'Me and Rach are looking forward to the wedding,' commences Carter, partially lying. 'Sure, it will be different from the usual toss speeches, Pimm's and overcooked chicken with prosciutto wrapped round it.'

'Don't hold your breath, mate!' slams Deepak, necking his wine like a man on borrowed time. He's stressed about installing new servers at work. Always a hint with Deepak that he gets through life bullshitting rather than bravado. His standard response to any crisis is control-alt-delete.

'Why not?' retorts Carter.

'There might not be Pimm's and overcooked chicken but it will still be a sentimental piss up. My family know how to handle their beer and whisky. We don't call our old man McCallan-ji for nothing!'

'Still, I'm sure the service is going to be different and a bit more colourful. Rachel's thinking of getting herself some kind of Hindu outfit. Been talking to a girl at work. Just to warn you guys that a Frida-lookalike will probably show up.'

'Weren't she Mexican?'

'Whatever.'

They smile, order another glass, toast. Usually drinks were reserved for Fridays, although on special occasions they would Skype each other the code word 'JOAM'. Jars On a Monday.

'How's Rachel doing these days? Still on your back?' continues Deepak, eager to change the subject.

'Got a bit better. Had to make some promises, didn't I?'

'Like what?'

Carter sucks the life out of his grapes.

'She wants to me to sort out stuff with my family.'

'Like be nice to your mummy?'

'Basically. Probably that as well but more finding out what happened to certain people and trying to answer a few questions I've always had. She's pissed off at having not met my family. Keeps saying four years is embarrassing.'

'You thinking of looking for your old man?'

'No, got no real interest in meeting him. Never been that curious. If I'm honest though, when Leanne said she saw him about ten years ago, I felt a bit narked.'

Carter recounts the story to an attentive Deepak who's keen to free his mind from fire sacrifices and endless John Lewis gift lists.

'Would like to find out what happened to my dad and my Uncle Alan and perhaps understand why my mum is like she is, maybe build some bridges with my aunt and my cousins,' says Carter, unconvincingly.

'Sounds like a right laugh….'

'It's going to be a bit of a car crash but Rach's probably right, it might go away again and come back and fester. I'm fine not having too much contact with my family, if anything life's better for it, but just want to know a bit more about my own story.'

'Well if you need anyone to talk to and the odd beer or five…'

'Thanks, pal. You'll have your hands full in no time, though.'

Carter heads back to his desk with a dull headache brought on by lunchtime drinking and induced by overcompensating with afternoon espresso shots. His mind drifts freely from his design palette. He's not ready to face the wall that is his mother. To negotiate with her, he needs more information, a more solid base to start from. Carter contemplates visiting Aunt Hev or scratching the surface with his cousin Paul. Same age. Same situation. In a word. No dad and uncle who left, only in reverse order. Paul may have some clues, some frustrations, some suspicions. Something. He's never ever broached the subject with Paul.

Carter opens Facebook. Paul Jeavons. 'Send friend request'. Carter hits okay and sends an adjoining email.

'Hi Paul, just your cousin here. Thought it was about time I found you on this thing even if it seems you are Villa scum. Lol. Haven't seen you in a while, if you're ever in town and fancy a pint then let me know. My shout. Catch ya later boss.'

Carter hopes that Paul was not a regular Facebook checker. That way he could linger for a while waiting for a response and have some time off not thinking about it. At least Rachel would be off his back for a while. He could simply tell her that he's waiting for Paul. In any case, Carter felt he'd done the right thing. Best to approach Paul before meeting those who knew more.

***

Two up, two down. Spending some of their retirement money, the Shirleys. Paul's on a quick stop off in Dorridge. Shirleys just back from a week, staying in a soulless all-inclusive hotel in Miami. Paul's accepted a cup of tea. Too weak and too milky. Leslie Shirley and her neat brown perm and large earrings purchased with the last of her baht from Bangkok airport are giving him the tour of the house. Paul's struck by two things. No dustbins, no books. Leslie says they are not big readers, prefer magazines and *The Sun*. If you need a book, go to the library. Just clutter the house. Paul's drafting a quote, eight new windows, ten percent discount as they went through a friend, three-hundred pound deposit, job done in two weeks. Michael Slater will be round on Monday.

Paul's made it good. Got his dad's talent for building and fixing things but a savvy business brain too. Set up his own company almost three years ago after working for Autoglass at seventeen and then for a DIY company. Specialises in double glazing. Work's gone well. Twenty-six-year-old entrepreneur. Started out on his own but soon had too much work and then hired a few technicians. Michael, Ian and Des The Drunk. They all call him

'The Kid'. Paul concentrates on invoices, paperwork and the initial client meeting. Promised to offer ten percent off any competitive invoice and for word of mouth. Made enough money in the first year to buy a first home. Second year had himself a brand new MG. Target for the third year is turning the two-bedroom flat into a three-bedroom home in time for the wedding. Paul's on target. Paul's always had a good heart but developed a ruthless and focused streak. Nobody's done him any favours, got no favours to return anyone. Borrowed money from the bank, paid it back. Disowned his violent, sadist, lout of a brother doing time for various putrefying crimes. Embarrassed by his mum crippling in self-pity, depression and alcohol. Tried to reason with her, can no longer bear the sight of her. The token weekly visit, sometimes every two weeks. Like going to church for a non-believer. A necessity, not a choice. A philosophy in the spirit of everyone else in the family. Let the roots rot.

Paul's meeting with the Shirleys goes well. His three technicians have a full agenda for the next ten days. More money coming in. In this time of tightening the belt, Paul believes people are investing more in their homes. Paul's preparing to head home in the Land Rover. *'Paul Jeavons Double Glazing and Fitting'* engraved on both sides. Checks his Blackberry. Message from Facebook. Friend request from Facebook. Dan bloody Carter. Paul still thinks of Dan as a wiry, bowl-headed ten-year-old wearing oversized football tops with knobbly knees and rolled up socks.

Paul's on 398 friends. Challenged his mate Betsy a month ago to a free Chinese for whoever got to 400 friends first. Betsy's on 392. Paul's obliged to say yes. Friend request accepted. Paul's not a big emailer. Not when it's not business. If it is not instantaneous gratification like an SMS, Messenger message or a Facebook wall post he's not interested. He drops Carter a note back. *'Here's my new number. Give me a call for that beer'.* Paul's assuming the beer will never arrive, it's just that fake, bullshit talk people adopt when wanting a new Facebook friend.

Carter's got himself a new friend. Carter's had about fifty-four minutes of freedom. Now the ball has been smacked firmly back in his court. Carter leaves his desk. Made poor progress with the music festival fliers. Head still spinning from lunch. Heart skipping a space. Perspiring. Heads out to the front of the Colmore Row offices. Registers Paul's number, calls. Cuts the call before it connects. Does the same thing two or three times. After five minutes leaning against a lamppost outside the front of the office watching bony and impossibly high-heeled estate agent receptionists smoke and drink lattes from tall cardboard cups, he sends a message. *'Hi Paul, thanks for getting back to me. How about Thursday? After work? Can meet you up by Snow Hill if you want?'*

Carter's proposed The Hotel Du Vin. Thinks Paul will be out of his comfort zone.

***

Carter arrives early. Always does. Advantage of never having much to do. Paul's late. Carter doesn't know what to order. Starts with a dry white. Does the job. Loosens his mood. Tray of khaki-coloured olives and soft nuts provided. Carter's about to order a second glass as Paul marches in. Paul's lost a bit of weight but has still retained a chubby man's posture which accentuates his paunch. And the money's led to in-your-face designer labels, a Ralph Lauren polo shirt with a massive emblem and the number 7, a pair of Diesel jeans sagging at the heel and oak-coloured loafers better suited to a man twenty years older. Paul exerts himself immediately, offering Carter a firm handshake, orders a gin and tonic, tells Carter he was here last week and brings a warning that he has to be gone in an hour. Thursday is take-away night with Carmen.

Carter and Paul are not used to talking as adults. Spent first nine to ten years of their lives side by side with Lee, the famous three, kicking footballs around the green spaces of Selly Park and Kings Heath, re-enacting Wrestle Mania, demanding drive-thru McDonald's, running across railway tracks, throwing darts and conkers at each other. As Heather and Pat's relationship became strained and Hev moved across the West Midlands to various homes she could never settle in, the twins and Carter saw less of each other. The odd token appearance at grandparents'. As the teenage years advanced even these meetings became more irregular. The twins got involved with a bad crowd. Lee became terminally infected, Paul got himself out.

There's still some scant acknowledgment of a shared childhood but as adults they've taken different roots and Paul's displeasure in Aunt Pat abandoning his mother led to him, albeit subconsciously, distancing himself from Carter by association.

'Was a bit surprised to hear from you, Dan mate,' starts Paul.

'Thought it was time I got in touch. Been a while, wanted to see what you're up to. Saw our Leanne at the weekend and we were talking about you. Said I'd try and grab a beer and catch up.'

'How's she doing? Not seen her in a while either.'

'Grand, she's still at the salon, nagging at Leon all the time, they're trying for another kid but not much joy in that department. Otherwise same old. How's things with you?'

'Sound. Proper sound. Business up and running for two years now, going great guns, feet on the ground but been non-stop this year. Can't get enough work, man. Car's even hoping it slows down so we can take a holiday. Trying to get a bigger place for after the wedding. Best thing I've ever done. Business, that is. Wedding's a fucking rope around my neck! Things good though, thinking about all these plebs who've gone to uni, got a debt, can't get a job, nothing like real life work experience for getting you in the right direction.'

Paul has no problems talking about his business. He carries on for about ten minutes to the point where Carter's almost booked himself double glazing. It's the only passage of conversation which halts Paul from checking his BlackBerry, sending texts, giggling into his phone and half listening to Carter's waffle about Gorman and Rachel. Gradually Carter, fearing that time is elapsing, seizes on the opportunity.

'Actually also wanted to see you to go over some family things.'

'What's up? Everything okay?'

'Yeah, it's just....'

Carter bumbles for a while, trying to find an anecdote which would ease him into the conversation more readily.

'All of these twenty year Hillsborough commemorations got me thinking about things.'

Paul's brow widens. He starts twisting his glass, avoiding eye contact. On the defensive.

'Know what you mean but it's in the past, though,' snaps Paul, 'no point going over that. And it's our old man who went missing, not yours. Think enough pain has been caused. Sometimes things are better left as they are.'

Paul's very definite. Clearly bitter with Carter for bringing it up. Carter's not sure where to look.

'From my point of view, I've never really understood what happened. Not just to your dad but also why my old man walked out, why our parents fell out, why nobody gets on and everyone is bitter. Just been….'

'It's best not knowing. Spent ten years living with Mom driving herself and us up the wall with theories about where Dad is. Comes a point where there's nothing you can do. It can either ruin your life like Mom and Lee, or you get on with it like me.'

There's a sense of self-satisfaction in Paul's voice, like's he's come through the tunnel and prospered whilst everyone else stinks of vile shit because of their own inherent cowardish weakness.

'It's just, I think about it a lot and want to try and find some things out for myself,' tries Carter.

'Don't bother,' retorts Paul.

Paul's become quite angry. Necked the last of his drink. Like he's on the point of walking out and probably removing Carter as a Facebook friend by the time he gets to the exit. Bob Marley's *Redemption Song* is the only thing keeping the atmosphere somewhat calm.

'I can understand why you're being so hostile but this thing is affecting my relationship with Rach. She's from a conventional family where everything is rosy and assumes every family is and needs to be. It's hard to explain to her. I promised I would look into things.'

'She's going to have to understand that the subject is closed.'

'It's not just her. I've got to the point where I can't talk to Mom, where I look back into my childhood and even where there are some good things, I just can't appreciate them anymore. Like it was all a fuckin' lie. Or some dirty secret. I need to know why she's like she is if I am going to accept how we are.'

'I know nothing more than you, mate. I just know that I don't want anything to do with what happened. Nobody can tell you anything. Dad went missing. If he's still alive, he doesn't want to be found, so fuck him. If he's not, then the chances are that his debts caught up with him and whoever did it is long gone or far away.'

'It's not just about your old man, it's about mine as well.'

'Well talk to your mom about that, she must know why he fucked off.'

'She's always refused to talk about it. From the moment he left to today. Mention his name and she throws a spanner. Now it's like this almighty taboo that you never bring up. Mom is just in her own limited fucking world, devoid of anything to do with the past. It's like she was born in 1990.'

'Your mom is a funny old bird, that's for sure. Got her own agenda. Don't want to be out of place but she's not been loyal to our mom. Didn't stick around and help her out once the going got tough and now Mom is a fucking mess and beyond help.'

Paul's still steaming. Carter feels it best to nod and agree, even if there is a part of him feeling he should defend his mother's honour. He can't be bothered and hasn't been for a long time.

'How often do you see her?' prods Carter.

Paul exaggerates. 'Once a week mostly. Sometimes pop in when doing a job. I've tried to help her out as well but she's brainwashed and going through fucking depression, taken every anti-depressant going, she never eats, sure she is drinking loads and has been in and out of trouble with the police. Even got barred from the local. She ruined my childhood, can't let her ruin my adult life.'

To Carter's amazement, Paul gestures for another drink, anything to alleviate his flustered state. He's sweating at the temples to the point a vein is bulging. Carter's a bit more relaxed now that there's been some dialogue. He orders a third hefty glass of Sauvignon Blanc.

'But why did our mothers fall out, if they were such good mates before? You'd think both losing their husbands at the same time would bring them closer?'

'Not sure, just remember growing up, Mom used to curse Aunt Pat, said she was always jealous, never enjoyed Mom having any success, was already seeing other men the minute your dad was gone, that she never seemed to have any sympathy for our dad going missing. Mom used to call her a selfish cow. Just repeating what she used to say, like.'

'Don't worry, she is.'

'Mate, there's not much I can do,' continues Paul, 'If you want to see our mom go and see her. Just warn you that it's not going to be pretty and that you're not going to get any sense out of her. She'll spin you round like a tornado.'

'What about Lee?'

'He wouldn't ever know he had a dad. Chased the dragon for too long.'

Paul's receives a text and motions to leave. Shakes Carter's hand in a manner to suggest that he doesn't want to sit through that again. Mentions sending an invite to December's wedding. Paul's hoping that's the next time Carter shows up in his life. *Stick fifty quid on the John Lewis wedding list, enjoy your apricot panna cotta, drink your free champagne and fuck off.*

***

It's six o'clock in the morning, feels like eleven. Hev's been asleep, cold, for fourteen hours. Cocktail sponsored by Prozac and Smirnoff, with a scrap of dope lifted from a guy at the pub. Hev's not worked for four months. Temping jobs dried up as quickly as her reputation. More days off than on. Sending out memos with typos. Answering the phone with the wrong company name. Unwashed hair. Holes in tights. Unpresentable. Hev's been home since. Unless there's a supermarket trip, walk to the pub or fish n' chip shop, she's always in. Passes out early evening, wakes up early next morning. Morphs in front of children's morning TV. Sometimes has a joint at breakfast, attempts to read the paper in the morning, still got a feeling for a crossword. Beans on toast for lunch. Every day. Washing up only done when a pan needs cleaning. Piled up for weeks. Damp clothes everywhere. Befriended some of the older guys from the pub. Wes the window cleaner. Red cheeks. Fluffy white hair blowing off his head either side of his bald crown. Picks his ear wax and devours it. Wears football shorts ten months a year. Gets a sloppy blow job from Hev every Wednesday. Brings round a bottle of gin and a tenner. Hev's no longer interested in the tenner.

Hev's not even slept in bed. Crumpled on the coach, fell on the floor during the night. Glass coffee table full of cup stains, crumbs, fag ends, bottle tops and a spot of chalky powder which could either be coke Wes has left behind or sugar. Hev tastes. It's sugar. There's a note by the phone. *Dan visiting Saturday morning.* Hev's memory is soggy. *Who's Dan?* House full of post-its. Hev checks the TV for the date and time. Dan had called Thursday lunch time. In between hangovers. Hev had retained some composure. Agreed to him coming round, spot of lunch, no questions asked. Facing a second note. *'Dan, 11.30, Sat'*, she has no idea how these three items are connected. Hev's got a few hours to get things together. Late morning usually the only sober, productive part of the day. Only time when brain cells receive some oxygen. Only time when she is not numb to the pain. On the mantelpiece lies a wedding photo, a snap of Al on a Spanish beach in 1988 in sharp fake Ray Bans and caressing a Pina Colada, pictures of Paul and Lee don't develop from the age of twelve, last time Hev had any real control over them.

***

Carter's taken Rachel for breakfast in town before heading on the train over to Solihull. Reading *The Guardian* more from Rachel's influence. Likes the Saturday *Guide* section. Rachel offered to drop him over in Solihull and do some shopping but Carter appreciates the downtime on the train before heading over. Gather his thoughts. Rehearse his questions. Prepare what Heather's going to say. Carter picks up some sunflowers and a small box of Thorntons Belgian chocolates, hoping the presents will entice his aunt into giving some answers.

Carter's never seen Hev's place in Solihull. Been there four years, long after the kids grew up. Moved around all over the Midlands. Had a fella for a while over in Hockley Heath but he got bored, Sutton Coldfield, Dorridge, King's Norton, even back in Erdington for a while when Lee got messed up. Leanne lives a mile and a half from Hev, in a soulless but comfortable three-bedroom flat, but never visited, never bumped into each other. Neighbours yet strangers.

Hev's not in the leafy part of Solihull. Made a bit of money in the property boom, before the alcohol became the comfort rather than a comfort, and got a narrow two up and two down with a small garden. Carter waits for a few minutes at the door. Hev's says she's 'coming' from afar and eventually opens up. She looks like an old whore. About fifteen years older than Carter remembers. His vision of Aunt Heather always of a pretty but slightly plump thirty-something with a kind heart and cupboard bursting with sweets and fridge full of pop. Hev's face is masked by a wall of horrifically misplaced make-up, her shaggy perm the result of hair hurriedly and unsuccessfully dried. She's chosen an outfit unsuited to lounging round the house in or for welcoming your estranged nephew—high heels, tight jeans and a white silk work shirt with coffee stains on the sleeve.

'You look well,' says Carter, lying through his teeth.

'You too, bab, could have had a shave for your favourite aunt.'

Carter's been carrying a bit of stubble for a few months and a small strip of hair between his bottom lip and chin. Contrasted with the navy seal cut. Feels it makes him look a bit more interesting. And older. Hev invites him into the living room which has clearly been tidied in a hurry. A heap of old papers and magazines have been hidden behind the couch. The kitchen is visible from the living room and although the dishwasher is running at full pelt, there is still a pile of washing up to be done. The carpet is grimy, windows not been cleaned for months and a thick layer of dust on every surface. Carter vaguely recalls Hev's homes always reeking of polish and being fastidiously clean.

Hev offers him a cup of Nescafe. Carter accepts, not wanting to be difficult although he always almost drinks espressos or filter coffee. Hev's got some custard creams which look about three days old and some of those Kipling French Fancies which expired a few weeks ago. Carter plumps for a few soft jammy dodgers. Hev's talking rubbish, babbling on about being busy and not having time to clean up. Says she was out with mates last night and has been working again. Carter's heard a different story from Paul.

For an hour they chat away like old friends, Hev clearly entertained by the company, talking Rachel, work, the Brown government, Leanne and how well Paul is doing for himself. Lee barely gets a mention. Hev talks about yesterday's TV—although she's waffling on about programmes shown days, weeks earlier. Hev seems to liven up a bit and become more coherent across the hour. There's a sadness in her eyes which belies the false smile penetrating the heavily glossed pink lipstick. Carter's decided that he will try and ease into the conversation at the right time, rather than making the waffled statement he presented to Paul. Says he's in the area and was just passing by, nothing special about the visit.

Hev's offered to buy Carter pub lunch but he prefers to stay on home ground. As Hev prepares ham, cheese and Branston sandwiches and pulls a few cans of lager out of the fridge, Carter seizes the opportunity to inspect the photos on the mantelpiece.

'Paul's changed quite a bit since he was a kid, hasn't he?'

'Yeah, not the little roly-poly he used to be! Lee was always the skinny one and think it used to affect our Paul growing up but he's done well for himself. Takes after his old man.'

Carter feels that it's the moment to bring Al into the conversation, skilfully working the situation to his favour.

'Been thinking about Uncle Al recently, with all that Hillsborough stuff.'

Hev's wandering in carrying the plates on a Cadbury's tray and pops the thick sandwiches and two open cans of lager on the table. Carter finds it slightly strange seeing a woman in her fifties sip Carling from a can.

'I've tried to avoid all of that,' replies Heather, 'even though it was on the box all the time. Only so much you can take. Just provides so many reminders of the day.'

'We were round that day, me and the twins, weren't we?'

'Yeah, Pat brought you kids round. You'd been playing football, remember giving you all a right thick ear for bringing mud in the house!'

'Were we always trouble as kids?'

'No, just normal, nice kids. Paul and Lee got a bit wild in their teenage years. Probably a bit my fault for being lost.'

Hev's words tail off. It's the most sober she's been for weeks although the beer is giving her the taste for something stronger and although the conversation is uncomfortable, she's happy somebody wants to bring it up rather than treating her like a parasite.

'I remember Al more than my old man, that being a few years later and all of that,' replies Carter.

'Can imagine so, you were round our place a lot as well especially after your dad left. Your mom was moping around for a while and doing her own thing a lot so we took care of you and Leanne for a bit.'

'What was my old man like?'

'It's going back twenty five years, sure he would have changed!'

'What's that mean?'

'He was a man's man, your dad. Bit of a hard man, always frightening people, always life and soul of the party, liked a drink but if I'm honest I never really liked him. He could be selfish and aggressive and had a short fuse and no bloody patience. Plus, he treated women like shit.'

'Why do you think he left?'

Hev gazes out the window, perhaps looking for somewhere to escape, but Carter feels she is trying to find words which are becoming harder to express.

'Think he found some other woman and pissed off.'

Hev's definite but at the same time not that convincing. 'Think' being the significant part of what she said. Carter doesn't reply.

'Your dad was even stranger when he came back from the war and around the time you were born. Seemed to become even more aggressive but also distant. He joined the police for a while. The Tony Cole we knew would never have been a copper but being in the army seemed to discipline him.

Not sure how long he became a copper for. Know some of his mates weren't impressed. I've not seen your dad though since '87.'

'Was he different to Uncle Al?'

'Chalk and cheese in terms of looks, sorry, love! You take after your mom anyway. Your dad was a beast, those piercing eyes, big hairy moustache, paunch, he was like a bear. Al was a good-looking fella, liked to stay in shape, never had problem having girls…..'

Hev tails off, swallowing a harsh reminder of Al's adventures with various other women, the ones she chose to ignore and the ones she never knew about….

'…..but he was a good man. Very funny. Was a good dad, like….'

'What do you really think happened, Aunt Hev?'

Carter can't believe the way the words came out but at the same time relieved with his own unexpected directness. Silence beckoned for fifteen seconds.

'He was murdered, Dan. By who I don't know. But he's dead. And if you don't mind, any theories I have will stay with me and we will stop talking here.'

Carter survives another fifteen minutes of stilted, light banter. Happy he'd seen Hev but depressed at her state and ultimately not being able to leave knowing much more than he started with, perhaps aside from Hev's disdain for his father.

Hev returned to the flat beer which became a bottle of Smirnoff and Sunday morning.

CHAPTER 7
KINGS HEATH

(May – June 1982)

'*HMS Hermes Gone To Action Stations*'. Al's watching The World of Golf. Supping a can. Mind not on the tube. Not even enjoying the lager. Headache. Hungover. Carries on supping regardless. Hev's in bed. Been down for days. Al's not been home. Al's not been grounded. Al's not spoken to Pat. Not since Sunday morning. Crawling out of bed before sunrise. As the neighbours spilled in from the clubs. Covert. *Should never have done it. Tony's wife. Tony's at war.*

Al's finishing the bedroom tomorrow. Got to face Pat. More work to finish. *Forget it ever happened.*

***

Lounge door still needs fixing. Garden's a mess. Never ending job. Pat better have more envelopes. Money needs to come in. Pat's holding a telegram. Tony's well. Ready to strike. Missing you. And the kid. Al's up in the bedroom. Nothing but the sound of the radio. Nicole—*A Little Peace*. McCartney and Wonder—*Ebony and Ivory,* Bucks Fizz—*My Camera Never Lies*. Bit of Ed Doolan. Blues rebuilding. '*Salute To Saunders—Now The Hard Work Will Begin At St Andrew's*'. No struggle next season. *So they say.* Pat's left a cup of tea at the door. Pat's downstairs. On the phone. Playing with Leanne. Baking. Pat's not coming upstairs. Pat's quiet. *It never happened. Not with Tony's wife.* Al lets himself out. Back at the weekend.

***

Wayne Cole's left a message for Al. Busy doing deliveries. Local pick-ups. Not left the Black Country, Wayne. Not a converted Brummie like Tony. Supports the Baggies to piss off his old man and brother. Mad about his drums. Getting married next year. To Shelley Smith. Strawberry blonde hair. Buck teeth. Trap that's been round every dick in Wolverhampton. Tony's left Wayne some money. Emergency funds. Worst case scenario cash. Tony's told Wayne to bring some over. Money for the house. Al's doing a grand job. Wayne's going to meet Al on Saturday. Over at Pat's. Bringing some money, lending some tools, got some furniture. Don't tell Pat. It's going to be a surprise. Cheer her up.

***

'Fleet Stands By To Strike'. Time For Peace Running Out'. 'It Looks Grim - Says Thatcher'. Al's nervous. Diary is empty. Few hours here. Few hours there. Quiet week. Put ads in the papers. Been a few weeks. Al's bored. Al's spending money. Money he's not got. Last year not enough hours in the day to do all of the jobs. Now nothing. *Fat fuckin' zero. Nothing aside this fuckin' charity work.* Hev's at work and asked for work to be done around the house. Spare bedroom for a kid. Bit of tiling. Tidy the yard. Erect a new fence. Al can't be bothered. Not at home. Not right now. Al needs to keep his mind away from it. Away from Pat. Away from Pat's slender thighs. Away from the wrath of Tony Cole. *It never happened.*

Al's back to the grind. The silent walls. Leanne's tears. Leanne's screams. No drinks. No dinner. Finish at five. Off home. Home to Heather. Baby maker.

***

Al's got his head down. Stripping the walls. Got the roller out. Pat's at the door. Pussy cat Pat. Smiling. Pat's gassing again.

'You heard the news, Al?'

'What's that, bab?'

'Steven Baker's been arrested. That trouble at the Baggies the other night.'

'Might have known it. Sounded like the sort of ruck he'd be part of.' Al's avoiding eye contact.

'Says in *The Mail*, forty-seven of them nicked, all kinds of shenanigans. Glad Tony's been seeing less of him of late.'

'He's an animal, that bloke, nothing more to say on the subject. Some time in the slammer will probably do him some good. Do the rest of us some good too.'

Pat nods. Pat displays a faint smile. Pat's never been a fan of Tony's eclectic phonebook of arm-wrestlers, nutcases and hard jobs. That's why Pat likes Al. Al's not a brute. *Good-looking bloke, Al.*

'Tony's been in touch, Al. And sent a telegram to his mom and dad as well. He knows it's making me really happy having the home done up. He's asked if you could finish a few things, give the spare room a lick of paint, do up Leanne's room and the front porch. You'll have a nice cheque coming your way.'

'Happy to oblige, Pat, things are a bit quiet right now so can even come in during the week when you're at work, get it finished. Just leave me the key and things. Will be out of your way when you and Lea get home. Keep the house all tidy, not me making a racket all of the time.'

Pat's looking displeased.

'Not trying to avoid me, are you, Al?'

Al's uncomfortable. Al can't make eye contact. Al's mind's gone blank.

'No, bab. Just thought you'd want the job done quicker. It'll also help me free me weekends for the summer. If something comes up, then I'll take it, otherwise I'll be here in the week.'

'Coz Saturday night, Al. Nothing happened. We've agreed about that, yeah. We were just a bit pissed up. I don't remember what happened. Just remember that we had a few drinks and then you went home. If I need a cry then there's nothing wrong with that. No need to bring it up, nothing happened, so we've got nothing to be ashamed about. Have we, Al?'

'No, bab, no need to bring it up. Was wrecked myself. Don't remember a thing.'

Pat's cold. Pat's in denial. Al's crushed. Al remembers everything. Pat's hands on his cock. Pat's warm, vodka-fuelled mouth attacking his throbbing bell end. Pat bent over the stairwell screaming enjoyment. Pat's compliments. Pat's cuddles. Pat riding on top. From behind. Watching her pert arse straddle his hard cock. Al didn't sleep. Al doesn't feel guilty. Al wants to do it again.

Wayne always seems shorter than Al remembers. Wayne's got Tony's few good qualities. Dry humour and hard work. But Wayne's got a heart. Short and squat. Huge forearms. Means well. Wayne's offering a set of garden furniture. From a delivery. Left one place. Didn't arrive in another. Things happen. Things go missing. Picked up a heavily chipped, granite garden sculpture of a Greek god. Couple of chairs. An outdoor picnic table. Pat's made up. Wayne's got shelving. Al's got to put it up. Wayne slaps Al on the back. Good to see you, mate. Wayne slips Al an envelope. Pat's not seen. Three hundred quid. *Fucking sound. Bit for Hev. Bit for a wage. Couple of drinks. Fucking sound.*

'Let's just say I've been looking out for me sister-in-law,' boasts Wayne.

'You're a star, Wayne. Come and have a quick drink before you get on your way,' shouts Pat.

Wayne's having a can. One of Al's. Wayne's had a few already. On his way over. Wayne's got a gig tonight, drumming over at Smethwick social. Cover band—AC/BC. Invites Al and Hev. Al makes an excuse. *Night out with the missus.*

'Is that your motor outside, Al? The Cortina. Nice set of wheels. Pat must be looking out for you with all this decorating.'

'Can't complain, had a lot of jobs over Christmas. Made some fucking decent cash for a change, decided to get some new wheels, that way Hev could take the City to work.' Lying through his gambling teeth.

'Got a note from Tony. He's looking out for you Pat, even from down there. Looks like it's going to kick off soon, get messy, especially now that Seaking's gone missing.'

The room's hushed. Pat's contemplating her husband at war. Wayne's brought up the wrong subject. Al's got the money. Al's hoping Tony's not coming back.

Wayne's got some more stuff. Bit more shelving. Nice coffee table. Bedside lamp. Spic and span. Brand new. In this part of town in the week. Got a delivery down in Northfield. Pat lends him a spare key. Wayne can let himself in. Wayne's off. Back in his van to Smethwick.

***

Pat's gone and got *The Mail*. Not good news. *'British Felgate Sunk—Nott'*. *Shit*. *'HMS Ardent Sunk—20 Missing'*. *Shit*. Tony's not on Ardent. Tony's on Hermes. Hermes not too close to the action. Tony's okay. Pat's framed Newsweek. Tony's vessel on the front. '*The Empire Strikes Back'*. Pat's worried about the dead. Al's not interested. Switched on the TV. Cup Final. Extra time. Spurs v QPR. Al's not worried about Tony. Not yet.

Hev's on the phone. Pat's being charming. *Guilty conscious.* Worried about Tony. Bearing up well. Girls make a cinema date. *Life of Brian* rerun. Al's looking after Lea. Thursday night. Cup Final Replay.

***

Al's plodded all week. *Prison sentence nearly over.* Bedroom's done. Leanne's bedroom close. Door can wait. Garden can wait. Al's got some work coming in. Hev's called. Colleague needs a new kitchen fitted. Good money. Guaranteed cash in hand. Al's almost done with Pat. Al's going to make himself some lunch. Cheese and Branston. Cup of tea. Take the weight off. Door opens. Pat's back from work early.

'Wasn't expecting you back, Pat,' begins Al.

'Swapped a shift with a colleague. She's got a hospital appointment later in the week so going to work a full day on Friday and she's covering me for today. Thought I'd get some shopping done this afternoon and a few other things. Our Leanne's stopping off at her mate's after playgroup.'

'Wanna sandwich, Pat? Made myself a cheese and Branny if you want some.'

Pat's takes a glance at the sandwich. Cheese sliced thicker than the bread. Branston seeping through the thin white slices. Pat declines.

Pat's talking about some film. *On Golden Pond.* Or something. Says it's romantic. Al's thinking about the Villa. In the final of the Big Cup. *Villa can't win the Big Cup.* Two days to go. *Villa can't win the Big Cup. Life won't be worth living.*

Al's sandpapering the door. Garden to do last. Summer days ahead. Few tins, bit of real work. Sun on the back. Al can get his top off. Door's nearly done. Pat's gone missing. Al's finished the door. Good as new. Add a knocker and number. Dustbin of a house starting to look proper. Al hears a cry. Pat needs help.

Pat's in the newly decorated bedroom. Pristine. Door's ajar. Al knocks. Pat says come in. Pat's wearing nothing. Nothing but her knickers.

'Haven't stopped thinking about you last time, Al.'

Al's aghast. Al's dick is erect in an instant. Al's tearing off his belt. Trousers down his ankles before Pat could blink.

'We'd better use some of these this time, Al.'

Al grabs the box, puts it on the dresser. Pat's rolling around in the sheets. Big smile. Curling fingers massaging her thighs and opening up her black lacy knickers.

'Thought you wanted to agree that nothing happened?'

'I did for a few days. But if we've done it once, no harm in doing it twice. Think we can both keep a secret. I enjoyed your cock too much to not want it again.'

'Me too. You've been driving me crazy ever since.'

Pat's turned the photo of Tony around. Pat's washed. *Smells of coconut butter or vanilla.* Al smells of man. Of work. Of paint. Of varnish. Al preferred not using a johnny. Pat's got Al wearing a rubber. Al's inside before he knows it. Al's ramming Pat. One arm pressed against the headboard, the other on the bed. Pat's sucked his cock. Teased him. Al's inside. Ramming fast. Pat's cum early. Pat's screaming. Al's about to cum. Al's trying to hold it in. *Pat's gorgeous.* Al wants this to go on forever. Pat's flinched. Pat's heard the door.

Wayne Cole's let himself in.

'Anyone home?'

Wayne's wandering around. Wayne's seen the varnished door and Al's tools. The half-eaten sandwich. Noticed Pat's Mini parked outside.

'I'm home, Wayne. Al's just fixing something in the bedroom. Will be down with you in a sec.'

Al's cum on himself. Al's thrown the condom in the bin. Al's got cum on his leg. Pat's rushed to put her clothes on. Al's flushed. Pat's made the bed. Made it badly. Pat's cursing.

Wayne shouts from the bottom of the stairs. 'Got you those chest of drawers for the bedroom and a couple of other bits. Long mirror, if you want one.'

'Ta, love. Al's just mending the window. He'll be down in a second. Give you a hand with all of this.'

Al's trying to look like's he's been working. Al's opened the window. Al's not got tools. Al's rushed out of the bedroom. Al's checked his zip. Al greets Wayne. Al's still got spunk traces on his hand. Al and Wayne lift the items upstairs. Chest of drawers is heavy. Takes a few goes on the long narrow steps and low ceiling. Turn at the top. Al's out of breath. Al offers to leave it out of the bedroom. Need to clear some stuff out before. Wayne's having none of it. Wants to finish the job. Drawers go in the bedroom. Al's panicked. Trying to get Wayne out of there. Wayne's impressed with the job. White walls. Lots of light. Brand new carpet. Good job. Wayne's heading out. Wayne's stalled. Wayne's seen the johnny wrapper and a few tissues. Wayne's froze. Says nothing. Wayne's in a rush to get out. Wayne leaves.

Pat's cold again. Icy. Like the Queen of Narnia. Long drags on a Silk Cut. Lights a second before the first one's finished. Pat's nervy. Too close to call.

'We can't take risks like that anymore, Al. Would have been the end for both of us. If Tony ever found out, we'd both be dead.'

Al's quiet. Al agrees. Al's still gutted he didn't cum inside Pat.

'No worries, bab, we just got caught away in the passion. Think once the work is done it will be a lot easier for us both.'

Pat's taking another long drag. Pat's caught herself in the new mirror in the kitchen. Places fag to make a Q-shape in the ashtray. Applies some gloss.

'I'd like to see you again, Al. Sex with Tony is about as charming as with an ogre. Just think we should do it somewhere else, away from home, just for a few more weeks. Can't stop thinking about you.'

'We can always take the car out for a spin. Over at Hollywood bypass. Or down in Lickeys, Barnt Green or somewhere like that. Somewhere secluded.'

'Was thinking of something a bit more romantic than a car, Al? Maybe get a room somewhere. Just a bit of fun for a few weeks. You'll be finished in the house this week anyway.'

Pat heads out to get Lea. Al's working on the garden. Al can barely lift a slab. Al's starting to feel guilty. Guilty about Hev. Guilty about Tony. Worried what Wayne might have seen.

Wayne's back in the van. Speeding back to Smethwick. Wayne's trying to find an explanation. Al's had a posh wank on the job. Al's had some bird there. Pat's fucked somebody else. Wayne's thinking back. Pat looked like she'd thrown on her clothes. Looked nervous. Al was dishevelled. Bed barely made. Johnny wrapper on top of the bin. Two of them fucking when the cat's away. Wayne's got to block it out. Wayne's not taking the risk telling Tony what he doesn't want to hear.

***

'The last moments—ablaze and dying. Frigate HMS Antelope bombblasted'. Pat's got the box on. Watching Brian Hanrahan. Pat's smoked a load. Two boxes. Pat's not eaten. Pat's had some gin. Pat's stressed. Pat's worried about Tony. Pat's feeling sick. Sick with herself. Pat picks up the phone. Calls Hev, asks for Al about the house. Al's in. Al's feeling guilty. Pat tells Al the game's off. Blowing hot and cold. Finish in the garden and bugger off. Pat's already seen what Tony's hands are capable of.

Talk of propaganda victory. *'Red Alert—Argentina's Independence Day'*. Tony's in the firing line. Al's out of it. Al hopes Tony's boat is sunk. Al's supporting the Argies.

Al's lovestruck. Hev's suspicious. Down about lack of work coming in. Lack of money to spend. Bills to pay. Depressed reading the Villa preview. *'Villa all fit and ready'*. Villa twenty-four hours from being the crème of Europe. Al's never liked the Germans so much.

Al's off to finish the garden. Pat's out. Out all day. Double shift. Al's headed upstairs. Sprayed some of Pat's perfume. Looked at her knickers. Stared and swore at the snap of Tony. Headed downstairs. Lawn's mowed. Fence nearly erected. Shed built for Tony. Keep the chainsaw and the knuckledusters pristine. Al's hoping Tony's not coming home. Al's headed out. William Hill. Few wagers. Fiver. 8-1. Doncaster. Three quid. Bayern Munich. 1-0. Horse comes in. Anxious night ahead in Rotterdam.

'HMS Coventry Is Sunk'. Sister ship of HMS Birmingham. Twenty deaths estimated. Only *The Mail* could have a war reporter called Stanley Slaughter, jokes Al. Al's hoping Hermes is going to be blown up. Sunk. Tony with it. But Hermes is not even in the action. Tony got the easy gig. Al's fidgety. Quick pint in the Hibernian. Quicker chaser. Jameson. About to head out. Then over to Tommo's to watch the Villa lose. *Villa can't win. Not tonight.*

Al's taken the Cortina over to Tommo's in Longbridge. *Fucking sty, Tommo's maisonette.* Tommo's just back from a shift at Rover. Gavo's already there. Nursing his measly bag of weed. Butler's there too. *The lanky fuck.* Four Blue Noses. Twenty-four cans. Stash of weed. Four fish. Four chips. Four mushy peas. One result needed.

Brian Moore's waffling on. Butler's up and down. Shouting at the TV. *Come on, you fucking Krauts. Payback for fucking bombing the shit out of us.* Caught between a rock and a hard place. *Villa against The Krauts. Can be no winner.* Rimmer's off. Creaked his neck. Spink's warming up. Spink's on. *Fat fuck. Who the fuck is Spink?* Butler's spitting out his chips. Butler's got his fist raised. Butler's shouting Spunk at the TV.

Bayern are pressing but Spink's equal. Butler's thrown his can at the TV. Gavo's having a joint. Tommo's got his hand down his trousers, massaging his nuts. Spink's saved from Durnberger. From Rummenigge From Mathy. *Villa have done fuck all.* Villa are going to lose. *Villa can't win the Big Cup.*

Bayern are dominating. Durnberger's close again. Breitner's running the game. Not seen Morley. Not seen Withe. Villa are not going to win. Villa are being outplayed.

Swain's cleared off the line. Hoeness has missed a sitter. Villa are doing nothing. Al's had a few drags on the weed. Boys want to get some action later on. Al's not keen. Al's had enough for one week. Al's on his sixth can. Lost on the weed and the beer. *Villa can't win.*

'Shaw, Williams, prepared to venture down the left. There's a good ball in for Tony Morley. Oh, it must be and it is! It's Peter Withe'. *Peter fucking Withe.* Room's silent. Gavo's dropped his can. *Peter fucking Withe. Fucking Krauts. Good for nothing.* Tommo says he's going out for a hard shag. Butler's moaning. Xenophobic babble. Butler doesn't know who he wants to lose.

Bayern have scored. Roar of cheers. Linesman's got his flag up. Last chance. Ref blows on his whistle. Villa are the crème of Europe. Tommo's dashed at the TV. Switched it off. Lights out. Everybody out. Boys going for a fight. Not Al.

Al's speeding home. Al doesn't want a two-bob hooker tonight. Al wants Pat. Al's got his foot down. Al's drunk. Nine pints. Two chasers. Lungs polluted with weed. Al's charging down the Bristol Road. Just wants to get home. Al's jumped two lights. Al's into Selly Oak. Al's under the railway bridge. Drunk walks out of The Station. Drunk flies over car. Lands on the pavement. Al breaks. Breaks fast. Drunk's motionless. On the pavement. Al's reversed. Drunk's moving. Crowd starts coming out of pub. Al's drunk. Al's stoned. Villa have won the Big Cup. Al's run over a drunk. Drunk's moving. Drunk's okay. Al's sped home. Sped to bed.

***

Al doesn't want to read *The Mail*. Al checks *The Mail*. '*Aston Villa— European Champions '82—Salute Aston Villa!*' No fatal accidents, no incidents, no trouble. Al's in the clear. Al drives back through Selly Oak. Scene of the crime. No mess. No police tape. No damage. Al's in the clear. Al heads over to Pat's. Finishes the garden. No sign of Pat. Pat's out. Out past four. Out past five. Al's finished. Al leaves the keys. Al leaves a note. Al's fun is over.

***

'Man of Peace In A Time of War'. Pope lands in Britain. Pope wants freedom. Wants war over. Wants Anthony Cole home. Al's asleep on the sofa. Killer headache. Tired from the garden. Emotionally drained. Al wants the sofa to eat him up. Al wants Tony Cole dead.

Hev's home. Got a promotion at work. Five hundred quid more a year. Hev's done a good job. Fast typist. Great people person. Organised. Driven. Pleasant. Hev's chuffed. Hev's sent Al out to get some wine. Al's got a box of chocolates. Quality Street. Bottle of plonk. Al feels rough. Al's not got the energy. Hev wants to keep trying. Al's not got the energy. Not tonight.

Hev's perplexed. Sister's got a kid. Mates are all pregnant. Newly married. Things were happy. Husband at home. Having fun. Together. Al's changed. Ring on the finger, Al's out of the house. Hev's down. *Nobody to talk to. Nobody understands.*

Al's out of work. Nothing on. Charity job finished.   Kitchen   job cancelled. Week of boredom. Pure tedium. Hev's stopped putting money in the joint account. Too much been going out. Not enough in. Need to control the cash flow. Al's blown up in front of Hev. *Selfish. Paranoid. Bitch.* Al's got a hundred quid. Al's been pissing it up. Losing on the horses. Losing on the cards. Drinking too much.

'Victorious paras poised for final push'. 'Next stop Port Stanley'. Boys are moving in. Victory in sight. Tony Cole's fine. Tony Cole's going to be home in no time. *Fucking Villa parading on a bus.* Al's seen the bus. Gives it the two finger salute.

***

1st June. Al's birthday. *Twenty-fucking-seven.* Hev's organised a night out. Chinese restaurant. Heaven Bridge in the Bull Ring. Pat's going to be there. Tommo's coming along. Butler too. Few of Hev's mates. Al never remembers their names. Al doesn't want to see Pat. Faking it. Al's spent the afternoon at home. Al's had a wank. Al's had fuck all to do. Al's called the Dunhill fags hotline for a free box. Al's having a bet. Epsom. Derby Day. Persepolis. 14-1. Al's got a tenner. *Mail*'s tip. Al's had a few quid on Palace Gold 33-1. Al's reading the paper. Listening to the radio. Distraught Brummie families. Relatives lost in Falklands. Argentine's say 'surrender' is not in their language. No news on Hermes. Hermes is still okay. *As is their fucking reservist engineer.*

Al's sat away from Pat at the table. Next to Heather. Al's chosen a white shirt, brown trousers, slip-ons. Hev's made a big effort. *Smells like the ground floor of Rackhams.* Outdone Pat. Pat's in a baggy, creased shirt.

Al's not making eye contact. Hev's talking about work. Unigate. Promotion. Bit more money. Going to get some new clothes. Making pointers about kids. Al shrugs it off. All in good time. *Forget she is there.* Tommo's mocking the waiter. Tommo's telling Pat that Tony's going to be okay. War's nearly over. Tony's been a hero. Tony's coming home.

***

Al's got some work coming in. More colleagues of Hev's. Living room job. Few days' work. Al's back on the game. *'Argentine Toll 250'.* Goose Green battle. Seventeen British dead. Tony's not one of them. War's getting messy. Final stages. More casualties. No chance of peace. Thatcher's cry: *'If you really want peace, get your troops on the boat home'.* British have started shelling. Argentina napalm threat. British ring of steel around Port Stanley. British days from victory. Tony's going to be a hero.

Al's round at the Collinses' house. Nice couple, tidy place. Hev's colleagues. Can't mess up. Al's having some jam tarts with his tea. *Fucking scorching.* Seventy-nine degrees. Al's working in his shorts. Footballer's thighs. Getting a tan. Getting back into shape. Press ups in the morning. Lifting some weights. Getting back on his game. Al's in the car going home. Martin Campbell. Tony Butler. *7,000 Argentines moved back on the defensive. British incensed by cowardish napalm threat.* Al's home. Hev's been into town. Been to Brentfords, got new sheets. Pastel colours. Al's had a good day. Easy money. Thanks, Hev. Al's fucked Hev on the couch. Hev's hoping it's the lucky time. Al's opened a tin. Al's on the straight and narrow.

Al's got more jobs coming in. Drought is over. Word of mouth. Jobs over in Sutton. Big houses, cash in hand. No time for a flutter. Al's been scared. Shagging Pat. Wayne came round. Hitting the drunk. Al's not seen Declan.

Al's not had threats. Not for a little while. Al's enjoying the simple life. Enjoying it for now. Al's been staying in. Following the war. Reading the rag. *Diana Ross Special. Liz Taylor at 50.* Playing Spot The Ball. Taken Hev to the greyhounds. Hall Green. Fun betting. Hev's got a video recorder. Pay in instalments. Twenty-three quid a month. Al's ready for the World Cup.

***

War's nearly over. '*Peru threaten to give Argies exocets. HMS Sheffield destroyed'. '43 British deaths'. 'HMS Plymouth damaged'.* Argentine mirage fighters shot down. Crews of stricken ships heading home. Hermes is fine. Hermes not in the action. Tony Cole's still there. Al's got work coming out of his ears.

'It's All Over—14,800 men surrender'. The boys have won. Galtieri's lost. *Argentines' frostbitten. Exhausted. Mendez wants free passage to country of choice.* Coward, snaps Al. So much for fighting to the last bullet and last man. *Cowards have given up.* Al's gutted. Al wanted to lose the war. Midlands family wait on missing soldiers. *'Victory Day Meeting for Cabinet. Government to hold on to hostages for a while'.* Tony Cole's coming home. Home a hero. Home to Al's handiwork.

CHAPTER 8
REDDITCH

(Spring 2009)

Carl's a man of few words. And even fewer on the telephone. The Talking Clock has a wider range of conversation. Carter has never been able to digest his father-in-law's slow, ponderous and thick Small Heath accent without diverting his brain elsewhere. If Carl was an animal, he'd be a city pigeon. If he was an image, he'd be a monotone visual of a 1980s roundabout. If he was a sport, he'd be crown green bowls. Carl informs Carter with loveless precision that his mother will call him back and let him know if Wednesday night's suitable. Carl does his pools run on a Wednesday followed by two pints of piss in The Green Horn in Redditch. The one night of the week Carl leaves the comfort of suburban bliss, aside from the twice-monthly trip to the Chinese with Pat. An occasion where Carl doesn't need the menu. He's found what he likes and sticks to it. Carl's a tedious creature of habit.

Carter's not spoken to his mom. She sent a rushed and misspelt text saying Wednesday was convenient enough. No expression of surprise at her son's first visit since Christmas. Carter decided to take the car in case alcohol forced him to spend the night over in Redditch. Redditch, home of the needle. Carter never understood his mother's reason for moving over there. Except her desire to be isolated from the past but in the same laborious comfort zone. Other Brummies move to Spain. Pat moved to Redditch. It's as far as Carl Frogatt could ever venture. Carl Frogatt, who's never been abroad. Well, only once. To the Costa del Sol. Never been to London. Once described The Grand Canyon as an overrated pothole.

Pat's working part time now. Got a job in a shoe shop in the Kingfisher. She's well-liked by the customers. Pat does small talk. Very well. Carl got a large redundancy pay off from Rover. His attitude is to keep as much of it for the next life. Don't waste it now. Never know if you'll need it. Money's gone on a new fence, lawnmower and golf clubs so the cash is enough to keep Pat and Carl in their turgid, B-road to grave existence.

Carter's feelings always go through the same schizophrenic curve before meeting his mother, a marked downward curve of trepidation and a small incline of nostalgia and hope that they might draw some kind of pleasure in each other's company. Feelings which have no inbuilt justification, given the lack of attention and love his mother has lavished on him as an adult.

Rockets Road is in *Revolutionary Road*-esque suburbia. Thirty-eight identical semi-detached red brick houses with near perfectly mowed lawns and immaculate cream trimmings. Most of Carter's time in the house has been spent over Christmas, a period of the year when Carl is at his uninspiring best. The near bald Xmas tree stands in the same spot every festive period, with polished golden baubles always an equal distance from each other. Carl doesn't get much done in life mainly due to the excruciating and tedious precision he insists on every task. His existence is drawn out and time consuming. No rush to pack in every last minute. The festive dinner menu is always the same: bland, taste and condiment free, everyone receiving exactly the same number of sprouts and every piece of turkey cut almost identically. Carl treats spice with the same disdain that the police treat Class A drugs. The house is charmless. The off-white fluffy carpet that dominates the living room is always pristine, the very few books which lie slanted on the under-used drinks cabinet, housing a mere bottle of Scotch Carl once won at a golf tournament, are dedicated to vintage cars and fairways and adorning the walls are those dull paintings of scenes from village pubs.

Pat seems mildly indifferent to her son's arrival. She's on the blower talking to a friend about a cinema date and sharing an online order for anti-ageing moisturiser. Carter reclines in Carl's cherished lazy-boy and spitefully completes *The Daily Mail* crossword which Carl treats himself to following his two pints of piss. Enough to knock him off his schedule for years. Carter's never understood what his mother sees in Carl, and nor perhaps what Carl sees in his mother.

For all of Carl's failings, Carter feels he deserves someone equally as tedious and mediocre rather than a bitter, aggressive, hyper, loveless woman like his mother. Carter always wondered whether behind closed doors they devour a common passion for 1950s Italian neorealism films and gorged deliveries of Châteauneuf du Pape and collections of world cheeses, marking off what they'd consumed in their Oz Clarke wine book, before tying each other in leather straps and embarking on all-night rogering. He preferred not to understand the attraction or what secrets might lie behind the immaculate white door of number 37 and its polished brass knob.

'Must say I was surprised to hear you were showing up,' begins Pat, only after a further fifteen minutes spent on the phone. 'You planning on staying over? Not split up with that posh girlfriend, have ya?' Carter's used to his mother not calling Rachel by her name, spite mostly for not having met her.

'Not sure, was going to see how late it got and whether I fancied driving back.'

'You mean, depends on how much of my wine you were going to pinch.'

'Actually bought you a bottle so I'll be pinching that one.'

'Hope you're not doing the crossword,' retorts Pat.

'Wouldn't dream of upsetting Carl, would I?'

Pat seems intent on living her Wednesday evening as she normally would without Carter and Carl, settling down to a bottomless glass of two for five pounds bottle of wine, giant bag of crisps and behind the scenes exposés of reality TV programmes. Like a moody adolescent, Pat's incapable of coherent conversation.

'Nothing I like more than coming all this way and watching...' snaps Carter sarcastically.

'Well, it's never like you want to talk to your mom normally, is it?'

Pat always had a habit of blaming others for any breakdown or mishap. It only served to highlight her insecurities and failings as mother. If she'd been a bad parent, it was down to her children not being loving enough.

'You've not been in touch with me since Christmas,' replies Carter.

'Well after the way you stormed out, blaming me and your sister for everything then it's no surprise. You're an adult now, you can apologise.'

'I wasn't pissed off with my sister,' barks Carter.

'Well, whatever. Your behaviour ruined our Christmas Day so quite frankly I haven't been chomping at the bit to see you either.'

'I'm your son, you should have a little bit more patience and a little bit of curiosity to wonder why I may have been upset. Empathy is not in your bloody dictionary.'

Carter had stormed off on Christmas Day and headed back to Birmingham in a hastily booked taxi after a furious row with his mother which started off as innocuous conversation about the lack of family photographs on display, his mother's anaemic interest in his life and intensified by the number of off-limit subjects, finishing with his mother slinging his present—a thick charcoal-coloured jumper from NEXT—at a departing cab. The fire was further fuelled by institutionally racist remarks about Leon whenever Leanne and her husband were out of sight. Carl had remained passive and unaffected by the whole experience. Although Carter had been somewhat aggressive, vomiting profanities in his drunken state, his mother's six-month wall of silence has been extreme. She's proficient at raising the bar of hostility to an almost insurmountable level.

'And I'm here now, aren't I? If it hadn't been for me then how long would have we gone without contact? You'd have expected me to come round on Christmas Day this year with presents, a smile and for me to keep my mouth shut?'

Pat remained focused on the television, but only as a distraction to avoid accountability to her son's questioning. She'd developed into an even more impatient, bitter person, far more content dwelling in her selfish and soulless routine than engaging with people. People asked questions. Routine didn't. Pat Frogatt didn't answer questions.

'Listen, let's agree not to talk about Christmas anymore and just try and enjoy our evening. That's unless you've come around here just to talk about that.'

Pat's not cooking tonight. Pat only cooks for Carl and Carl's six different meals a week which work on the same monotonous rotation. Omelette on a Monday, chicken and chips on a Tuesday and so on. On a Wednesday, Pat usually dials herself a Chinese and offers to do the same for Carter.

Carter has no reference points in his mother's home. He never grew up there. Never lived there. So there are no corners which bring a sentimental smile, no weak spots, no happy memories, no association with his mother either. It's a soulless, charmless abode. A space which Pat has created as a microcosm for her conscious and memory. Clean, empty, functional.

Pat's ordered the Chinese without consulting Carter on what he wanted. Snapping down the phone, she ordered Carl's favourite Menu F2. Pat waffles on about what Carl had in his fortune cookie last time. Carter's got little time for banal chatter about TV and work colleagues. He's come for a fight and not to be placated over chicken chow mein. He's lacking the energy and the empathy to swim through the tide of trivia he patiently endured with other members of his family, those who tread the tightrope of the past with greater sensitivity and heartache.

'I'm not going to bullshit you, Mom,' starts Carter, serving himself a glass of his own wine as Pat empties the spotless tumblers from the dishwasher.

'I actually want to talk about what pissed me off at Christmas, about my life and about what I've been doing over the last few months. Do you know I saw Aunt Hev on Saturday? Don't supposed you do, seeing as you have no contact with her. Let her down, you did.'

Pat tuts loudly and mutters a swear word under her breath. Too apathetic to even argue. Before she can get a word in edgeways or assess how she wants to respond, Carter has ploughed on.

'I've always wanted to know why our family is like this, and the difference is now I'm not taking silence as no for an answer. If you don't want to talk then you won't see me again and I'll get the truth out of somebody else. I need to know who I am in order to live my life.'

Pat's searching for her box of Silk Cuts, smoking less than she used to but still hiding a few boxes around the house. Pat finds one behind the chrome bread bin, lights up and opens the door to the garage in order to adhere to Carl's rule about no fumes in the house. She stares intently and aggressively away from Carter, perched on the breakfast bar stool, and at Carl's fastidiously organised power tools and immaculately polished Opel Corsa.

'There's only so much that digging up the bloody past will work, son. Be careful about what you want to find out. There's a reason you don't know some things. Because nobody knows them. We went through an unhappy time in our family and we're all like this because we want to forget about them.'

'I just want to know a few things.....,' insists Carter, 'we've never talked about it, what I know is through hearsay, from eavesdropping and assumptions. Like why the fuck did Dad leave and never come back? And did you know Leanne saw him about ten years ago?'

Pat's stone cold. Taking a long drag, hoping that Carter too will evaporate like the fumes she's exhaling.

'You're both adults, if you want to go on a wild goose chase looking for that violent prick then it's your bleedin' choice. I guessed Leanne had done because she suddenly stopped asking questions. So your Dad is alive if you want to go and find him. Fact is, he fucked off and didn't want more to do with you. It's not for me to explain, is it?'

Carter's taken aback by his mother's brief lapse of emotion. Overcome by a momentary sense of guilt for putting her back through a situation that might lie deeper then he can comprehend.

'You must have some sort of clue why he left. Leaving you is one thing, fair enough, happens all the time, but never seeing your friggin' kids again is just either callous or there's something deeper.'

'Listen, your dad was not a nice man. He was selfish, always fucking about, looking for a fight or taking advantage of folk. He was even worse after the war and the police just turned him into a thug. He was unbearable, always drunk, never home, in scrapes, I couldn't put up with him anymore. He was a bully and the police just made him worse, gave him the friggin' justification to boss everyone around. I told him I wanted a divorce, for it to finish, he accused me of being with someone else which wasn't fucking true and that was it. He went. And he went straight off to the woman he was fucking for a year so there's only one victim in this and that's me. A fucking victim for putting up with him, and a fucking victim for being left alone with no money to support two kids.'

Carter contemplates moving over to give his mother a hug. He decides that he doesn't want the situation diluted by unnecessary bonding and emotion.

'So you never heard from Dad again after that?'

'Tony kept in touch with very few people from the old life, the family over in Smethwick, some of his mates and your Uncle Wayne. For about the next year, Wayne used to drop some money through the letterbox for the two of you but after a year that dried up, maybe because Wayne was pinching it, maybe your dad couldn't be bothered. I should have asked for more with the divorce but I wanted it done quickly to get rid of him. Should have fought for more for you kids.'

'And nothing else, Mom?'

'Not to do with your dad.'

'What does that mean?'

'I just mean there is no great mystery surrounding your dad. He left me because he had another woman. I don't know why he left you kids or never gave you any money. If you want to find him, then find him, but I don't want to know anything so keep me out of it.'

'I've got no intention of finding a dad I've never had, nor getting in touch with him. He disgusts me, I just wanted to know why we could never talk about it.'

'I was just protecting you.'

Carter detects a sense of sincerity in his mother's voice that he hadn't heard since he was about twelve years old. Also a sense of relief that some of her removed and frigid behaviour may have just been a shield. Pat's rather relieved when the takeaway scooter pulls in. An opportunity to move on.

'Do you mind if we eat in a bit, Mom? I want to finish what we were talking about.'

'I thought we had finished,' snaps Pat impatiently.

'I want to talk about Aunt Hev a bit as well. Like why you two don't see each other anymore.'

'It's complicated.'

'In what sense?'

Pat's reached for another fag and refilled her glass of wine, mixing grapes from bottle number two. In her panic and fluster, she's smoking in the house and flicking ash into a seldom-used espresso coffee cup.

'She's messed up. She's fucked herself up. There's only so much you can help someone before you realise you can't help anymore and you'll end up losing your own marbles as well.'

'Why did she get to this stage?'

'Look, if you want to know everything then here it is, but it's the last pissin' time and if you walk through my friggin front door and start talking about this I'll throttle you, whether you're my son or not.'

Carter senses this is a once only opportunity to extract anything from his mother.

'Look, our Hev was great after Tony left. And sorry if I call him Tony but not your dad but he never was very good at that. She was round all the time and you kids got on very well. Then like a flash the thing with your Uncle Al happened and she turned into a monster. First she never accepted he was dead, didn't even go to the ceremony they had and then got lost in trying to find him and bullshit about where he went.'

'And do you think he's dead?'

'He's definitely dead. He wouldn't just leave his kids. He loved them. He was a better man than your father. Problem was he was weak and liked spending money as much as he liked chasing skirt. The loan sharks and gambling dens had been round a few times over the years. He'd been warned off it. Chances are someone got violent with him and it went too far. I really don't think he'd run off. He wasn't bloody intelligent enough to carry it off.'

'What does Hev think happened?'

'Well, I imagine you were there at the weekend asking her the same thing.'

Pat's defensive, uptight at any mention of her sister.

'I didn't want to trouble her. I was passing through the area, wanted to say hello after I mentioned it with Paul. She's a mess, Mom, she tried putting on a front for me but it only made things worse. I think she needs help, need you.'

'I've already told you about walking through my door and giving me advice.'

'Sorry....'

'She won't accept he's dead because they never found the body. There was a phase when she did and for a few years she went back to normal. But then something changed and she filled her head with theories again. Someone must have told her something or wound her up. She's hired private detectives, I've had to talk to all sorts of people about it because of her rummaging...'

'Why did they come and talk to you?'

'Because I knew your uncle, guess they were trying to work out his character, know more about him.'

'And what did you think of him?'

'He was alright.'

Carter's rather taken back by the term, which seemed to suggest his mother was hiding a disdain or something else for Al.

'What's alright mean?'

'He was a better man than your dad, it's twenty years ago, Daniel, there's only so much I can remember about him and it's all changed. We've all changed.' Pat's now shouting.

'Is there anyone who will know anything more?'

'More about what! You came here to ask about your fucking dad, I've told you. Leave this alone. Leave this alone! What happened to Al doesn't concern us or your life so drop it.'

'So, nobody else would know anything...'

The atmosphere is pungent and neither Carter nor his mother have the stomach for Menu F2. *Probably best heading back to Moseley before anything worse happens....*

'Anyway, Mom, I'll drop it, I just hope you and I can be a bit more normal and maybe you can see it to check up on Aunty Hev once in a while.'

Carter's back is turned; as he heads through the door-less walkway to the living room a pan flies over his head. His mother's yells begin in earnest.

'DON'T YOU COME HERE AND TELL ME WHAT THE FUCK TO DO. FUCK YOUR DAD, FUCK YOUR AUNT AND FUCK OFF OUT OF HERE. IF YOU'VE GOT NOTHING ELSE TO TALK ABOUT THEN THE SHITTY PAST THEN FUCK OFF. CLEAR OFF. GET OUT.'

Carter feels like a rabbit caught in headlights, shocked at the violence of his mother's outburst and the irrationality of it, her failure to hold a normal conversation without losing it. He knew there was more to the saga, more which wouldn't come from his mother. Not now, perhaps not ever.

CHAPTER 9
LONGBRIDGE

(June – July 1982)

Scotland tonking New Zealand. John Wark's netted his second. Al's on the couch. Drifting off. Ready for bed. Phone rings.

'Is Hev around?' whispers Pat. *No idea why she's whispering.*

'No, gone to bed, why you want her?'

'No, wanted to speak to you. Heard the news about Tony, coming home?'

'Yeah, bet you're relieved. No more worrying and late nights. Will be good to have him back.' Al at his bullshitting best. Pat knows it.

'I want to see you, Al,' she hits back.

Al's frozen, surprised. Pat's voice is very forceful.

'Just one last time before Tony's home. Just to say thank you for being a mate.'

'I thought…'

'He's going to be back mid July, they reckon. Take me for that ride you promised. Then that's it. Gotta go, Al. As soon as we get a Saturday free if you still want to.'

Al's hung up. Hev's not heard the phone. Al's been doing fine. Work coming in. No gambling. No straying. Early starts. Early nights. On the sofa. In front of the World Cup. Now Pat's resurfaced. *Using his dick to warm herself up for her husband. War fucking hero.* Al's not sure. Al doesn't want to go. Got his head sorted.

Gotta go. One last chance with Pat. Then everything's sorted.

***

The Carters are inspecting Al's efforts. Say Al's done a grand job. Al's always scored more brownie points than Tony. Preferred son-in-law. Al can turn on the charm. Unlike Tony.

Arthur Carter's moaning about the strike. Trouble with the railways. *'500 railway men could lose job if strike goes ahead—British Rail threaten sack.'* His pal Roy's not going on strike. Roy says fuck the unions. Roy's not missing a day off work. Gladys tells Arthur to go ahead. Arthur's not worried. Says Thatcher's worse than Hitler. Tells Pat her husband's been wasting his time fighting the war. Waste of time fighting for Thatcher. Pat's got the date of Tony's return. 21st July. Family going down to Portsmouth.

'4-star Slashed by 20p in War. Petrol prices plunged by more than 20p a gallon in parts of the Midlands today.' 'Tories Home in a Cliffhanger'. 'Conservatives won the by-election in Birmingham's Sheldon yesterday—but only just'. 'Government enquiry into Falklands crisis, Ted Heath in attack on Thatcher 'cover up''. 'No support blow of Falklands aid dance—Dance organised to raise cash for HMS Coventry appeal cancelled due to lack of support'. Post-Falklands Britain all over the place.

Taken a few weeks to get things sorted with Pat. Leanne's been sick. Hev's had Al rushing around. World Cup's got in the way. Al and Pat have to settle for an escape on a Friday. Pat pulls a sickie from the salon. Al postpones the Simmondses' kitchen until next week.

***

Al's spreading damson jam on thick buttery toast, waiting for Hev to disappear to work. Says he's got a late start. Preparing for his day with Pat. Three weeks waiting. Northern Ireland get a draw with Austria. Billie Jean King against Chris Lloyd at Wimbledon. Al's nervous about England against Spain on Monday. Al's nervous about just about everything. Al's not concentrating.

***

Al hits the claxon. Motor freshly polished. Pat's skipping out of the front door. White, sleeveless top, bra straps caught round her arms, short white skirt, heeled shoes. Al's gone heavy on the cologne. Ironed his shirt. Trousers uncomfortably tight.

'Where do you want to go, Pat?'

'Gotta be back late afternoon, take me out in the country. In the fresh air. Just away from the roads. Maybe stop for a little drink on the way.'

Al's headed through Longbridge, passed The Lickeys, down into Barnt Green. Nice drive. Stop for a pint. Bit of courage. Pat has a gin and tonic. Pat's sat on his knee in the pub. Let Al grope her thighs. Promised him a great time. Needs to be the last time. Al agrees.

Al's found a lay-by. Taken Emma here before. Saw Emma a few years ago. Eighteen. Lovely barmaid. Just before the wedding. One last taste of freedom. *Lovely breasts, lively girl.* Pat's pulled down her knickers in the car. Had one leg on the dashboard. Pat's climbed on Al, pulled open his zip. Al's forgot the johnnies. Pat doesn't care. *One last fuck. Just to say thank you.* Pat's gyrating. Pat wants to go on the bonnet. Al slips outside. Pat's on the bonnet. Al's got his Levi's round his ankles, arse out in the open pumping Pat against the Cortina. Pumping her hard and fast. Hot summer's day. Al's cum. Pat says thanks for the good times. Al's cum for the last time. For the last time inside Pat.

Drive home is near silent. Pat's fallen asleep on the passenger side. Head pressed against window. Al looks at her lovingly. Listening to *Why Do Fools Fall In Love?* Pat's starts talking about Tony coming home. Party for the hero. Forgotten about Al already. Al was good company. Al's over. The war hero's coming home. Al's heading back to Hev. Back to the easy life. Pat's says it was just a bit of summer fun. Can't happen again. Al should go back to try and make babies.

***

Pat's a liar. Pat's been blowing hot and cold. Had Al round again. During the England against West Germany match. Al's said he's gone out with the lads. Al and Pat at it as Schumacher saves from Coppell. Wilkins has a go from distance. Leanne's upstairs. Leanne could wake up at any time. Brian Robson's header pushed over. Breitner loses Mills. Shilton saves. Al's back watching the box. Game loses edge. Al and Pat are lying on the sofa. Sharing a bottle of cheap Sancerre. Coppell shoots over. Rummenigee hits the crossbar at the very end. England almost out. *'And it finishes a point a piece. Match not appreciated by locals in Madrid.'*

Al's round again on Monday. England against Spain. England need a win. *'Goalden Chance'* says *The Mail*. Shilton. Mills. Thompson. Butcher. Sansom. Francis. Wilkins. Robson. Rix. Mariner. Woodcock. Al says King Trev will make things happen. Al says he's got a fiver on England going through. *Ron fucking Greenwood*. Al says he can't screw during the match. Comes round earlier. Pat leaves Leanne locked in her room. Al's mind's on the game. It's over with quick. Pat's making hot dogs in toasted buns and oven chips. Al's caressing his pack of beers. Woodcock shoots wide. Al shouts at the TV. Sansom blasts wide. Robson times his run. Not his header. Spanish keeper saves again from Woodcock. Butcher's slips. Spain miss a sitter. King Trev denied from distance. *Alonso's useless.* Misses a sitter again. Pat's trying to distract Al. Al says wait until later. Brooking and Keegan on. Brooking's shot at the keeper. Arconada's stopping everything. Pat's annoyed with Al. Start arguing. Keegan heads wide from the six yard box. England are out. Sad end for Ron Greenwood. Pat's says Al's a rude fuck. Pat says it's definitely the last time with Al.

***

Al's painting away at the Simmondses'. *'Shattered! It's Sad England'*. *'World's End for England'*—*Pathetic as chances are missed, like in training.'* Greenwood says players have a lot to be proud of. Even the Stan Miguel cartoon in *The Mail* doesn't bring a smile. Al's dejected. Summer's over.

'British Rail confident workers are heading back'. Arthur's had a few days off. Roy was one of twenty-five to work through the strike. Ghost trains they called them. *'600 paras flying into royal welcome at RAF Brize Norton'. 'Hermes on its way home. Docking in a couple of weeks'*. Tony Cole's got an easy fucking cruise ahead of him.

Al's persisting. Pat's not answered. Pat's not answering again. Knows it's him. Eleven pm. Two am. Once at half-four in the morning. Phone rings repeatedly. Pat's unplugged it. Posted messages through the door. Al says he will leave Hev for Pat. Says he wants to see her again. Can't stop thinking about her. Three weeks since the Diana Ross-soundtracked car romp. A week since England headed home. A week until Tony Cole's back. Al didn't get the message. *Was just one for the road, Al. Now get on with your life. Fuck off, Al.*

Pat's got Leanne full-time during the summer. Juggling hours at the salon, leaving Leanne with friends. Leanne's playing up. Kid's a nightmare. Been given too much freedom. Been spoilt. Pat's mind's occupied. Tony Cole's coming back in a few days. Hermes landing in Portsmouth. Pat, Leanne, Arthur and Gladys heading down. Pat's organising a home-coming party the following weekend. Everyone's coming round. Family and friends. Al included. Pat's got a bag full of Union Jacks. Balloons. Mr Kiplings. 'Welcome Home Dad' banners. Weather's decent. Pat's going to set up a table outside on Sunday. Everyone's bringing some nibbles and booze. Neighbours told to pop by. Pat's even ask *The Mail* to run a little piece on Tony. *Mail* don't get back to her. Pat's worried Al's going to have his head under the grill. Worried Al's going to speak out.

Pat fucks Al again. *One last time.*

Tony Cole's been at sea a hundred and eight days. Hermes spent longer at sea than any WWII ship. Pat and the family watching on. Took seven hours to get down from Birmingham. Left at the crack of dawn. Arthur drives as miserably as he mumbles.

Patrol boats rounding Hermes. Helicopters flying past. Leanne's scared by the cannons going off. Carnage at the harbour. Huge, grey warship crawls back into shore, oppressively cutting through waves. Partisan crowd. *Welcome back Hermes* they chant. Banners everywhere. John Craven's patrolling the harbour with a microphone. Gladys says Pat should try get on TV. Pat's too shy. Sea of Union Jacks. Dogs, grannies, kids, the lot. Thatcher's on board. Inspecting the ship. Thanking the crew. Tells them to write down their unique experience. Most wonderful crowd of people she's met in a long time. Record-breaking military campaign. Chapter of pride for our country. Tony Cole catches a glimpse. Tony Cole knows that the words are for him. Tony Cole's on deck. Waving his hat at the onlookers. If only his mates could see him. *Looks like a proper cunt.* Tony Cole in his uniform. All proper and proud. Tony Cole doesn't want to head home.

***

Pat wells up on seeing Tony. All trim and smart. Gladys and Arthur shake his hand. Tony says he's exhausted. Proud of seeing the PM. Arthur bites his tongue. Head for a pub sandwich and a few pints of lager. Tony's not coming back up straight away. Going to have a night down in Portsmouth with the boys. Invites them to stay. Arthur says they need to go back. Pat barks at Tony. He's had a hundred and eight days with the boys. Time to come home. Arthur rolls his eyes. *Al wouldn't have been this rude.* Tony says just one night. Will be back in Birmingham in the morning.

***

Tony spends the night down at the docks with the boys. Pub full of fellas with Aviators and lamb chop sideburns. Gets messy.

Tony rises late. Couldn't face heading back. Going to miss the fellas. Even the boredom. The hours spent on deck, tanning away, trying crosswords or playing hangman. Tony enjoyed the war. Liked being away. The focus. The camaraderie. Was even off the beers. Serving his country. Making people proud. Doing something. Tony's been thinking hard the last few days. Needs a change. Contemplating joining the navy full time. Or the police. Hates the pigs. But would like the work. The respect. The power. The banter. Discipline.

Pat turned up for the eight past twelve train. Waited outside New Street. In the Mini with Leanne coughing away. Missed Tony's call to say he was going to be late. Pat headed home. Dismayed. Tearful. Disappointed. Worried. *Tony doesn't appreciate shit.* Tony's not ready to head to Kings Heath. To see Al's handiwork. Takes his time. Has a jar in the Station Bar. Looks out back onto New Street. All feels too easy. Too simple. Plebs walking around doing their shopping. Biddies with their cheap fresh fish in dirty plastic bags from the market. Dull, grey, dirty New Street. *Folk who've never made a sacrifice. Had it easy.* Tony feels removed. Misses the lads. Misses the isolation. Misses his bunk. Has a chat with a WWII veteran at the bar. Cliff. Got a limp Cliff. Worked in the Royal Air Force. Best years of his life. Tony heads back on the fish-stenched 35 before he drinks himself into trouble. Or back to Portsmouth.

***

Al's tetchy. Drinking even more than usual. Hev knows he's had something on his mind. Presumes he's had trouble with the bookies. But Al's always got money in his pockets. Doesn't seem distracted in the same way. Never wants sex. Never gets physical. Hev says she's going to get Tony a present. Some of those Union Jack dice for his motor. Maybe a

162

bottle of Sapphire. Al's drained of enthusiasm for Sunday. Al can't stop thinking about Pat. Al spent twelve quid on a night with a Cheddar Road hooker called Stacey on Thursday. Long blonde hair, bony legs and freshly trimmed. Got bored half way through. He's not sure how he'll cope on Sunday. *With fucking Tony Cole panting around Pat like a proud fucking lion.*

Hev's getting ready to get the 45 into town. Wants Al to come in with her. Have a lunchtime pint. Al says he's got some work on. Can't make it. Al's going to work on his arms. Dust down the dumbbells. Go for a run down the Rea, up through the woods. Run Pat out of his system.

'Seen that Nissan have pulled out of that car plant,' shouts Al, changing the subject and lowering the paper as he finishes his brew. 'Fucking government, fucking recession. And Thatcher's got the balls to say everything's great and the war shows that. Telling us we should be fucking proud of the victory.' Hev nods passively. Hev's been doing well recently. Got a promotion last month but now also an interview with the council. Decent pay rise. Could go places if she put her mind to it. Hev wants to focus Al's mind on kids. Wants Al to be bringing more money in.

***

Tony Cole ambles down Addison Road. Struggles to ignore the lure of the pubs. Morale lifted slightly when he sees Pat and the kid. Or maybe when the drinks start going down easier. Pat got Leanne a present on Tony's behalf. Giant tiger. Tony's impressed with Al's work. Done a good job. Everything nice and neat. *Turned out alright, Al. Good sort. Wasn't sure at first. Into the birds too much.* Al's been a loyal friend. Pat agrees. Tony says he will take him out on the lash. Pat's shown Tony the framed *Newsweek.* The newspaper cuttings. Says she was nervous. Upset. Hard. Tony says it was fine. Had a good time. Pat says she wants another kid.

Leanne needs some company. Tony and Pat spend the afternoon in bed. In the bedroom Al decorated.

Pat orders Chinese. Sweet and sour chicken and a big bag of chips. Tony's beer starts to taste like a headache. Tony finds Pat hard work. Pat doesn't understand the war. The submarines. The assault helicopters. The strategic, often ponderous maternal role of Hermes. Pat doesn't get the banter. Tony feels a void. Felt a void during sex. *Maybe it will just pass. Maybe it will never pass.*

***

Pat's told everyone to come round for two o'clock on the Sunday. Make the most of a nice afternoon. Hev turns up without Al. Al's making his own way up. Tony's chuffed with his presents, the attention. Made to feel special. Passing neighbours shake his hand. Stop for a drink. Tony says he'd go back. But wants to be closer to home. Talks about police. His mates laugh. Tony doesn't find it funny. Tony Cole seems different. To everyone. Grown up. Distracted. At the same time focused.

Al's turns up an hour later. Walked up from Selly Park. Kill a bit of time. Put off the inevitable. Up through Highbury Park. Al hugs Tony like an old friend. Wayne Cole looks on suspiciously. Catches Pat's glance. Pat looks away. Pat stays clear of Al. And Tony. Gaz has turned up with a throwaway BBQ. Tells Pat he'll do the grilling. Gaz and Tommo flipping skinless Kwik-Save sausages and cheap frozen burgers. Hev tells Gaz to put out his fag. Dripping ash all over the pork chops. Kids playing hide and seek and street football with a flyaway.

Tony's taking a deep sip from his can. Looks genuinely pleased to see Al.

'You did a great job, fella. Looks proper mint in there.'

'Was my pleasure, chap. Nice for you to come home to something.' Al tries changing the subject, 'How was it out there?'

'Fucking sound. Not much sleep, it's fucking twenty-four-seven when you're on board. Great set of lads though. Couple of fellas from the Midlands. Might be coming round later.'

'Ever worried you were going to be blown up?' shouts Tommo.

'Fuck off. I'm not going to even respond to a twatty comment like that, friggin imbecile,' barks Tony.

'Waste of time that war, if you ask me,' laughs Bob the toolsetter, winking at his son.

Tony ignores the bait.

'Anyway, how was it here?' replies Tony.

'Bit boring,' replies Al. 'Just been getting on.'

'Cheers for everything, fella,' says Tony again, patting Al's shoulder, 'having a nice new house must have kept the wife sane. Owe you one.'

Al smirks and reaches for another Carling from the cool box.

Arthur Carter's spent most of his time inside avoiding the Coles. Checking out the new look house. Still unhappy Tony convinced Pat to flee Erdington after a year in the place Arthur paid for. Made a tidy profit. Paid nothing back to Arthur. Gladys tells him to grin and bear it. Become more sociable. Arthur's nursing a half from a proper pub tankard. Gladys is carrying a full pint.

'Getting drunk under the table by your missus again, Arf,' mocks Bob the toolsetter.

Arthur shoots back a mean look. Bob the toolsetter's oblivious to it.

'What about them trains. You fellas had a few weeks off by the sound of it. Everyone wants a bloomin' pay rise these days.'

'Think they're overdue a pay rise,' replies Gladys.

'Easy fucking job if you ask me, cushy number. Sitting on your arse all day,' laughs Bob the toolsetter, leaning against the low brick ledge at the front of house, his beer belly accentuated by a terrifying posture.

'So fucking easy, how about you do it,' replies Arthur.

'Prefer working for a living,' barks Bob the toolsetter.

Bob the toolsetter and Arthur have had their run-ins before. Never come to blows. But close. Including at Tony and Pat's wedding when Arthur accused Bob the toolsetter of being tight. Bob the toolsetter just thinks its banter. Treats everyone the same. Same disdain. Arthur takes everything too personally. Wayne says his dad's just having a laugh.

'Go and sharpen your fucking tools!' replies Arthur.

'Did do you hear that?' continues Bob the toolsetter, mockingly putting his hands around his ears.

'He fucking speaks!'

Arthur Carter scuttles back inside.

**

Al notices that everyone's outside. Spilling onto the street. Blocking passing cars. Lager cans all over the pavement. Small Union Jacks decorating the table. Everyone's outside apart from Pat. Al heads inside for a slash. Crosses Pat on the stairs. Looking like she's had a few too many already. Al gets a flash of her long legs as she descends.

Al's hushed.

'I've been trying to call you, Pat, left some notes, why've you been ignoring me?'

Pat looks annoyed. Pat doesn't want to stop and speak to Al.

'You should fucking stop it, Al. It's fucking finished. You know that. Don't want any more of that. If Tony finds out he'll crush your neck, so stop the calls and the notes. You should spend more time with my sister.'

'But I'm in love with you, Pat,' whispers Al, 'Can't stop thinking about you.'

Pat looks Al in the eye as she glides down the stairs. Pat points her long, manicured nails into his face.

'Fuck off, Al, just fuck off and die, will you.'

Before Al can get another word in, Pat's gone and Hev's heading through the front door looking for a Chardonnay refill.

'Everything okay, bab?' she enquires tipsily.

Al's mildly irritated and nods. Al knows he can't come back.

***

Pat's got a day full of perms. Wendy's tried to undercut the market offering £7.95 with a cut and blow dry. Offering £9.95 at Rackhams. Salon's full for weeks. *Alright for Wendy. She's not the one doing the donkey work.* Pat's got a sore head from last night. Feels sick. Few late revellers came. Tina and her new fella. Car crash of a chap called Lennon. Blitzed out of his skull. Tony fell asleep watching USSR and Poland. Then got up and carried on. Then put on *My Way*. Pat's struggling to focus on Mrs Doyle's perm and Mrs O'Connor's rancid split ends. Hands shaky, head heavy and annoyed with Al Jeavons. Al who can't just leave anything alone. Al who couldn't get the message. Al's who's going to keep coming back. Pat thinks back to the sex with Tony. Cold. Unemotional. Impassionate. Boring. Not like with Al. Adventure and excitement. Tony's mind was somewhere else. Pat asked Tony for another kid. Not even sure why. Tony said yes. If it keeps her quiet.

***

Tony's had to get up early. Pat's planted Leanne on him for the day. Kid's lively. Jumping on the bed. Threatening to colour the walls with large coloured Crayola crayons. Al's shiny white walls. Demanding biscuits and TV. Dog's going wild. Nobody's fed him. Charging up and down the stairs. House is a shit sty from the party. Tony Cole's not come back to this

168

headache. *Not come to clean up this fucking sty.* Tony Cole wants to get the train back down to Portsmouth and be free. Free from the fucking mounting bills. Free from his nagging missus who wants to head down to Lanzarote for a holiday they can't afford. Only fifty quid, she says. All inclusive. Wants a second kid. Can barely cope with the first. Tony Cole needs action again. Promised Al a night out for doing up the house. Agree to head to Tommo's and then for a few jars. Al says he wants a quiet one. Tony Cole needs a messy one.

***

Summer carnival season at Cannon Hill. Tony prefers Leanne when Pat's not around. Kid's quieter. More playful. Adores Dad. Pat's smacking and shouting only make her play up. They chase Pop along the river. Temporary moment of family happiness. Leanne dives into the brook and plays with the dog and chucks pebbles. Tony sits on the bank staring at the sky and the passing ladies in their strapless, spotty summer dresses. Wishing he was somewhere else.

***

Tony picks Al up on the way down to Tommo's. Al wants the radio on. Looking for a big winner at the 6.40 at Wolverhampton. Game Dame USA. For Your Eyes. Al's only gone and bagged twenty-five quid. Al's says he's having a lucky summer. Conversation's a bit lacking in the car. Al doesn't want to talk birds. Tony Cole's going on about the ones he saw in the park. Says sex becomes boring when you're married. Al wants to punch him.

Tommo's place is still the pits. Not cleaned it since the European Cup Final night. Got himself two golden retrievers. Place stinks of piss. Al's swallowing floating dog hair. Tony Cole can't stomach Tommo's shanty town. Boys head down to The Old Hare and Hounds. Al's quiet. Says he's depressed about work. Says Hev's always nagging. Doesn't feel comfortable being with Tony. This new, friendly, matey Tony Cole. Feels suspicious. Tommo's bored too. Tommo wants to be elsewhere. Tony Cole insists they drown their sorrows. Tony Cole starts chatting to the girls at the bar. Can't be older than sixteen. Seventeen. Talking about the war. Playing up. Regaling stories. Come and polish my medals, he says. Al and Tommo keep their distance.

'What's up with you, Al, Hev got your dick above the mantelpiece or summit?' laughs Tony.

'Just feeling a bit flaky,' replies Al.

'For fuck's sake, what's happened to you boys since I've been away? That bird with the long curly hair is well into you.'

The girl is. She's winking at Al. Trying to get his attention. Flirting around him. Al's passive. Al has a joke or two. But Al doesn't want it to go further. Tony's getting himself in trouble. Tubby girl called Leslie. Squat nose, nice smile, everything on display. Boys turn around to order and Tony's gone. Gone into the parking lot and let out two minutes of frustration. Comes back in. Necks a shot of Smirnoff and drives home.

***

Tony wakes up. Barely remembers coming home. Rolls over and sees his jeans and pants on the floor. Pat's doing the late shift. Pat asks him if he recalls having sex with her. Tony says yes. Tony doesn't. Tony's forgotten about Leslie as well. Tony's reading through old copies of *The Mail*. '*Interviews with Marines. Survived terror on SS Canberra. Emotional homecoming.*' Nothing for Tony. No interview. No emotion. No terror.

Kids screaming. Wife's miserable. House is the pits. Tony just wants to leave. Back to his Selina Scott poster. *Eight thousand miles to come home to this. Monotonous bullshit.*

CHAPTER 10
SUTTON COLDFIELD

(Summer 2009)

Deepak ensured that his in-laws' mammoth wedding budget extended to cover the cost of a piss-up. It's one the Joshis have hijacked, erecting a large tent in the vast back garden of their Moseley home. Two Indian chefs have been prised away from one of the city's top restaurants for the evening. Fresh paneer, giant baltis bubbling away, industrial size bags of turmeric, cardamom pods and garam masala, copious barrels of beer and a free bar to cut the legs off the most ardent sailor. Between the Guptas and the Joshis, near on two hundred people are filling their faces. Garden's packed to capacity, house rammed with giant gift-wrapped boxes from Rackhams and John Lewis, endless rails of suit jackets and overcoats. There's a sprinkling of Deepak's mates from school, from work, from the band. Revellers posing for group photos, couples taking selfies, bride and groom doing the rounds, opening gifts. It's an orgy of spice and family pleasantries.

Carter and Rachel headed back for a change after the service. Excuse for a quick bonk. Bracing themselves for the kind of party in which they will have to keep each other company, avoid polite conversation and well-meaning relatives. Carter's enjoyed a good few weeks. Been able to put the incident with his mother behind him, convince himself of the futility in pursuing the past, enjoyed the summer evenings and band practice. Rachel's placated by seeing him happy again. She's not insisted on discovering the results of his research. Status quo.

Music's blaring. They say it will go on for days. Deepak's complaining he's not had enough time to get the drinks in. Queues for the food immense, generous guests making sure their wedding gifts are

173

compensated by large plates of food and multiple glasses of booze. Carter's found the beer tent and poured himself a pint of Cobra. Deepak explains he's under fire from his parents and in-laws. Needs to find a proper job, earn more money, reach the family standards. Computer technician at a small time design studio not good enough. Not now he's married to a Joshi.

Rachel's escaped from small talk with Virali's group of assorted accountant and back office bank worker friends. 'Imagine if we ever get married, not sure we know anywhere near two hundred people,' she begins, on discovering Carter craftily serving himself further Cobra.

'Don't get started on that sort of talk.'

'Don't worry, not going to get all emotional about getting married. Just think this is insane. How much do you think it cost?'

'Heard something from that couple in the corner that there's not much change from a hundred grand. All things included.'

'Wow. I don't think we'd pull in fifty people.'

'Well, not with my family, no way. But sure your mum would have enough friends pulling in! There would be no stopping her.'

Carter often feared about marriage. Or rather about a wedding day. How Rachel's conventional Middle England family with their solid roots and network of upstanding, childhood friends would easily fill a charming countryside church, visioning his side of the aisle as empty as the Railway End in the late 1980s. It's a spiral of thought Carter doesn't want to delve into any further. Not at this point.

'Yeah, I'd imagine there would be a few people that she'd just have to invite. What about you, how many would you consider?'

'None of the fuckers, if I could help it! Do it on the sly, in that place in Scotland. Beyond my sister and a few friends. Keep it small and all of that.'

Rachel's sensing that it's not the time to delve back into the subject. Not in front of two hundred people and an explosive cocktail of free booze.

***

Saturday's often quiet. Paul usually does something for himself. Round of golf. Few jars. Vacuous shopping in The Mail Box for designer polo shirts. The lads are busy on projects and don't need any guidance. Paperwork taken care of. Few loose ends tied up. Paul decides to pay the customary monthly surprise visit to his mother. Although the visits have become more surprises than monthly in recent times. Seeing his mother is an exercise in relieving Paul's conscience. He draws scant pleasure from it anymore. He usually calls ahead, best from experience to give his mother the chance to sort things out and avoid any nasty revelations. Usually a futile mission as Hev can make no sense of her post-it reminders.

Calling before means she might at least scrub up, ultimately less of a weight on his mind. Avoid seeing something he doesn't need to. However, today, perhaps out of morbid curiosity, Paul arrives unannounced.

Hev's had a spare key cut but Paul seldom uses it. Paul knocks twice on the door. Door bell is broken again. No response. Knocks again. Hears a male voice groan and a shadow amble towards the door. Catches a glimpse through the letterbox. The guy's clearly hungover, sporting a semi-soiled vest and a pair of loose, grease-stained jogging bottoms. Paul's never seen him before. The guy has no recollection of his own name.

'What can I do you for?' says the voice at the door.

'I came to see my mom,' replies Paul.

Pause.

'Man, for fuck sake…you'd better hang on a minute then, lad,' is mumbled back.

The guy attempts to close the door but can't stop Paul barging in. Paul makes it as far as the living room. A veritable pit. There's junk everywhere, piles of takeaway boxes, half empty bottles of vodka and gin, a stench of week-old cigarettes, crumbs all over the carpet.

'I'll just see if I can find her,' says the guy, still to introduce himself.

The guy shuffles up the stairs. Farts as he moves. Paul's not sure why he has bothered, beginning to regret not going home and enjoying an easy afternoon. Knows it's not going to be a simple five-minute stop over.

The guy's gone for about ten minutes. Paul flicks on the TV. Some coverage of far-away pre-season friendly football tournaments and transfer rumours. Doesn't want to go upstairs. Is happy to play ignorant. Paul can hear rummaging and some movement. Eventually there's some stirring on the stairwell.

Paul hears his mother before he can lay eyes on her.

'You'd better let yourself out, Wes,' she tries to whisper.

The bloke walks out. In the same stained vest and saggy jogging bottoms.

Hev ambles towards the door in creased jogging bottoms and a jumper slipped carelessly over her frumpy chest. Her hair is unkempt and greasy, her slippers have been hurriedly put on and she's clearly not attempted washing in days.

'Son, you should have said you were coming round, would have had things prepared.'

'Just wanted to surprise you, seems like I've only ended up surprising myself. Who the fuck is Wes?'

'Wes is the window cleaner.'

'Didn't look like he was cleaning the windows to me.'

There's a pause. Paul's not really mentally prepared to face any more of the truth. Hev's too tired and intoxicated to lie.

Paul picks up a chipped cup carrying last week's tea as a symbol of the wreckage.

'What the hell's going on, Mom? The place is a shit hole. You look a mess and there's some random bloke answering your door.'

Hev shakes as she tries to light one of the cigarettes lying on the coffee table. Wes has left them behind. Paul's never seen his mother smoke. He pulls the fag from her mouth.

'Do me a favour, Mom. Get in the shower. Get yourself cleaned up, and I'll work on down here. Then I'll drive you to the shops and we can get some food in.'

It's a role reversal. The kind of passing of family responsibilities that Paul didn't envisage happening for another twenty years or so.

Hev's gone for an age upstairs. Shower's running. Paul's just assuming it's taken a while to wipe the grime off. In the meantime, Paul scans the lounge and decides to get Carmen to organise a cleaning lady. Going to take someone half a day to clean this shit up. Paul throws as much in a black bin bag as possible, including crockery and cutlery beyond repair. The dishwasher is piled with last week's scrubby plates, a heavy stench of mould and layers of fat. The cleaner's coming round on Monday. Paul now needs to work on cleansing his mother.

Hev's resurfaced looking more normal, although her hair is still dripping wet, her red puffy cheeks advertise the vast amount of alcohol consumed, and bags under the eyes the lack of good sleep. Paul beckons her into the Land Rover for a trip to the local Safeways. There's little chat en route. Paul's finds it easier to engage on a practical rather than emotional level. Despite Hev appearing more interested in filling the trolley with three-for-two on the wine and the crisps and chocolate aisle, Paul's collected sixty pounds worth of relatively healthy food, non-perishables and tinned supplies. Sort of stuff that will survive a gas attack. Tinned beans. Macaroni cheese. Tea bags. Long-life milk. Eventually they sit down for a cup of tea in a nearby Starbucks, populated by the wholesome breast-feeding brigade and young couples gorging on impossibly creamy concoctions. Paul feels like he's out with a special needs patient.

They've both gone for the cheap drip coffee. As bitter as the mood.

'Everything okay, Mom?'

'Just been a bit down. Me demons and everything.' Hev's slowly sobering up but the departure of a week's booze is replaced by a heavy tiredness and the depressive comedown of reality.

'Anything I can be helping you with?'

'You're fine. It's nice of you to do all of this for me......,' Hev breaks off, '... You've turned out well. Wish your brother had your breaks. I know you have your life and it's not easy finding time for an old has-been like me....'

'I can come round more often, I don't like seeing you like this.'

'I'm fine. It's just I have these bad days. Bad weeks.'

'When's the last time you were working?'

'A while.'

'What's a while?' snaps Paul, unintentionally.

'Couple of months.'

'Couple of months! What've you been doing in the meantime? Has no work come from the agency? Thought you were doing bits quite regularly?'

'They got tired of me missing days. I'm too old now for a lot of the work. It's all computers now.'

'So what've you been doing? Sitting in the flat drinking and hanging out with the fucking window cleaner. Mom, what the fuck is this about? For fuck's sake.' Paul's failing to keep his voice down.

Hev's silent.

'Are you still on the medication, still meeting your groups or you stopped that too?'

'I just need some time. Got myself into a rut, promise on Monday I'll get everything sorted. Back on the right track....want you to be proud.'

'I've got a cleaner coming round on Monday, you should get out for a few hours and see the doctor, get some help. Call one of your proper friends, speak to someone. I'll come round whenever I get an hour off work. I can't see you like this, Mom but you need to help yourself as well. Get back to work. Get some bleedin' structure in your day.'

Hev's sobbing into a tissue and sobering into a reality as every bit dark as the extreme drunken binges and lock-ins.

'You know your cousin came round a few weeks ago?'

'Who? Dan?' replies Paul, knowingly.

'Yes, came by to say hello.'

'What did he want?'

'Nothing, just a chat, I think, was being nice.'

Paul keeps his thoughts to himself, salvages a tearful public meltdown and drives his mother home.

***

Paul struggles to sleep on Saturday night despite the four cans of Guinness and a few miniature Jamesons stolen from a stag weekend hotel mini bar to wipe the day down. He's called his mother at midday on Sunday to make sure she'd got up and began organising her day. She sounded sober. Heading out for the afternoon and tidying up. Paul's seen Beryl the cleaner and handed over fifty quid and his spare key for Monday morning. Everything seems a little better.

***

Carter's nursing a lingering hangover. Twelve o'clock and still in bed Rachel's cleaning up around him, making enough noise to try and stir him into action. She took it characteristically easier at the wedding and is itching to get ready for the annual summer afternoon BBQ, organised by her ostentatious boss. Carter's phone has rung a few times. They've let it go. Phone keeps ringing. Rachel picks up. It's cousin Paul, can he call back when he gets up.

Carter knocks down some Vitamin C, stumbles around, spreads himself on the couch, is forced into the shower, knocks back a few espressos and is bullied into calling his cousin back. Paul's sounding tense.

'Sorry if I got you up out of bed.'

'No worries, just a bit hungover from my mate's wedding last night. Bit surprised to hear from you, to be honest.'

'Yeah, went to see Mom yesterday.'

'Okay.'

Carter's fearing the worst.

'She wasn't doing too well, to be honest. Place was a pigsty, she's a mess. Managed to get her out and sorted a while back, seemed to do some good…'

'Sorry to hear that.'

'Anyway, reason I'm calling is that she said you turned up a few weeks ago.'

'Yeah, swung by for a few hours, was in the area, just wanted to say hello.'

'How was she when you went? Hope you weren't asking the same questions you were bugging me with….'

'No, no, she seemed okay, place was a bit skuzzy, she seemed to be making too much of an effort to let me know she was alright. But it was fine.'

'And did you bother her?'

'I went to have a chat but didn't get anywhere, didn't seem right, so I left it. Why?'

'Just don't think she needs bothering right now. Trying to get her help.'

'Anything, I can do?'

'No, don't worry'

'Let me know if there's owt I can do.'

Paul hurries the phone call as if he's been caught doing something on the sly.

'Okay, will be in touch for that beer.'

Receiver. Dead.

***

Beryl's not done home cleaning for a while. Been on a nice part-time number assigned to offices and businesses. Easy money, easy cleaning. Pulled this as a favour for Carmen, her goddaughter, and offered to help Paul out. And money's not bad. For a few hours' work. Been told Hev won't be there but knocks the door a few times out of customary politeness. After a minute or so she lets herself in. The place has an eerie stench of dust, stale liquor and having not had fresh air for weeks. It's unloved. Despite Hev's frantic attempts at tidying things up, the place looks worse. Worse in the sense that this is the best someone can manage.

Usually Beryl would settle down, make a cup of tea and pop on a Daniel O'Donnell CD or daytime TV. But she wouldn't risk drinking anything from that kettle. Or the cups. She decides to take a look around, assess how much damage there is. Been told she can take thirty quid for an extra couple of hours. Looks like a long day job. She's about to call Paul and advise him to tell his mother to stay away longer. The living room carpet bears months of grime, burn marks and stains. The plants probably haven't seen daylight since being brought into the home. The curtains unopened. Despite the presence of a resident window cleaner, the large double glazing windows fitted by Paul's team remain stained and the rims and ledges full of grime. Beryl opens as many windows as possible, letting in the faint summer breeze. She's realised that her bag of products will barely cover one room.

The downstairs is essentially one huge room, the divide between the kitchen and the large, narrow living room knocked through. The small backyard is overgrown and all three dustbins full with bottles everywhere and housing all kinds of junk that's not been thrown away. Old boxes of Christmas presents and white goods, a broken washing machine and, mysteriously, three wheelbarrows.

Beryl takes a trip up the stairs littered with old newspapers, a precariously placed telephone and clothes which have fallen from the landing rail. It's a classic two up, two down house. The back bedroom has never really been habited, instead full of plastic boxes stuffed with items which once had space in a larger house but are now just sitting waiting to be thrown out. Nothing really has its place in the house. The boxes resemble Hev's memory, stuff which lives on, in the way, never out of sight, but no longer serving a constructive purpose.

The bathroom is the worst kept of all of the rooms. Wet towels stick to the floor, a filthy bath and shower curtain survive in their own micro-climate. Shit stains cover the toilet and lid, dozens of used toilet rolls spill over the small, square plastic bin, a mirror full of soap marks and long, black hairs and pubes all over the floor. Losing any will to start the project, Beryl moves into the bedroom, which seems warmer, darker but somehow more cynical than the rest of the house. The bed is set against the wall on the far side of the room, facing the street traffic. There are a few suitcases, which have exploded clothes all over the room and a dressing table full of out-of-date and empty bottles of make-up. Beryl notices that the bed's not been made. On turning on the light, she realises there is a body in there as well. She knocks on the door twice. No response. On moving closer, she nervously and fearing the worse pulls back the sheets. Hev's got her head turned towards the wall and is fully dressed. A bottle of Gin and a couple of pill boxes are spilled over the dresser. It takes Beryl a few seconds, seconds which seem like minutes, to pluck up the courage to check Hev's pulse. There's no response. No hope. Hev's not going to respond. Hev's been dead for a good eighteen hours.

***

Beryl called the police and ambulance first. Asked the police to get in touch with Paul and Lee. Couldn't face being the one who found the body and broke the news. Beryl agrees to stay in the apartment until Paul comes over. It takes an hour or so for the granite-coloured Land Rover to pull in. Paul's being strong. Not really let the news hit him. Remaining practical and proactive. Carmen holds his hand and hangs in the shadows. Police say that a note was left for Paul.

Paul moves into a corner of the kitchen. The two police offers remain seated passively on the sofa. Beryl, not the world's most demonstrative woman, gives petite Carmen a wrap-around hug in the corridor. All wanting to give Paul his space. The note's squeezed into a cheap envelope and written on Paul's company notepaper. It's scribbled in erratic capital letters, like somebody in a rush to beat the slipping sand of time.

LOVE,

IF YOU FIND THIS BEFORE I WAKE UP, I AM SORRY IT ENDED LIKE THIS. I AM SORRY I TOOK THE EASY WAY OUT. BUT IT'S BEEN TWENTY YEARS THAT I'VE BEEN FIGHTING.

I DON'T WANT TO TURN INTO A DRUNK OR END UP IN A HOME. I COULDN'T LET YOU SEE ME LIKE THAT AGAIN.

LIVE YOUR LIFE, BE HAPPY, LOVE YOUR CHILDREN AND TAKE CARE OF YOUR BROTHER.

I HOPE WHERE I'M GOING, I'LL BE ABLE TO FIND YOUR FATHER AND THE TRUTH.

I KNOW HE WAS TAKEN FROM US AND KNOW IT WAS SOMEONE IN THE FAMILY WHO DID IT.

BUT DON'T GO CHASING THE TRUTH LIKE I DID. LIVE YOUR LIFE, LIKE YOU HAVE.

LOVE YOU.

MOM

Paul stands motionless. Looking out the window at two erratic sparrows on the edge of the fence and the apologetic excuse for a Solihull summer afternoon.

***

Paul's had the police tell the rest of the family. The few of them left. Gladys Carter. Pat. Lee's been informed in prison. He'll get a few hours leave for the funeral. Pat informs Leanne, who calls Carter. The news left Carter feeling numb. The visit to Hev. The shock news. Everything so real. Carter started to panic, realising a funeral will be on the horizon, and a rare unison of the family. It's going to involve Rachel and everyone coming together. It's going to evoke and provoke sensations and his discoveries. Going to plunge him back into it all again.

Carter's not said much over dinner and before Rachel can get more than a sympathetic word in edgeways over jacket potato and chill con carne, Carter receives a call from Paul. He moves into the lounge on the sofa. It had been a few hours since he'd heard the news, but he'd not had time, nor the strength to get in touch with Paul.

'Guess you've heard the news?'

'Yeah, I'm really sorry...only found out this afternoon, been a bit of a shock. Was going to get in touch later.'

'Don't worry.'

'How's it going?'

'It's going. Just trying to focus on the funeral and getting stuff sorted.'

'Did your mom get in touch?'

'No, we're not really talking. Leanne called. Not spoken to Mom yet. We had a benny a few weeks ago and to be honest not got the strength to fight that.'

'Are you going to be alright with everyone being at the funeral?'

'Sure it will pass. Are you?'

'It's going to be a small thing. Mom didn't really have many friends left so a few old colleagues, and the family, whoever wants to turn up.'

'Is Lee getting out?'

'They're giving him a few hours. But he'll be in cuffs.'

'Anyway, really got to go and just wanted to say, once this is settled. I want to talk a few things over with you. Like what you were talking about last month. Mom left me a note. I guess things have started to make me a bit curious.'

'Okay, we can talk after the funeral.'

Paul's hangs up without saying goodbye and Carter realises there's no turning back. The funeral's going to pit his mother and the rest of the family together.

***

Carter doesn't hear from his mother before the funeral. He contemplates calling but loses the will whenever he flashbacks the flying saucepan. Leanne acts as the informant between the two parties. She explains Mom's too upset. About her sister. About the argument. Decide it's best to see each other on the day.

***

Funeral's held at the red-bricked St Mary & St John's in Erdington. Second week of September. Thursday afternoon. There's a pleasant breeze in the air and Paul's offered to house the reception back in Sutton Coldfield. The turn out's bigger than expected. There's been a word of mouth movement amongst Hev's old colleagues. Those who remember her when she was full of life and slightly repressed ambition. A few distant cousins, acting like extras in a film, lurking in the shadows of more immediate relatives.

Pat's the very embodiment of sobriety. Dressed all in black like a Sicilian widow, leaning against Carl, in his grey, off the hanger suit. Colour matches his pencil-thin moustache. The introductions with Rachel were simple and pleasant enough. Given the occasion, Carl seemed almost animated and personable even apologising for having been out when Carter appeared a few weeks earlier. Gladys Carter has been driven over by friends. She seems a lot older than last time Carter saw her, two years ago at Arthur's funeral. Carter spends a bit of time with his grandmother, finding some comfort in her thick Welsh accent, feeling guilty he's not been to visit in so long. The general atmosphere is of guilt and missed opportunities. Gladys tells her grandson he's turned out alright. Carter can't help feel how old and frail she's beginning to look. She's come along with her brother Wilf, who's hiding behind a thick pair of sunglasses. Leanne's turned up late. And alone. Everyone's keen to get this over with.

Cousin Lee arrives with two fresh-faced prison officers. He's given time to greet his brother. An embrace that stretches to a rushed, cold handshake. Prison time only seems to have perfected that aggressive stare, and regulated diet accentuated the meanness of his wiry frame. Carter nods from a distance, unconvinced Lee knows who he is. He'll try and pluck up the courage to have a word after the service.

The funeral's quick and impersonal. The sermon mentions the difficulties Hev faced in later life. There's a brief mention of Al, a misguided and revisionist view of the closeness of the family, a few words about one loving son, less about another. Paul and a burly former colleague by the name of Brenda read psalms and the service is over before it begins. A shitty life summed up in about twelve minutes.

Lee's not given permission to attend the reception so Carter has a brief exchange before he's taken away. A series of nods and grunts. Lee is still haunted by limited social graces. Says he will be out in a few years, got some plans, been working on his boxing. Paul's very much the man of the day though, beckoning people into cars, providing instructions for directions to the reception. Remaining calm and strong. Carter's feeling anxious and finding himself regularly checking his mother's posture, gestures and emotions. Pat's the embodiment of grief-stricken, sobbing away, tissues permanently mopping her tears. Carter refuses to sponge any of her sadness.

Paul and Carmen's pristine and minimalistic abode is tested by the presence of around twenty people all wanting to sit down. There's the uttering of small talk and memories but nobody really wants to talk about the deceased because the deceased has been gone for about twenty years. Nobody's really got a fond or amusing anecdote about Hev since April 1989. Dead woman walking. The missing husband a taboo subject every bit as huge as the drinking binges and lost years spent chasing conspiracy theories. The elephant in the room is colossal. The desire to have a few drinks and get out as mammoth.

Carter exchanges a few words with his mother but he makes sure Rachel and Carl are in attendance to avoid the conversation moving onto their problems. It's cordial yet hypocritical. Nothing more. Pat's shunned both by Hev's friends and Paul, and barely engages in any discourse with her parents. She lasts about thirty minutes at the cold finger buffet and heads home from exhaustion. Carter knows it's the last time she'll see a lot of these people.

As Pat ghosted away, Paul beckoned Carter towards the BBQ patio area out the back where a few mourners are smoking but generally minding their own business.

'Hope today's not been too bad for you? Think you've handled it very well,' offers Carter.

'Can't say it's been easy, especially seeing certain folk.'

'You mean Mom?'

'Well, among others. Just find the whole thing hypocritical. But guess she had to make an appearance. You know they'd seen each other about twice in five years? And only then when she had to...Grandad's funeral....Fucking cheek....'

'....she should have been there. It's her fucking sister, for Christ sake. Know I could have done more. But look what happened when I got involved. Had I not gone round on Saturday, had I done things differently, she might still be alive....'

Carter, not knowing what words to offer, rests his arm on Paul's shoulder as he chucks down the dregs of a can of funeral beer.

'In these situations, I guess we all think we could have done more. You can't blame yourself, it had been a mess for a long time, she had help, you were there, it just wasn't enough, I guess....'

'I know, guess it just doesn't feel like that right now.'

There's a silence as if those words kind of summed it up.

'Let's have that beer later in the week. Like you, I think there's stuff we can find out. Even just scratching the surface. I'm going to have a sort out of Mom's stuff at the weekend or whenever I can get round to it, see what I can find. Come along and help if you're interested.'

'Do you think it's still right I'm getting involved? I've argued with Mom, your Mom's gone, not sure who else can help anyway.'

'Think it's worth us talking about what you've found, see what Mom has. If there's nothing we can just leave it but who knows? The note she left me said something about getting on with my life but in the same sentence that someone in the family knows something. So, in the same breath she wants me to find out. Fucking typical. And if it's someone in the family, it's surely got to be Aunt Pat.'

'Sounds good,' agrees Carter, suddenly feeling a huge weight of expectation. 'I just don't want to get involved with Mom anymore but I'm up for doing anything around seeing her.'

Paul simply nods. Carter realises he's plunged back into this dark hunt. The sense of support is going to make it easier. Possibly.

CHAPTER 11
TOWN

(July 1987)

Pat's powdering up in front of a hand mirror. Girls' night in with the lassies from the salon. Siobhan, Karen and Linda. Linda's in charge of Ann Summers nights. Underwear modelling, giggling over sex toys, getting a bit boozy, carry-on style gags. Leanne and Dan have been dispatched to Aunt Hev's to play with the twins. Not that Tony gives a shit. Tony's staring intensely into the long hallway mirror hung under a 1976 Blackpool Tower temperature reader. Preparing for a night shift. Preparation limited. Intimidation total.

Pat's flicking through *The Mail*. Quiet day. Advert for West Midlands police officer. Recruitment drive. Individuals like Tony Cole have put people off joining.

Pat's in a teasing mood. It's rare Tony and her are in the house at the same time. Tony's almost begged for night shifts and when he doesn't get them, pretends he's on them. Nobody on the Force doing so much overtime. Tony's unable to conceal an increasing dislike and distance from his wife. They've not had a regular conversation or a meal together in a year. Not had sex in months. Not had consensual sex in even longer. They bark and bitch at each other. Pat's bitter, repressed and emotionally uninterested. The problem is terminal. Tony's always somewhere else. Lost interest in the marriage. Only hanging around for the kids. Drops Leanne off at school every day, looking forward to taking Daniel down the Blues. Can't stand being around the kids when Pat's there. *Loveless bitch.* Tony's been head over heels for Jackie Barnes, a busty, lippy barmaid with no baggage except the two jugs that propel from her chest. The offer of cheap encounters on Broad Street and in Digbeth cure any nights when Jackie's not up for it.

'Says here there are five things that make a good copper,' beckons Pat, insisting on reading the advert out loud.

'*A genuine concern for what is going on in today's society.* That's hardly you. *The desire to play a key role in the local community and an awareness of local issues is essential.* Not you again. *Plenty of stamina and courage and also fair play and understanding.* Well, I'll give you courage and probably stamina as well, just not at mucking in round here. And forget the fucking understanding. *The opportunity to operate as part of a friendly, caring team, always ready to lend a helping hand in any situation.* Fuck that too. *The desire for sheer challenge, variety and job satisfaction in a well-paid career where there is ample opportunity for promotion.* That's really not you! Remind me, why exactly did you want to be a fucking copper?'

Tony's polishing and re-lacing his ankle-cut Dr Martens. He's only caught half of what Pat has said and remained stubbornly uninterested.

'Well then, cat bit your tongue?' barks Pat.

'Suits me, like friggin' cutting hair and gossiping suits you. Maybe I like some order, bashing a few fucking heads together. I'm doing something I fucking enjoy and making a difference. It's bringing the money home so get off my fucking back.'

'We'd all love a job spent in a pub, wouldn't we, Tony?'

'If that's where they want me to work, that's where I work. I'm just following orders.'

Pat's polishing her nails, feet balanced out on the chocolate-coloured pouffe. Tony tweaks his moustache in the mirror, spreads a lump of green gel in his greying hair and leaves without saying a word. As is custom.

***

The Porters' protestations that the spare bedroom's not finished has fallen on deaf ears. Al doesn't give a toss that they've got guests coming in a few days. Al's behind. Al's not focused. Al promises a twenty quid discount. Al's two weeks late paying off Wayne Cole. Washing machine, couple of bookshelves, microwave. Fell off the back of a lorry. Fell into Al's hands. Wayne and Al shook on four hundred. Al was ripped off. Wayne's not seen anything. Al's been pissing it away. Small bets. Lots of bets. Nothing but torn slips. Storming out of the betting shop as fast as he marches in. Even Brian the bookie is starting to feel apologetic.

Wayne's impatient. Keen to get his money back. Tiny envelope. Hundred quid in five pound notes. Rest by the end of the week. Al's not got a clue where to find the rest. Al's been a slippery bugger. Again. Al's crashed off the wagon.

Al's tuned into Slater at 7. *Brummie hero Mansell's won at Silverstone. Seen off Piquet. 2,000 runners finished Sandwell marathon.* Al hates going over to Smethwick. Hates the area. Hates the Black Country. Hates Yam Yams. Hates Wayne Cole's small time sarcasm and condescending cracks.

Wayne's pissed off. Promised Shelley and the kids a holiday. Some sun on the Costa del Sol. Paid the deposit, waiting on slippery, bull-shitting Al to come up with the rest. Wayne doesn't trust Al. An uncomfortable, slippery nuisance. Always sure of tomorrow's winning bet. The next big thing. Gagging for a favour. Big mouth, small return. Wayne sees Al out of necessity, whenever there's a family piss-up or bit of money to make.

Wayne's done a week of long haulage. Across to Hull. Down to Swansea. Bit of overtime. Got four days off. Been jamming down The Legion with the new band. *Thrash Thunder*. Occasional gig in the Black Country's heavy metal clubs and a few too many pints. Enough to ignite his temper. Wayne's not accepting less than the full whack.

Al's parked with the engine running and knocked the door in a hurry. BRMB booming out of the speakers. Wants to say his piece and get away.

'Alright mate, how's it going? Gotta get off somewhere so can't stop.'

'As long as you've come with what I've been waiting for,' snaps Wayne.

'Nearly there, mate.'

Al takes a step backwards, reaches for the thin, heavily-folded brown envelope from the back pocket of his paint-splashed Levis and hands Wayne the light wad.

'Doesn't look much like four hundred.'

'There's a hundred in there, fella. Rest will be with you at the weekend. Been breaking my balls, work's been slow.'

Wayne's about to blow a gasket. Final straw.

'You better park your fucking car properly and come in as you and I need to talk about this.'

'Give me a minute.'

Al feels like speeding off. Wayne could take him out. And Wayne looks like taking him out. Short, fat bugger, Wayne. Needs more to wind him up than his brother but could still squash a man like a fly. Especially a pretty boy like Al Jeavons. Al parks and prepares his bullshit excuse.

Shelley and the kids are out. Wayne's waiting, arms folded at the front door, his paunch accentuated by a tight blue vest and fat legs breaking through his fluorescent yellow Baggies' away shorts. Been a hot day. Wayne's been working out. Muscles struggling to break through the winter podge.

'I thought we said four fucking hundred. It wasn't easy getting you that fucking stuff and I need the bleedin' money to go on holiday.'

'I've got a hundred together, you'll get the rest soon.'

'How soon? I've heard soon for the last fucking two weeks. You've been pissing it all up again. Don't fob me off about not working because your Hev says you've got work up to your eyeballs. So you're either lying to her or to me.'

'You'll get another two hundred at the weekend, mate. No bullshit. If not I'll give you my bleedin' car until you've got it. Done and dusted.'

'I'm gonna call it another fifty with the interest.'

'That's fucking harsh.'

'You want harsh, mate? How about I tell your bird about all the customers you shag?'

Al's turns ashen-faced, taken aback by Wayne's rash statement. Al pretends he doesn't know where Wayne's coming from. Brushing the comment off. Wayne's rapidly losing his patience.

'Don't think I don't know about what you were up to during the war. To my brother.'

'What the fuck are you talking about?'

'Talking about the fucking time you and Pat were at it just before I came round. Could smell the sex on you and saw your fucking spunk in the bin. So, if you want to avoid fucking World War Three, then you'll get me three hundred and fifty quid by the weekend. Otherwise it will be my brother on the end of this.'

Al's trying hard not to hide his panic. Al's shitting himself. Been five years and thought he'd got away with it. Almost forgotten about it except whenever he caught a glimpse of Pat's slender legs. *Coast clear.*

'You'll get your money but you're wrong about what you're saying and you'd better be careful of the fucking enemies you make. I'll have you for that.'

In an instant, the door's slammed in Al's face and he's back down the Dudley Road.

***

Al's not going to get four hundred quid. Got another hundred coming in from the Porters and then a fat void for the summer. *Never much work in soddin' August.* Hev's reading *The Mail. 'Looking Good for Brum'. 'City wanting to shed concrete jungle image, raise standard of architecture, become leisure centre of England.'* Bollocks.

'Think we should send the kids to some of these play schemes.' Paul and Lee have been bored and acting up.

Al's twitchy. Al's half paying attention. Paying less attention than usual. No card schools organised for a few weeks. Never going to make that sort of money back from the gee-gees.

'Are you listening to me?'

'What was that…?'

'Think the boys would like to do some of these activities the council are offering, look swimming, running, footie. Will get them out of the bleedin' house during the summer holidays. Can see if Pat wants to send Daniel.'

'How much is that going to cost me?'

'Not much, couple of quid a day…'

Hev's only been part-time since the twins were born. Thursdays and Fridays. Big salary cut. Al'd kept his head above water for a while. Just. Not been easy but took on some cheap help to get jobs done quicker. When he's been off the gambling, the jobs have been completed faster.

'Going to need to take some money out from the savings. Not had a chance to pay bleedin' Wayne for all of that stuff.'

'Thought you'd paid him all last week?'

Al had bent the truth. Again.

'Paid two hundred. Cash from the last job not all in. He's on my back for the other two hundred, off on holiday with the kids. Told you we shouldn't have got all that junk.'

'You said we could afford it!'

'We could…we can. Just not all at once.'

Savings are low as it is. Mortgage and kids have seen to that. Plus car's regularly packing in. Al's not seen the savings for a while. Hev's kept it from him. Hev's wised up to him.

Hev switches her attention to *Points of View*. Planning to watch Carrott's *Stand Up America*.

'I'm not letting you chip away into our bleedin' savings again. Need that money for a rainy day. Can get fifty quid out for Wayne, not giving you any more. The money left is all what I've earned as well. As soon as you get some cash in your pocket it goes down the bookies!'

Al retreats and scuttles out of the room.

***

Al's had a rough day. Doing a slapdash job on the bedroom, trying to drum other work. *It's A Sin* emanating from the radio. Got nowhere. Racking his brain trying to find cash. From somewhere. Exercised and exhausted all of his mates. Too many debts paid too late with too much hassle. Could sell the video or washing machine. Hev will crucify him. Would only be able to flog it on the cheap anyway. Thinks about going into TSB, get a loan for the business. Credit history already abysmal. Al's in a corner.

Some jammy bugger's won on Littlewoods. 1,339,358 quid. Biggest ever win. Al'd take the 358. *Just need a little friggin' slice of the pie.* Another reprieve. *Last time in trouble. Last time owing money. Got to be clean. Got to stay in.*

'Blues back in training'. 'Cram running on Brum's big race night at Alexander Stadium'. Terrence Trent D'Arby on the radio. Al's distracted. Al's not got much choice. Heading to the bookies. 14.10 Newmarket. Twenty quid on 8/1 favourite. Few simple bets. Sure-fire winners. Will get Wayne off his back. 8/1 favourite comes fifth. 6/1 favourite at Haydock finishes second. Al's out of forty quid. Al's spent half the eighty notes coming to him on Sunday. Al's in a hole.

***

Tony Cole's plain-clothed and on a mission. Drug monitoring in the pubs and bars on Broad Street. He enjoys the night shifts. Check out the birds. Bit of rough stuff with junkies and abusers. Occasional bribe. Odd hooker with Hudson. Power to pick on anyone.

Hudson, his new right hand. *Got rid of that flaky Cockney Braithwaite.* Braithwaite's back down Pebble Mill. Behind a desk. *Hudson's a Villa fan but he's alright.* Hard as nails. Wiry build, pencil-thin moustache, questionable breath, oversized leather jacket and too much cologne. Hudson just needs to give a glance and a stare. His sheer presence radiates violence. Hudson carries a Stanley knife and knuckledusters like others do a wallet and keys. Regularly gives the odd non-payer a slice or a heavy tap.

Cole does the talking. Pair got more enemies than friends on the Force. Sent to plainclothes owing to looking more like crooks than the crooks themselves. Hudson's been on warnings, head-butted a fellow officer, glass fight in a pub ended up with two fellas in the Queen Elizabeth for a week, too much back talk to his superiors. Force about to split the pair up. Not enough arrests being made for all of the cages being rattled, all the hours being paid.

Late nights allow Tony to see Jackie. Jackie Barnes. Huge tits, sparrow-like body. Part share in an Ansell's pub near Aston. Wants to get her own place eventually. Tony's there on the beat regularly. Often when covering, and contributing, to some of the football violence. Met a year ago, Tony's seen her fanny more than Pat's over the past year. *Everything Pat isn't.* Tony's going to be out soon. Jackie's an authentic redhead, collar matches cuffs. Sharp sense of humour, sharp mind. Likes hard knocks like Tony though. Men who lead from the front. Jackie wants Tony to move in with her.

Tony's got a few mates heading over to Edwards No 8 after a routine shift on the streets. Wayne, Steven Baker, Gaz Hartley, Mick O'Brien. Usual hard drinking before winding up at a Riley's snooker club for some winner takes all games. Al's no longer invited. Al's a bore. Al's a big mouth. Al's owed everybody money. People have got tired of Al.

Wayne should be getting his cash tomorrow. Still pissed off. Wayne's been getting smashed all week. Isolating himself from Shelley's whining and fish n' chip dinners. Wayne's going to have enough beers to start talking. Madonna's *Papa Don't Preach* booming in the club. Boys move for a smoke peering at the underage school girls and a gathering of students celebrating a Friday night on the town. Tony Cole's made some good money tonight, taken a cut from some of the bars to keep things quiet. Has to make the odd arrest but keeps it low profile, low charges. A win-win situation.

Wayne's hyperactive, shooting his mouth off at everyone and anyone. Ogling girls and spilling drinks on innocent passers-by. Eventually finds himself alone with Tony. Had something on the tip of his tongue all night.

'That cunt Al should be over tomorrow with the rest of the fucking money. Going to fucking flatten him if it's not the three fucking fifty he owes me.'

'You wanna put the fear into him. He's owed every cunt in this city money, he'll just continue taking liberties. Fucking liability. He's a shit, that bloke.'

'Don't worry, I've got a fucking feeler on him. He'll have the money. But I'd like to see that cunt suffer.'

Wayne's trolleyed. Enjoyed two-for-one on the shots even more viciously than happy hour. Been given too many warnings for fondling young girls. Ready to say anything to anyone who will listen.

'Need me to get involved?' asks Tony.

'Maybe. Hasn't surprised me that you haven't twatted him already.'

'He's never had to owe me money, always been careful about that. Slimy little fuck.' Tony takes a large sip of his rye and coke and mutters 'cunt' a few times under his breath.

'It's not just his wallet that wanders, it's his fucking dick as well. Sure he's fucking always getting it off on the job. Cunt and the bookies, that's all he ever wants.'

Tony's stroking the top of his tash, enjoying seeing his brother so riled. Happy to observe the one man slanging show.

'And you're a fucking saint all of a sudden? He's really got into you.'

Wayne's not holding back. Proverbial rush of blood to the head.

'Got pretty good evidence of him fucking around on the job. Seen it myself.'

Tony's amused. Fondles his moustache again. Takes an aggressive and long drawn out drag out of his fag, glances at the bountiful rear of a passing girl who's probably no older than seventeen.

'You been spying on him, you perv?'

'No, but caught him at it once.'

'Fuck me. Where?'

'When you were away fighting the fucking war.'

Tony's not made the jump in his head. Tony's still smiling. Wayne carries on. Trying not to smile through his teeth.

'Sure he was knobbing your missus.'

Instantly, Tony grabs his brother by the throat and smashes his shaved head against the cigarette machine. Wayne's receives an open gash behind his ear from the impact against the coin slot. A packet of Rothmans slips out, almost in slow motion. Almost comically.

Tony's charging with the violence and the force of a runaway freight train.

'What the FUCK are you trying to say? You better just be talking out of your fucking pissed arse.'

'Let me fucking go, you twat. I'm just telling you what I saw.'

Tony headbutts his brother. Wayne's nose is cut in two, blood swamping down his rodeo denim shirt. Security are on their way over. Tony's pulled out his West Midlands police badge. Security backs off. The two scrap against the toilet doors, swinging arms against innocent bystanders while the remainder of the gang try and break it up. Pushed outside, they continue to wrestle. Steven Baker, as hard as and more psychotic than them both, manages to intervene, break 'em up, throw a few wayward punches. Not because it's necessary. But because he likes it. Wayne's trying to pick himself up off the curb, now slurring his words.

'Tony, go and have it out with that fucking slag of a missus. I saw the fucking johnnies in the bin. Caught them at it. They were fucking dead suspicious. Al was getting his dick in. Fuck you.'

Tony Cole kicks his brother hard in the stomach. Wayne roles over the curb. Wayne's too pissed to respond. Wayne knows the money might never come his way now. Tony hails down a cab and threatens to murder the petrified driver if not back in Kings Heath in ten minutes. Cab's there in nine.

***

Cunt. Bitch. Fucking slag. Going to fucking knife her in the cunt. See to her proper. Knife her in the cunt. Smack her about until she's fucking numb. Nobody gets on the wrong side of Tony Cole. Nobody. At the fucking war, fighting for my country and she's knobbing slimy Al. Going to fucking smack her and fuck Hev. Going to fucking finish Al. Hard and painful. Slice his dick off. Cunt. Bitch. Fucking Slag. Die.

***

It's 02:42. Pat's woken by Tony breaking into the house. Not the first time. The beast regularly left his keys on some hooker's bedside table, in the pub, at the station. Leanne and Dan are fast asleep. Pat's promised to take them to Drayton Manor with some mates in the morning. Pat hears her husband screaming and charging up the stairs. Tony's fallen over twice on his way up. Tony's drunk and on a violent mission. He's in the bedroom before Pat can peel her head off the pillow.

'You fucking slag. Fucking dirty bitch. Fucking slag.'

Tony's words coming out so fast he's spitting all over himself. He's got Wayne's blood all over his shirt. He's the definition of a violent nightmare.

Within seconds, Tony's pounced onto the bed and got Pat by the throat.

'You fucking cunt. Fucking about with that cunt Al? When I was at fucking war.' Tony's spitting blood. Literally.

Pat tries to fend him off but Tony's squeezing her neck so hard that she can barely breathe. Pat fears death. Pat's choking. Tony relents and smashes his fist into the headboard with such force that it reverberates for minutes.

206

'Tell me the fucking truth, you slag!'

Pat can't answer. Pat says nothing. Just looks at Tony with disgust and feels the energy to lie or respond is drained out of her. This is her way out of this loveless, violent, cancerous marriage. Tony reaches again for her throat, glances into her eyes and smashes her with a firm right hook across the face. Tony's still got his brother's blood on his hands. Pat's jaw makes a cracking sound and Tony's gone hard under her eye. Tony swears that he'll never see Pat again, drunkenly threatens revenge and before leaving embarks on a violent spree destroying almost every piece of glass and furniture in the house. All to the roar of 'YOU FUCKING SLAG.'

Treading through the glass shards of his own wedding photos, Tony grabs a framed picture of himself and the kids in front of the wolf pen at Birmingham Nature Centre. Leanne as stroppy-looking as her mother, Daniel with that cute, charming glance. Coles don't do charm. Tony Cole no longer recognises the boy.

***

Wayne Cole's nursing a severe headache. Got a split lip, black eye and partially broken nose. Kids have cried on seeing him. Shelley's taken them to their grandparents for the day. Banning him from late nights. Wayne couldn't give a shit. Wayne feels sick. Feels like only a drink will sort him out. His head's spinning and he can't keep anything down. Wayne's been on the lid all morning. And to make matters worse, the Beast is on the phone.

'How much does cunt-face owe you?' directs Tony.

'Three hundred and fifty.'

'Do me a favour, kiddo. Don't contact him. Let it fucking go. I'll tell you why one day. I'll get your fucking money later. Meet me down in Digbeth at the bus station. Four hundred quid. Just forget about Al, I'm taking care of him. Just going to ask you to go round and get my stuff once this settles. It got messy last night. I'm not there anymore.'

Tony half apologises for smashing his brother's face. The money covers the other half. Wayne understands. Shelley will be off his back about the money. Al's got it coming.

***

Pat hid in her room for hours after Tony left. Shaking, chain-smoking and sobbing. Glad Tony has gone. Fearful of the consequences. Tony's not done as much damage as his hating hands are capable of. Not to Pat. Pat's got enough make-up on to be presentable to the kids. Going to send them off with their mates to Drayton Manor. Pat's not going to make it. Not like this. Pat will lie low for a few days. Bit of time off work until the swelling is down. Al might have had it himself by then. Pat's anxious to find out how far Tony's reach has got. If Tony's got to Al, then Hev will know. Hev can't know. Not now things have been going better.

The house is a mess. Tony's kicked through every bit of wood, the glass cabinet's smashed to pieces, plates and glasses shard everywhere. The kids slept through it. Pat tells them a burglar came and Dad's at the police station. They need to go away while things get cleaned up. Pat's just not sure how long it will take to clean this up. Days, weeks, months, a life.

***

Al's sheepish. Middlin' July day. Been down Stirchley for a fry up. Tried to read the paper. '*Ali blames boxing for his Parkinsons*'. '*Council want to set up computer bus timetables*'. '*Dunlop shopping centre 5,000 new jobs*'. '*10% of Birmingham city council employees have a drink problem*'. Al doesn't see the panic. Ducked in and out of mates' houses seeing if he can borrow some cash. Most mates hard up as him. Morley's even offered him a 1982 Fiesta for eight hundred quid. Got their own issues. Own debts. Own problems. Hev's out getting a Van Heusen suit. *Spending her fucking cash.* Got a wedding at the end of the summer. Al doesn't know how to face Wayne Cole. Al's heading home to make the call.

Al's back to an empty house. Hev's gone into town with the twins to pick up her suit. Phone's ringing. It's Pat. Sounding panicked.

'Is Hev there?'

'No, she's gone up town, back later, want me to leave a message?'

'Is she okay?'

'Of course she is, why wouldn't she be?'

'Coz, Tony found out what happened. About me and you. He went berserk, smashed my face and the house. Wondered if he'd come for you yet.'

The line goes quiet for about half a minute, Al's been crippled with panic.

'How the fuck's he found out? How can he prove it? BOLLOCKS.'

'I don't know, he just knows. Supposed you must have blabbed about it to one of your mates.'

'Out of the question.'

Silence. Pat's sobbing.

'What shall we do?' asks Pat.

Pat's voice is wobbly.

'Let's see what happens. I can deny it to Hev, not going to tell her, that's for sure. Tony's got no proof. Nobody saw us at it. Nobody knows. Tony just flew off because he's fucking paranoid.'

Al relents…

'Do you think Tony's going to come over?'

'Surprised he hasn't already, just watch your back and protect my sister. Tell her to call me back about taking care of my two for a day or two. House is a mess.'

Al puts down the phone and sinks in the armchair for what seems like an hour but is about four and a half minutes, to be reawaken by the sound of the phone again.

'Al?'

'Yeah?'

'It's Wayne.'

'I was about to….'

'Fuck it. Just listen to me. I don't want your money. We're through so just stay the fuck away.'

Phone dead. Al's got no idea what just happened. Al just knows it's not good.

CHAPTER 12
YARDLEY WOOD

(October 2009)

It's taken a few weeks for Paul to sort things out. Carmen's pushed him into setting a wedding date for the end of the year. Help focus their minds on something else. He's buried himself in work, even turning up on jobs. Couldn't face rifling through most of his mother's affairs, piles of unused or unwashed clothes, crap accumulated and never thrown away.

On a crisp October Saturday morning, he plucks up the courage to throw the furniture and junk mercilessly into a skip. The local hordes were out in no time. Sooner it's out of the way, sooner things can move on. His mother left very little of use bar a small, potential profit on the house, which Paul has decided will go towards the honeymoon and the rest to Lee as a start-up fund for when he gets out. Following his mother's wishes. Carmen organises getting the clothes down to a charity shop. There's a box or two of paperwork, books and photo albums which Paul takes back to his place.

There's a few rare treats in there. Wedding photos and snaps of himself as a child which had been lost in attics for years. And threatened to be for further decades. In amongst the photos, Paul discovers the most rigidly organised item in the entire house—a green spiral folio full of cuttings and letters related to Al. Paul skims through it to gain a general feel for what's in there. There are *Mail* and *Gazette* articles, notes from friends, some old photos of Al, invoices from private detectives, lists of agencies written down by Hev, some formal notes from West Midlands police about the investigation being closed and then a dozen or so typewritten notes from Bob Rowntree, *Evening Gazette* Crime Reporter.

Paul packs it up and decides to invite Carter to plough through the documentation, if it marries any leads he's already followed. Or if he wants to take it further. A seed has been planted in Paul, a desire to justify and terminate his mother's futile emotional and financial investigation.

***

Carter's early. Work's been somewhat quiet, he's waiting for feedback from clients so he's been able to enjoy a day bantering over coffee and distracting himself on the internet. He's equipped with a stack of Peronis and a Domino's pizza voucher, a reward for advertising finished last month. Paul's lost some weight since the funeral and looks cheerful, sporting a more genuine smile than during their meeting a few months earlier. He mocks Carter's 'fanny magnet' beard.

Carmen's lingering as she's preparing to head out to the cinema to see *Up*. She's a remarkably pleasant, conventional, somewhat old-fashioned girl and seems very much part of Paul's mantra of self-improvement. Carmen's suggesting that Rachel and Carter come round for dinner, that they should see more of each other. Paul's enthusiastically in agreement.

After about half an hour of drinking and dancing round the subject of the evening, Paul hands Carter the folder recovered from his mother's house.

'To be honest, there wasn't much of use at Mom's bar this folder, but it's pretty detailed. Seems to have got most of her leads about what happened to Dad. It's all there newspaper cuttings and all.'

As Carter starts scanning through the articles and deciphering various bureaucratic notices, some research regarding a death certificate and old bank statements, Paul suggests he cuts to the notes at the back, written across three years between December 1989 and December 1992.

'There's about twelve notes from this Rowntree guy. It's about the only thing in there that seems to have any weight. He was the guy at *The Gazzette* who followed the story. I've read through his letters, seems he's one of those investigative reporters or something, sniffing round what the police didn't do.'

Carter takes the twelve double-sided letters out of the A4 plastic file they've been kept in.

'Do you want me to read them now?'

'Maybe take them with you, have a look in your own time. Will take ages now. I've been through them a few times, there's a few interesting things. He gave Mom the name of a private detective he knows, some guy who used to work for West Midlands police. Seems like he was working on behalf of Mom and Rowntree. Like Mom was paying for this guy and then feeding Rowntree stuff for some stories.'

'How come nothing more got published if he was still investigating stuff?'

'Says in the letters his bosses weren't keen. Seemed the investigations just led Rowntree to slag off the police for being lazy and dropping the case. Papers weren't keen on that by the looks of things. Also says Dad went missing in Yorkshire so it was for the police up there to deal with as well. But there's some interesting stuff in there….'

'…..Mom had the private detective follow members of the family. Including your mom but this didn't get anywhere very fast. But this guy managed to find your dad and was on his trail for a while. He was over in Coventry working for the police until he quit in the early nineties. Had him followed, checked out his connections.'

'Anything?'

'Well, had a lot of mates who were criminals or near-criminals. Mentions this guy here, Steven Baker, ever heard of him?'

'Vaguely,' replies Carter, lying.

'Well they put the feelers on him, see if he knew anything about what happened to Dad. Just says this guy was not to be trusted and either knew more than he was letting on or would be prepared to for some more money.'

'Anything else?'

'Well, they checked out your dad's brother, a few of his old colleagues, this bent cop called Kevin Hudson and a few fellas who were ready to testify against him, about misconduct during his time in the Force. But he quit and starting running a pub with his new bit of skirt before they got close.'

'Do you know if these people are still alive? Rowntree? This Baker guy? Think this is where we need to start. Can't help think there's a connection between our dads disappearing. Mom might know more, might know why Dad left at least, may even know what happened to yours, but it's going to go way beyond her.'

'Not sure if most of these guys are alive, to be honest. It's nearly twenty years,' adds Paul.

'What about your dad's family?' continues Carter. 'Is there anyone left?'

'Dad was an only child, remember. That side of the family went with him...' drifts Paul. 'He had a few uncles and aunts. His old man died when he was young, really young. About four or something. Had a massive heart attack on Christmas Day coming out the pub. His mom passed away just before he got married. Circumstances were funny there too. Went down as suicide but nobody was convinced.'

'Fuck me, your dad didn't have much luck......in that case I'll call *The Gazzette* tomorrow and see if I can get hold of this Rowntree guy,' offers Carter.

'Sounds like a plan.'

'Then I'll maybe get in touch with my old man's family and see what connections they have. As much as that puts the fear of God into me.'

'Sure you want to do this?'

'No, but I've got a feeling we're heading somewhere.'

Whilst Paul devours the giant Hawaiian pizza, Carter goes through the letters. They read like a James Elroy novel, an intrigue of nicknames, undercover findings and mystery from another era. In the West Midlands, admittedly.

***

Carter's found the editorial desk number of *The Mail* and headed out of the office to give it a try. It's a fairly bleak October morning, and he's having to lurk in the entrance to the offices to stay clear of the rain while the girls from the recruitment agency downstairs gossip and violently puff on their cigarettes. Bob Rowntree's no longer full time. He carries out some part-time sub-editing but is retired and only comes in once a week. Carter is given an email and a desk number for Fridays, when he helps with the weekend edition. Going to have to wait a few days.

Carter hits Google. A search for Tony Cole, Anthony Cole and the lady he is reported to have married, Jackie Barnes, is in vain. There's a few other names in the folder. Steven Baker is just too common, most leads divert to a pastor in Missouri. Hardly likely to be the same one. Kevin Hudson likewise draws blanks. These fellas carved their teeth when the internet was not around and hardly likely to be on it now. Bar a few links to *Mail* , *Post* and *Gazzette* archives, Bob Rowntree is hardly conspicuous. Andy Braithwaite, one of the officers mentioned in Hev's notes, draws a blank. The other—Earl Beckford—is everywhere as a motivational speaker. Yet nothing on the past. Michael Hartley, the private detective hired, is lost in cyberworld as well. Carter's not seen his dad's side of the family in over twenty years. He can't for the life of him remember the name of Wayne Cole's kids and Wayne himself is nowhere to be found. Apart from the address of his grandparents, assuming they are still in the same boxy Smethwick house, he's going to find it tough enough getting close to the Coles. It's going to take pre-internet powers of research and dedication to get anywhere.

Carter's unsure of how to approach Bob Rowntree. Whether a cold call or an email. In the end he decides for the latter and will follow it up with a call if nothing's back in a week.

Dear Mr Rowntree,

Apologies if this email is rather out of the blue. I am the nephew of Heather Jeavons who you had vast correspondence with in the early 1990s.

Sadly Heather passed away earlier in the month and on organising her belongings, I and her son Paul found the various letters you exchanged. If you were willing to meet me for a coffee at your convenience, I would be very interested in discussing some things further.

I understand fully if too much time has passed and you don't want to discuss an old case.

Best regards,

Daniel Carter

An out-of-office reply follows almost as soon as Carter hits send. He decides Bob Rowntree's his best bet for now.

***

Bob Rowntree's working on a new walking tour guide of Birmingham for the city council. Bach's *St Matthew Passion* is turned up to an impressive volume. Rowntree's keeping busy, editing a few books for local historians and producing a small photobook on the prefabs in Hall Green. Ever since Colette passed away five years ago after an illness as long as the Bristol Road, he's been rejuvenated. Time passed him by on the newspaper, email, internet, cut out the need for proper reporting. Local papers shut down, more and more stories from agencies. Just didn't suit him anymore. Not like the heydays in the '70s when there were allegations of a corrupt police force to attack, when the criminals would call the newsdesk, when he was every bit a detective more than a reporter. That never sat well with his superiors. Rowntree always a believer in the truth, even at the expense of cutting the hand that fed you. Wrote a resignation letter fifteen times during his twenty-five-year career. Was never accepted, always coaxed into coming back. Rowntree still enjoys breezing in on a Friday, sympathetically bullying young reporters about their poor grammar, berating the advertising team as talentless buffoons, enjoying a pint, and always just one in the Old Joint Stock on the way home. It's a link with the past, a vital anchor in his week.

Rowntree's not really an emailer but his only child Michael has set it up so it's easy enough to master. The paper sometimes asks for opinion pieces or some editing in the week. It's rare but he has to keep his email open. There's still a lot of readers who write in about old cases, or enquire about one of his tours. Rowntree likes feeling important, wanted, helpful. The email from Dan Carter's troubled him for a few hours. The name Heather Jeavons flashed like a neon sign on Las Vegas Boulevard. One which had flickered apologetically and lingered longer, a case as wide open the day Rowntree closed the file as when it arrived. The semi-tragic woman, mourning like a Sicilian peasant, spiralling into her liquid demons. Pushing out theories, repeating the same story. A voice which fell on deaf ears.

Rowntree agrees to meet Carter in his local, The Covered Wagon, on Yardley Wood Road, just a mile away from Carter's in Moseley. Carter's a little nervous about the meeting. Rachel reassuringly tells him it's an interesting breakthrough and there's nothing to fear. Paul keeps blowing hot and cold and pulls out at the last minute. Pressure from the girlfriend. Things have become raw again. Carter respects his decision but is anxious about going alone.

***

Rowntree's attacking *The Guardian* crossword when Carter arrives. Although there's no formal meeting place and the pub is relatively full with post-work revellers, Rowntree's an immediately easy figure to point out. Thick glasses attached to a green cord running round his neck, a late 1980s M&S knitted jumper and thick-hemmed mustard-coloured cords. He has the aura of a nice man. Carter introduces himself and offers to get Rowntree another half pint of Spitfire.

Carter talks passively about his aunt's death and mentions the disappearance of his own father which started this chain of events. Rowntree's a good listener. He's not writing notes but always gives the impression he is. He nods in the right places, smiles at important junctures, makes journalistic prompts. He possesses a warm Black Country twang which becomes more evident when he mentions that he's a West Brom season ticket holder.

'It's always best with these things to start from the top. Devil's always in the detail. That's the motto I've always tried to ram home to some of the halfwits I've had pushed on me over the years. I remember hearing about your uncle's case as it was a terrible week on the paper. Bleedin' pain. All that Hillsborough stuff. When something like that kicks off, which is not local news, it always puts a lot of pressure on the rag. Your uncle going missing just happened on a really busy week. Had it been on quieter weekend, it may have had some more coverage, sort of coverage that would have got people involved. Unfortunately, from a paper's point of view it just faded quickly. I tried many times to bring the case forward, but there was never any great evidence. Just evidence of the police's failings which those upstairs were not keen on at the time. Brown-noses that they were.'

'What were your first impressions when you started covering the case?' asks Carter, hesitantly.

'Well, once the dust settled and he never reappeared it was unusual. And unfortunately, as it most likely happened up north, and not on our own territory there was not much I could do from a paper point-of-view in terms of pushing the police or heading up there. There was some coverage in the South Yorkshire press but nought that really developed. Once he'd not come home, you have to assume he's dead. He had a wife, two kids and a business. It was only when we dug deeper that you could give credence to him having running away.'

'You mean the gambling stuff?'

'There was that, but there was always something else that didn't sit right. He'd been in a gambling mess before, in a bigger mess. You wouldn't mess with these people. The Irish Jacks, they were called. Nasty buggers. They're all dead or inside now, thank heavens. I can see them having done him in, to give a warning, but I'm not convinced that he ran away.'

'Did the police ever find anything on these people?'

'Your aunt was convinced at first that they did it, so the police went in hard. But they all had alibis. Good ones. They could have had someone else do it, easily, but there was not much evidence of it. And on the Monday and Tuesday after he went missing, they were round at your aunt's, so they were either good actors following through with a plan or unaware of what happened. To be honest, the card thing has never sat with me. And they kept bothering your aunt for the money. Until the police stuck their noses in.'

Rowntree breaks off, sips his pint and is mildly distracted by twelve across on the crossword.

'Couldn't help me with this could you....it's been on my mind all afternoon.'

'Lucky In The Way Things Develop (3,2,3,5).'

Carter looks at the half-filled clues and without hesitation replies, 'Rub of the Green'.

'Not as thick as you look,' smiles Rowntree.

Almost in order to take a respite, Rowntree passes the conversation back on Carter.

'So, you must have been what, four or five when your uncle left?'

'Yeah, about that, six, I think. I'm the same age as his twin kids.'

'Paul and Lee,' shoots back Rowntree with no hesitation.

'That's them.'

'How've they turned out?'

'Paul's done great, considering everything. Got his own business, become a real entrepreneur. His brother's inside, all kinds of stuff. Probably out in a few years but I think it's going to be hard for him. He was the emotional one, got in with the wrong crowd too young...'

'And what about your own folk, remember meeting your mom once, quite the firecracker.'

'Mom's still around, we don't talk, to be honest. We've not really got on since I left home, she's always kept a distance from me. Dad disappeared when I was four but guess you know that...'

'...Well, yeah. Your aunt was convinced your dad was involved. In fact she made that clear to the police and to anyone who would listen for a while. That whole thing was always shrouded in mystery, that part of it...' Rowntree pauses for breath.

'....well the relationship between your mom and your aunt. It was great when your dad left and then eroded quickly after Alan went missing. They just seemed to be chalk and cheese. Your aunt thinks Alan owed your dad money or he was jealous of him or that he even had it on with your mom but we never found anything concrete. And your aunt was drinking by that stage and had plenty of hysterical theories. I approached your mom with these theories once and she nearly knifed me so I left it. Scary lady. She had a temper. No doubt about that.'

Rowntree smiles as if reminded of his lucky escape.

'Do you think my dad leaving was in some way related?'

'I'm not necessarily convinced about that either. Not without a motive. Your dad had moved on, was remarried I think, had his job in the Force.

By all accounts he hadn't been close to your mother ever since he'd come back from the Falklands so I just saw a guy who had moved on....Al was nothing to him.'

Carter interrupts....'Did you ever meet him...?'

'No, I got very busy with stuff in 1990. Big year in politics, that one, they had me move onto different desks to help out. I told your mom to use this guy Hartley I knew, who'd set himself up as a detective after leaving the Force. Great guy. Great brain. The dog's bollocks.'

'And how did that go?'

'He basically mapped out your uncle's life from about five years earlier. Met or followed almost everyone you could imagine. The Irish. Your dad. Family. Extended Family. Friends. Even people he did jobs for. He met your dad, that's for sure. But going back a bit, I'm convinced your uncle is dead, there's no way he's alive. His accounts were never touched, he never got in touch, there were no sightings. He's gone, son.'

There's a brief pause, as Carter decides whether to interject.

'My man didn't get a great impression of your dad. He's met a load of old contacts on the Force. Your dad was basically a racist, corrupt bully. They were down on officers in the mid 1980s, so too many of these twits got in. The Serious Crime Squad era. Most people despised him and he didn't last long. His one ally was this horrid skinny guy whose name escapes me, nasty piece of work who's still there, apparently. Or was last I heard but that might be longer than I think. Anyway, your dad was running a pub in Coventry with his missus and threw Michael out one evening, almost took his jaw out. Michael didn't press charges. He should have. But he didn't want to upset the case. There were just not enough leads from your dad, not a firm motive. He'd cut himself off from his old life.'

'Do you know where he went?'

'Last in Coventry, I heard. Michael passed away in 2000. Some drunk ran into him. Got away with murder, that guy. Tragic. The dog's bollocks, that bloke. We talked about the case a bit but I finished in '92 with your aunt, I couldn't handle her anymore.'

'Why not?'

'She started treating me like her own personal reporter, turning up at the office half cut, getting angry and aggressive that more wasn't done. She didn't have a sympathetic ear in the police so when she did get one she abused it. But she seemed to be getting better a few years later, gave her a courtesy call one day as we ran a piece in the paper five years on, she almost seemed to have accepted it.'

Carter finally gets a word in. 'Did your guy find anything else out? I'm kind of looking for myself now to see what happened….if between the police and your reporter nothing came out then I'm not holding my breath, but I'm thinking that I need to get hold of my old man and look him in the eye. Irrespective of Al, this is why I started.'

'Just be careful lifting old slabs. Some of them don't want to be turned, and the ground isn't always softer underneath. Your dad abandoned you, and if he's still with us then he's a nasty, aggressive man who doesn't want to be bothered. Just brace yourself for that. And from what I can remember his sort weren't good people.'

'I appreciate that, I'll be careful,' says Carter, sounding unintentionally naïve.

'I'm here if you've got more questions or want to talk about your findings. There's still part of me that wants to know what happened.'

'Cheers,' breaks Carter….'Do you know much about this Steven Baker guy or his sidekicks? Where I could find them?'

'I'll run a check with the police for you. I still know some people there…Hudson, that was his name, Tony Cole's mate. If he's still there he must be what, fifty-five by now? So probably pushing paper until his retirement if he is. I'll get you a number but then it's up to you. Steven Baker's a tough one. I know of him through the football, he was one of the chief Baggies hooligans in the 1980s. Always in trouble. Was involved in that big ruckus in the mid '80s. I'd be surprised if he was alive or not in jail. Let's see where we get with Hudson first. But I wouldn't go alone to see somebody like that. In any case, I'd suggest seeing the fellas Beckford or Braithwaite if you can. Nice guys from the Force, they may have something or at least have a few stories. I'll see if I can find them too. But so many moved on. They had a clear out.'

'What do you think about checking in on my dad's family?'

'If they're still in touch with your dad, they'll warn him off. Your call, Hudson and your old man may have grown apart. Could just be worth checking to see if your old man's parents are still alive. Or trying his brother. From what I remember he wasn't such a bad sort, at least compared to your dad.'

Rowntree looks hurriedly at his watch and puts on his jacket. The Albion are on Sky tonight and Rowntree doesn't miss a Baggies' kick-off. Never.

'Need a win tonight. Keep the run going. Newcastle are breathing down our necks. Always listen to it with the wireless on, mind. Can't bear those idiots on the box.'

Carter smiles. It's been like a lesson with the history teacher. More anecdotes than leads or conclusions. There's some old addresses on Hev's documents so he decides he's going to do a recce of them over the weekend, before approaching anyone, establish a map of where they all are, waiting for the possibility of meeting Hudson or the other coppers from the late 1980s.

***

A few days pass before the weekend. Carter's still waiting to hear back from Bob Rowntree but in the meantime has put together some addresses: Bob and Lynette Cole. Wayne Cole. They're twenty years old, though. In addition, there's Tony Cole's address at the Margaret's Arms pub in Coventry, Hudson and a few numbers of old police colleagues.

Carter decides to head over to Smethwick first. Paul's busy with wedding arrangements but agrees to tag along for anything 'interesting'. Rachel's signed up as a companion to pass away any idle hours in a car. She seems positively excited about spending hours watching people pass down a Smethwick side-street. They've packed a flask, some blueberry muffins and reading material.

The Coles were last noted living in Gladstone Road, Smethwick. A phone number is included in the precise address book created by Michael Hartley. Carter's tried the number out of curiosity, even taking into consideration the additional '1' added in Birmingham during the 1990s to the prefix code. The Coles have either moved on, died, or simply changed their landline. Likewise Wayne Cole's number for Ford Street, parallel to his parents, is answered by a Pakistani-sounding family. Carter presumes that Wayne and his family moved somewhere bigger.

There's no plan. Carter's not sure that he's prepared to meet anyone today. More a case of piecing everything together.

**

Smethwick's changed greatly since his last visit. Fried chicken takeaways and Asian grocery stores dominate the landscape.

There's a small gap on Gladstone Road for Carter to reverse park into. It's opposite the address given for his grandparents. He vaguely remembers the house but not sure whether it is old photos playing tricks with his memory. Whilst most houses on the street give the impression of being populated by Indian or Pakistani families, number 23 has the distinct feel of being habited by old, white folk. The downstairs net curtains look yellow and fag-stained. Faded Neighbourhood Watch, Labour Party and British bulldog stickers adorn the windows. Upstairs the lime green curtains are partially drawn. The small front garden is better tended than the neighbours and recycling boxes empty and ordered.

'I reckon it's still them,' says Carter, adjusting the volume down on *Fighting Talk*.

'Do you want to knock? Pretend you're lost or something,' suggests Rachel, who has taken to the mission like a girl guide on a Duke of Edinburgh award weekend.

'They'll recognise me, I'm sure. Even if it's been twenty odd years. Families are like that.'

There's a suggestive pause as Rachel gets the hint.

'I reckon you should knock. Just say you're looking for a garage or if the Smiths still live at number 29.'

Rachel's out of the car in a flash as Carter positions himself at an angle where he can see the door more effectively. He's borrowed Mace's Canon EOS 500 and paparazzi-style lens kit to take photos of the occasion. He's dreamt about setting up his own murder investigation board. Too much time watching *The Wire*. Carter observes as Rachel waits outside the front door. After a minute or so an old man opens. Practically walking on his knees. The old man's sporting a blue cardigan over a white shirt. He's well-dressed, small, stout and doesn't smile. It's definitely a Cole. It's his grandad for sure. He's pointing, gesticulating and within seconds has closed the door. Rachel's managed to get in the way of most of the photos. Carter shoots a few of the house just for his records.

'What did he say?'

'Well, I've only gone and got your uncle's address!'

'How did you manage that?'

'Said I was a friend of Wayne's and was wondering if he was still in the area. Pretended we worked together.'

Carter's chuckling.

'He was a truck driver. How did they fall for that?'

'Not sure but he said that he's about two miles up the road in Oldbury. McKean Road, it's called. Living there with his girlfriend.'

'Nice work, babe!'

'See, I have my uses.'

Carter takes a look at the map as they prepare to move on to follow the Wayne lead. Unaware of how best to negotiate the situation. Wayne was married, according to the files. To Shelley. Two kids. Seems life has moved on differently for him as well.

McKean Road is slightly more upscale version of the Cole's terraced house. The area's a shade greener, with a row of hedged gardens battling with an impressive amount of For Sale and To Let signs. Seems like the neighbourhood is expecting the rag and bone man. Plenty of junk in the front yards. Wayne's abode is no exception. There's an old fridge waiting to be taken away and a litter of damp newspapers lying in the open porch. The white-painted house appears cold and uninviting. There are shadows at the window.

Carter sits back listening to the early team news on Five Live. They wait to see if anyone leaves the house. Carter can remember his uncle as a short, solid, bald man but little more. After half an hour, a woman who seems only a little older than Rachel, long-legged, with an overgrown bob and goofy teeth, leaves the house. Presumably the girlfriend. Carter takes a hurried picture.

The amateur detectives hang in the car for another twenty minutes catching curious looks from dog walkers. Eventually without saying a word, Carter leaves the vehicle and gesticulates to Rachel to stay put. In the style of 'sometimes you need to take matters into your own hands'.

Carter has no speech prepared and no idea what kind of reception he's going to get.

He knocks the door. A thick, unmistakably Black Country voice replies 'Coming'.

A few seconds later, a squat, red-cheeked, skinhead sporting a Londsdale t-shirt, grey jogging bottoms and a big throstle tattoo on his right forearm comes to the door. He gives the look of recognition but can't quite get there.

'What can I do for you, lad?'

'Wayne?'

'The one,' replies the bald man.

'I'm Dan Carter, your nephew. Can I come in?'

There's a silence as Wayne beckons him in, uttering 'for fuck's sake.'

CHAPTER 13
SMETHWICK

(March 1989)

Tony Cole's taken a sharp detour to St Andrew's. Bagged a pair of tickets for June's UB40 concert. Birthday present for Jackie. Together with the rock. Cold, distant divorce from Pat's come through. Plan hatched. In a few months Tony Cole will be free to go back to St Andrew's. Watch the Blues again. *In the third fucking division. Against Northampton bleedin' Town and Wigan fucking Athletic. No risk of running into scummers like Al Jeavons. Not then.*

Tony's spent the morning finalising his 'Two Year Plan'. Grafted, stolen and pimped the money. *Plan's concrete.* Jackie's heading out to watch some film called *Rain Man* at the Odeon in town. Tony Cole's cruising over to the Black Country. Off to communicate the plan. Meeting the fellas at the Red & Cow. Morgan, Hudson and Baker. The tyrant trio. Three men you'd trust with nothing outside of mindless violence.

The fellas are already there. Hudson's suspended. Off for a few weeks. Racially abused a black officer called Beckford. *Ideas above his station.* Young and ambitious. New face of the Force. Hudson's acted out the monkey chants. Just for a laugh. Hudson's squashed bananas on his desk. Just some banter. Not for his superiors. Not for Beckford. Been getting a bad press. Need to put things right. Hudson's days are numbered. Hudson's on a last warning. Last warning from being kicked onto the streets.

Steven Baker's just done a month for burglary. Breaking and entering into an electronics warehouse. First van pulled away in time. Morgan's van. Baker's got blocked in the yard by two cop cars alerted by the alarm.

Alarm Baker set off. Baker's never been too sharp. Been in and out of the slammer. Returns home when he runs out of money. Life possessions in a bin bag. Loving mother losing patience. Spread his rotten sperm about. Abandoned several pregnant conquests. Rarely not doped up. Brain's mashed. Got his own bed down Smethwick station. Almost every Friday night. Baker's future's inside or on the streets. There's no alternative. Not for someone like him.

Morgan's not done a day's work in his life. Never been inside. Record as clean as a weekday Christian. Right place, right time. Insists on being called the 'King'. Tattooed across his knuckles. Homemade effort. Full of confidence in everything he does. Hardly surprising. Morgan's made decent money. Done some big hits. Sticks to once in a while, well paid, high risk jobs. *Too many jobs, your odds aren't good.* Gets his planning right. Can work ten days a year. Got enough money to please himself the rest of the time. Sometimes connections have tried stitching him up. The cops have tried taking him in for questioning. Morgan's above that. *Long live the King.*

Morgan doesn't like having Baker on a job. Liability. Leaves the light on, door unlocked, sets off alarms, turns up half cut, leaves traces. Sloppy and drunk. But Baker's the kind of man you need if you want to send somebody down. The scapegoat. Baker's loyal enough to keep his mouth shut. Stupid enough to keep his mouth shut. Baker's just bait for the cops. The cops have even got bored of booking Baker.

Tony Cole's not yet made the pitch. Hudson's called the fellas together. Says there's an interesting job on. Good money to be made by everyone. They've been steadily drinking since twelve. Hudson and Baker going pint to pint. Talking wenches. Bantering over football. Baker's blagging about cars he's stolen, wheels he's going to nick, fanny he'd wished he'd had. '*A machete attack in Birmingham. 50-year old man attacked.*' Hudson says he had it coming. Morgan's more measured. Morgan doesn't like losing his edge. Morgan's tried talking about the budget hike. Price of petrol. Wants to hear the plan with a sober head. Morgan's carrying a copy of the Communist Manifesto in his pocket. *Joy Division* plays in his head. Morgan's a Trotsky. Big quiff and holed jumpers. Morgan needs nobody. No friends. No ties. Lives alone in a converted attic. Musty, vintage paperbacks. Notes. Sketches. Criminology course. Communism. Morgan's trying to make enough money by the time he's forty. Get out. Write. Read. Learn the piano. Morgan's the archetypal delusion of grandeur. *Morgan's from Walsall. Not fucking Warsaw.*

Heavy arms force the pub's double doors wide open. Tony Cole beckons the barmaid to bring his pint over. Light banter over the Blues match with Walsall. Micky Burton making his debut. *Micky fucking who?* Villa. Blues. Baggies. Represented. Morgan hates football. *Bunch of oafs kicking a pig's bladder in the mud.* Morgan peeks at his Casio. Tony Cole tells him to be patient. He's not calling the shots. Tony doesn't know Morgan so well. Knows of him. Doesn't trust his superior intelligence. Or his motives. Signed on reputation. Never been caught. Professional.

'Here's the deal.' Tony Cole leans forward to draw the conversation in.

Hudson's put an hour's worth of *Madness* on the Duke Box. Conversation will stay where it is.

'I want a hit. I want it clean and I don't want to be involved. This conversation and this meeting does not go beyond us four here. Fucking clear?'

Nods in unison. Steven Baker's got a rolly in his mouth and is shakily fingering his tobacco. Not had a sober day in years, not had a good day in longer.

'Kev's doing the planning. Going to get any tools necessary. But he's out after that. Bakes, you better be fucking listening. You're the link to Morgan. I don't want to see you after today, fella. Bakes gets you the money, Bakes answers your questions. You fuck up, you answer to Bakes. You fuck up, you go down. You never met me, never spoke to me.'

'I'm not in the habit of 'fucking up',' replies Morgan. Eerie. Aloof. Composed.

'Baker is your right hand man, if you need one.'

Morgan shakes his head as if Steven Baker was not there. 'I'm not bringing him along.' Uttered with the disdain usually reserved for dog turd.

'It's the four of us or nothing,' affirms Tony Cole.

'I've got my own man. No offence, but your chap here is just out of the slammer. He's linked to you as a mate. I'm guessing he's linked to the guy you're after. When this fella goes missing, they're going to sniff round his past. Sniff round you. Sniff round your mates. There's links to me and Steven. Even if the fucking pigs will probably never find, no offence meant. So, if you don't mind, Steven can bring me the money but that's it. And after this, we won't work together any more. The past lies like a nightmare upon the present. That's Marx, if you didn't know.'

'Stuff that commo shite up your arse,' snaps Hudson.

Tony Cole's impressed, although he's not showing it. Surprised Bakes has brought such a professional to the table.

'Can we trust your man?' adds Cole.

'Big coloured lad. He's cheap and he does what I say,' affirms Morgan. 'Just get me the money, tell me how you want it done and you'll never hear from us again.'

Tony Cole's scribbling on a fag box lid.

'Not sure what Bakes has told you but the split's this. Kev's taking five hundred, Steven a grand and you've got three and a half coming your way. That covers weapons, petrol and your man. Manage that how you want.'

'Sorted. What do you want done? And when?'

The group is hushed as Trisha brings round another three pints, a bag of pork scratchings and a vodka orange for The King.

'It's got to be fucking clean. Fucking flawless, got it? This plan is not to be discussed with nobody. You don't discuss it. You don't tell anyone where you're going.'

'I'm not sure you've twigged but I'm a professional. It's my living. I work alone or with people I trust.'

'You're a bit full of your fucking self aren't you?' says Hudson, mildly distracted by two peroxide blonde twenty-somethings noisily arriving.

'The guy you're after is called Al. You don't need to know my connection to him. Just that he's a gambling cunt. A fucking snake. One thing you can guarantee about Al is that he will fuck anything that moves and he will be down the Blues. Rain or fucking shine.'

Tony continues, caressing his wet pint, as if he's drawing inspiration from it.

'I've got my brother and a few people over in Selly Park keeping an eye on his movements. Nothing suspicious. They don't know why and don't know the order comes from me. On the 15th April, he'll be going up to Barnsley for the game. The guy he usually goes away with is going up early so he'll be going alone. Think he'll drive and not get the Blues coach, but we'll keep an eye on that. Expect he's staying up there for the weekend. If he's with someone, it's mission aborted and we will work on another time. Got that?'

Tony Cole's grabbed the attention of his assorted audience but he's on edge and his words are coming out rushed.

'He'll stop off because he's got a weak bladder and will need a drink. At the stop off point and if he's alone, you get him in the back of your van. Gag him and take him for a drive.'

'And if he meets someone up at the services?'

'Unlikely, but if there's contact with anyone else, it's off. If the services or lay-by or wherever he's fucking going is busy or you get seen, then leave it. Go up to Barnsley and see if you can get him there before he meets his mates. After you get him, clear the crap from his car so it looks like he's abandoned it. Once you've gagged him, taken him away, I only need two more things done.'

'All ears,' replies Morgan.

'Staple a card to his chest. So in the very unlikely possibility that this body is found, it will look like it's a gambling thing. He's been losing big recently, in another fucking crisis, so it's a good time to get him. He's making enemies. And you can give him one in the bollocks too.'

'I'm not a fucking surgeon,' throws in Morgan, 'think we can call that an optional extra. Three hundred please, kind sir.'

'Two fifty,' pipes Tony Cole, expecting the bargaining.

'Deal. Any preference where the body goes?'

'Somewhere it doesn't show up. If it shows up, it will be yours next. Not now, not in five years, not in ten. Just take it a long way from the Midlands, long way from Barnsley. Somewhere he's got no connections. I don't want to know where or how, just that he's gone. Burn him, bury him, chuck him into the fucking sea. It's up to you. And make sure his stuff is burnt about a hundred miles away. Hundred fucking miles away from the body.'

'Got it. Any other business?'

'Just make sure it's done properly. If it doesn't work out in Barnsley, if you get seen or it's too bleedin' risky then we meet here the Monday after at three o'clock and Kev and I will have worked out something else. You'll get fifty quid for any aborted mission. Make sure he doesn't see you until you've got him in the van.'

Morgan stands up, slips on his parka, stuffs his battered and over-read *One Day in the Life of Ivan Denisovich* into his pocket, shakes Tony's hand and heads off to buy his niece an Easter egg.

Al's put the twins to bed. Promised to take them football on Saturday. Had a bash at Spot the Ball. Said goodnight to Hev. Assured he's not gone to spend money, just a few pints with the mates from Sunday league. Going training, few pints afterwards, easily done. Al doesn't wash his kit. If Hev checks he's got the grass stains and stench of someone whose been playing. Al's over to Handsworth. *Fucking pig of an area.* Race riots. Hollyhead Road. Al's had his highs and lows recently but been feeling like it's all under control. Fifty minimum spend.

Al had a big win in February. Took a grand. Went on the Rover 200. Didn't need a new car. Told Hev he got more from the part exchange than reality. Been steadily pissing and losing it up since. Enjoyed the win. A grand in his pocket. *The look of those Irish cunts.* Their respect. Their fear.

Al's walking down the steps and into the Den. Face slightly flush from the cold March snap. Got a hundred in his pocket. Open top shirt, Levis and slip-ons. Al's mere presence is enough to rally the Micks. *If he had the balls of man, he'd spend his time licking them.* Al's baiting the Micks. *Going to take home another grand. Sure you want to play. Go home now, you pussies.*

Carney's at the table tonight. On a personal mission to make sure Al's money is coming back. Carney's in charge. Carney's not even a Mick. But Carney saw off Declan. Carney's not scared of smashing a few heads. Al's having twenty-five on a game of pool, then twenty-five on the table. There's some new geezers there. Carney's brought in some of the sharks from down Perfection. Big players. Take fifty percent cut of winnings. Al's won the first game, won it easily. Nobody can get Al off a roll. Stakes for second game raised to fifty quid. Geezers win by a squeak. Al's not seen the bait. Hundred on the last game. Al loses by a rat's bollock again.

Al's coaxed into a double your money game. Within forty-five minutes, Al's two hundred and fifty quid down. It's not money coming back from the pool table.

Al's moving over to the card school. Palms starting to sweat from the pool loss. Big players on the table. Good blackjack players. Al endures a torrid night. Can't get his ego out of the game. Can't keep his addiction down. Can't stop chasing it. Al's left owing nine hundred and fifty. That's a good month at work at the moment. Mere weeks after paying off his last debt. Al's barely got anything to pay them back with. Micks are going to be knocking on the door. Al's given a slip for nine hundred and fifty. Plus interest. Al has to have it returned in two weeks. No games until them. Rules. Al's in trouble.

***

Tony Cole's nervous. The drinks have not calmed his feelings. Only made his heart race, and mind discover holes in the plan. It's been two years in the offing. *Never been more patient.* An obsession that's fuelled every drunken binge, random shag, violent thrash at work. A personal vendetta that's forced him into near-hiding. Cutting almost all ties. *Al has to go. Couldn't give a shit about Pat. But not in my house, when I'm at war, in front of the kid. Crossed the line. Gambling little shit. Fathering his bastard kid for years.* Tony wants to be there. Do it himself. See him suffer. Thinks about joining in the van. Kicking the crap out of him. See the job through properly. Tony's mind is wandering. Knows it's not a good idea. Needs to stay away. Protect his job. Protect himself from the risk. Tony reaches for another can. Number eight had rolled for mercy under the couch. Pulls back the ring, picks up the phone. Hudson.

'Sure we can trust these people?'

Hudson's passed out asleep. Takes a while to realise who's on the other end of the line.

'……Bakes is what he is. The other guy's a bell-end but seems to know what's he's doing. Comes recommended. Think about it, as part of the deal he takes any fall for the crime. It's a no risk situation for you. He's caught. Him and Bakes go down. No link to you…no trouble. You're free and whatever our friend's out of the picture.'

'You done your homework on this Morgan? Sure you've done it properly?'

'He's cold, calculated, stays sober, done it before and never been caught.'

'Do me a favour?'

'What?'

'Make sure Bakes gets him the fucking money. Don't want that fucking cunt messing this up.'

'Sorted.'

Hudson hangs up. Tony Cole lies back on the sofa. The receiver pressed against his stomach. Can of Castlemaine XXXX between his thighs. Counting down the days and hours until this is done and he's free again. *Al's got to go.*

***

Al's been in some scrapes. Borrowed money at the last minute. Pinched, stole, done anything to get brass together and pay his debts. Even grafted.

Wrestles with his mind. The dragon. Work's dry, trying to balance out the money. Al's a bad gambler. Bad on the horses, worse on the tables. Carney's not going to spare some damage this time around.

Al's mind's not on Wigley's goal. 1-0 enough to see off Walsall. Inevitable put back. At least for a few weeks. *Third fucking division.* Al's home on a Saturday night. Hev knows things must be bad. Al's picked at his corned beef hash. Watched his chocolate and mint Viennetta melt. Tells Hev he's feeling crook and heading to bed. Al's got two weeks to find the cash.

***

Queen's made it to Brum. Hev and Pat have gone into town with the kids. Liz is in fuchsia pink. With the Duke of Edinburgh. Freezing in town. Al's reading the fruit machines being removed from Birmingham cafes. Al feels sick. '*Wigley's not going to Portsmouth'.* Al still wants to vomit.

Al's arranged to meet Tommo. Down The Camp in Kings Norton. Going with his begging bowl and best excuses. Tommo's his best mate. Liked the same things, did the same girls. But Tommo's grown up. Got a line manager's job at Longbridge. Got himself married. Al was best man. Gave a filthy speech. Involved the bride having given him a blow job. Tommo's on the straight and narrow. Away from the gambling. 9-5 in the factory. 6-11 at home. Tommo's been saving money. Got a new place on Wychall Lane, getting the kitchen done. Al wanted the job, Tommo gave it to a superior's brother. Playing the right cards at work. Al's held a grudge since.

Pub's near empty. Only distraction is the lone guy drinking at the bar. The lone guy who's always drinking at the bar.

Al's not got small talk in him.

'Listen, Tommo mate, that kitchen job, if you've not given that job over, I'll do it for twenty percent less and have it done in half the time.'

'Sorry, mate. Too late. He's already cracked on with the job and got him on the cheap anyway.'

Al's beyond hiding his disappointment and deluded sense of loyalty.

'You could have fucking helped me out.'

'Why are you a fucking charity all of a sudden?'

Al spins his pint in frustration, drenching the surface of the table.

'I've got myself in a situation. Was on a run and then those Micks sharked me again.'

'Thought you were staying clear of that lot after last time. Told you about fucking getting involved?'

'Work's been too slow. All you lot are fucking indoors all the time. Best way of distracting myself and making some extra cash.'

'Thought you were alright now Hev's back at work. That's what our Trace's been saying.'

'What man wants to earn less than his fucking wife?'

Al's detecting a gap from his friend. It's not the first time. Tommo's newfound maturity and sensible advice is not what he needs. He needs some of Tommo's cash. Some banter, few drinks, money in his pocket. Like before. To pay off the Micks. Just to keep them at bay a little longer.

'Mate, I'm going to be straight. Whatever you can lend me is going to sort me out. I'll get it back to you in double time. You're doing alright for yourself, it's the last time. As a mate.'

'If I'm a mate, I wouldn't help you out. Maybe it will do you some good to get a kick in the teeth to deter you from going back. Maybe your Hev needs to know where the money's going. Sorry, Jevvo, but not getting involved this time. When you're straight let me know and we'll have a pint again.'

Tommo necks his pint and despite Al's brash expletives, taps his old friend on the shoulder and is on his way.

***

Tony Cole's woke up in a sweat and still can't get the plan out of his head. Needs some reassurances. Wants it done right. Regrets getting Baker involved. Regrets trusting someone he doesn't know. Wishes he was there to witness it. Mind is wandering all day. Tony Cole's back on football duty. *At the scum*.

***

Al's been through every drawer in the house. Found twenty quid. Got another five from the kids' piggy bank. Pocket money. Enough to put on a bet. Al heads down Hall Green for the evening. Meets Challenor. Lanky fella. Does the windows on the street. Lisp, big smile, kind heart. Challenor knows his dogs. In every sense. Al's hoping to make up to two hundred. Will be a first deposit for the Micks.

Challenor's already been there an hour. Made a steady thirty quid. Challenor's not in it for the money. Likes the banter, time away from home, the lights of the track. Had his fingers burnt making big bets. Fingers burnt too many times, you stop enjoying the sport. No use trusting dogs. Knows they're as unreliable as people. Put small bets on percentages. Gets enough extra cash a week to buy the kids a treat.

Al's turned up all pumped. Masking his desperateness. Done his bar trick. Laid a twenty on the counter, ordered two pints, and switched the twenty for a five. Got change for over fifteen back. Trick never failed him. Learnt it from some late night film. Boys settle down for scampi and chips served by old birds in hairnets. Stench of smoke and newspaper print everywhere. Challenor runs Al through the paper, how to spot a winner. *Brought a fucking cashier's calculator.* Challenor's told Al to follow his first two bets. Keep stakes low. See how it goes. Two wins both on 6/1. Al's regretting not putting the whack on it. Third bet goes badly. Favourite comes fourth. Al'd put half his stack on it. The fourth race is a winner, Al's sixty quid up. Challenor's off soon. Had a good night. Made as much money as he wants. Tells Al to quit here. Last race wide open. No form, no favourites. Al agrees. Challenor leaves. Al puts his stack on the second favourite. Spotted Triumph. 5/2. Second favourite gets off to a great start, leads until the final stretch then runs out of Pedigree Chum as the finish approaches. Al shouts expletives, knocks punters out of the way and heads towards a desolate and uninviting car park.

The Micks are coming round tomorrow. Not unless Al makes contact or heads over with the envelope. And at least half. Four hundred quid. Al's got loose change. Made terrible decision after terrible decision. Not stuck to the Challenor approach. Small, calculated bets. The Micks know where he lives now. Know how to put the squeeze on. Al's off to Leicester tomorrow. Off to see The Blues. Needs to see the Micks before.

Al's heading home via Moseley, through the top of King's Heath. Passed Tony and Pat's old place. Past old punters. Al parks behind the Kings Arms. The Frains. Old couple did a job for. Used to leave stuff lying about. Bound to be asleep. Lights off. No alarm. Al's tempted. Seize the day. Al's bottled it. Heads into the pub. Orders a double scotch. Drinks, pays, got twenty pence left in his pocket.

Al's heading back to the car. Street's silent. In an instant Al's headed down the side alley, bolted over the fence and finds himself at the Frain's back door. Still not got it fixed. Al told them about the dodgy lock and paintwork. Offered to do it. Too cheap to have it done. Wanted to wait for the summer. *Two fucking years ago.* Al's fiddled with the lock in the dark, lights a match, and within seconds is in. Place got a stench of Dettol, everything sterilized. Kitchen in order. Nobody's home or if somebody's home, they're in bed. Al wishes he had a torch, a balaclava. Turned up as a proper burglar. Al's flicked on the tall lamp above the armchair, starts searching around. Newspapers, pipes, library loans, knitting kit, unfinished mug of tea. *No fucking cash.* Al slips into the front living room. Coats laid over the sofa, lady's bag. Al's dived into the purse. Emptied the coins over the sofa, rifled through the purse and found seventy quid. *Seventy fucking quid.* Start. Al's feeling shifty, wants to get out. Lays his eye on nice looking Omega watch and a spanking new clock on the mantelpiece. Puts them under his arm. Heads back old. Closes the door. Frains need to get their door fixed.

Al's had little sleep. Got to drive to Leicester. Agreed to pick Martin up. Heading to the pawnshop, back of Jewellery Quarter on the way. See what he can get for a watch and the clock. Al's in a corner. Shop run by elderly couple, frail in body, strong in mind. Know their stuff. Clock is worth a few bob, watch worth next to nothing. Fake. *Fucking Frain*. Al gets eighty quid. Clock's a two hundred and fifty pound retirement present. Gordon Frain only retired six months ago. Al's been conned. But Al's got two hundred quid together. Leaves the shop. Heads to a phone box. Tells Carney's man Whitley that he's on his way over. Whitley says make it sharp.

Al's late for his meet up with Martin. Told him to hang tight. Al knows the envelope's not thick enough but he's got a few other break-ins planned for tonight. Sure-fire winners. Easier than gambling. Risk next to nothing.

Whitley's come to the door. Half-caste fella. Heavy set, drinks stout for breakfast. Him and his crew are the ones going to be knocking on Al's door. Al's nervous, apologetic, almost sincere.

'I've got you two hundred and twenty here. I'm back on Monday with the same. Got a cheque coming through end of next week with the rest and your fifteen percent.'

Whitley goes quiet. Wants Al to walk into a verbal trap.

'You have my word.'

'For that insult. We'll call this the deposit. You know it's your last fucking warning. We're still calling it nine-fifty from now. So, half by Tuesday, half next weekend. Otherwise we'll smash your head in front of your kids and fuck your missus senseless.'

Al smiles nervously, turns around and heads off to Filbert Street.

Mind's not on the game. Nor on the players'. Blues lose 2-0.

***

Carney's not been happy with the envelope. Not even happy it's an extra two hundred and twenty quid. Whitley's been sent round on a week night. With a baseball bat and sharp tongue.

Al's slipped out. Blues versus Shrewsbury. Hev's channel-changing, Top Gear with Woollard, Thatcher in Middle East Peace talks, party political broadcasts. Kids just got to bed. Hev hears a knock on the door.

Whitley's balanced the bat against the front gate. Hev's taken aback by the size of the shadow at the door. Peels door ajar.

'Is Al there?' booms the faint Irish voice.

'No, he's down the match.'

'You his wife?'

'Yeah.'

'Well, do me a fucking favour, love. Tell your man if he's not got us the nine hundred by the weekend, we're coming back and I won't be alone. We're going to smash his pretty face in until we get the money and when we're done with him, we'll start on you.'

Whitley strides off, Hev's slams the door. Is too shocked to cry, heads to the sofa, numb, sick and waits for Al to come home.

Blues lose. Again. 2-1. *Step nearer the third fucking division.*

CHAPTER 14

OLDBURY

(October 2009)

'You know I shouldn't really be letting your kind in,' announces Wayne as Carter shuffles into a bare terraced house in the process of being re-plastered.

'You've caught me off guard, never thought you'd be over here again,' he continues, seemingly irritated as much as confused.

Wayne's tone is direct. Carter's not expecting any kind of hospitality, at least until Wayne sets his tool belt down and offers a can of warm Carling. Carter politely refuses. Wayne keeps one for himself and leans against the kitchen work surface.

'What brings you round here, son?'

'Not sure if you know but Heather passed away a while back, just taking care of some family affairs with her son.'

Wayne still seems flustered, anticipating an awkward moment on the horizon. Guzzling down his beer like an athlete refuelling on hydration supplements.

'So what the fuck do you want?' he returns aggressively. 'Not seen any of your family for about twenty fucking years, son.'

Carter's a little nervous. Wayne has a threatening, sketchy demeanour about him like he could throw a punch as easily as a pleasantry.

'Wanted to know why we lost touch, I guess?' offers Carter, nervously.

'Because your mom and dad got divorced. That's what happens.'

'It's not so normal for the dad to abandon his son,' fires back Carter, more directly than he intended.

'That's a beef between you and your old man, not my business.'

'Where can I find him?' as Carter drops the pleasantries.

'Couldn't tell you. Haven't seen him for about five years. He was over in Coventry, Warwick, somewhere like that. Blue Nose twat, my brother. We just drifted apart, he had his own world, own plans. Know he was talking about buying a bar in Spain, not sure he ever made it. Can't really help you, kiddo.'

'You got an old address, last contact number?'

Wayne's breathing heavily as if irritated, and repeats, 'Leave it alone, leave it alone. Nothing but trouble, all of that.'

'I won't say it came from you.'

'Listen, kid, if I give you this number then it's the last thing I'm helping with. I'm enjoying a quiet life as well. I don't want to be fucking bothered again.'

Wayne punches a few buttons on his dusty Nokia and writes down a mobile phone contact for Tony Cole, warning it might not be the latest number. The handwriting is, intentionally, barely legible.

'He doesn't want to fucking see you, kid, I know that for sure so whatever it is you're after, be prepared for a hard time.'

'And,' Wayne continues, 'why do you exactly want to see him?'

'I want to know why he left, and if he knows what happened to Al as well.'

Wayne's goes deathly quiet.

'Murky waters, son, murky fucking waters, be careful where you swim.'

'Is there anyone else I can speak to, help me out, anything you can tell me?'

'Am I talking?' responds Wayne rhetorically, putting his hand over his mouth as if to silence himself. 'No, because I know shit. Don't come round here again, don't come fucking bothering me, I've given you what I can. Now piss off.'

Wayne still offers Carter a handshake and an unexpectedly sympathetic squint on the way out.

As Carter heads through the entrance, a lady who introduces herself as Catherine walks in. She's every bit as polite as Wayne is coarse.

***

'Wow, if that is the nicer of the two brothers, don't dare imagine what Dad is like,' remarks Carter to Rachel as he gets back in the car.

'What was he like? Did you get anything?' she eagerly responds.

'Let's just drive out of here first, don't want him seeing me.'

A few blocks down the road Carter and Rachel stop off in the Mad Hatter, the sort of the place Rachel would not usually be seen in dead, but she's so wrapped up in events that she's barely noticed the aggressive and curious looks from lonely Saturday drinkers, fag-stained curtains and stench of piss emanating from the adjacent toilet. They order orange juices and sit, hidden in a corner.

'So?' prompts Rachel.

'He scared the shit out of me, to be honest. Without doing or saying anything really. He shouted a few times, but just had this manner about him. Fucking nasty bloke.'

'So tell me what happened?'

Carter runs back through the conversation, slightly exaggerating some of Wayne's aggressiveness to render himself braver.

'What do you think you'll do next?'

'I don't know. I don't want to go into it all like a bull in a china shop. It was kind of weird seeing my uncle again, bit raw to have your own flesh and blood turf you out after five minutes after some twenty years apart. I kind of want to go back and reason with him.'

'Want to drive back?'

'No, best to let him dwell on the fact I've turned up. I'm not sure what he knows, he seems keen to be isolated from the family as well. Like him and Dad had some kind of bust up.'

'Are you going to call your dad?'

'Find that weird right now.'

'What's that?'

'Calling him Dad. He's never been that. Doesn't feel right yet it just keeps coming out of my mouth.'

'We can call him TC,' jokes Rachel.

'Twat's better!'

Carter looks up at the screen as Jeff Stelling and the Sky Soccer Saturday gang kick into gear.

'Think calling TC or twat or whatever his name is should be the last resort. Need to know more. I'm not going to get anything from him unless I go with something. But I'm in a rut. Mom doesn't want to talk and not really sure what she knows. Wayne scares the shit out of me. He'd probably sooner put my teeth through than tell me anything else… but he definitely knows something. Then there's all the leads from Rowntree but he's gone quiet.'

'How about getting in touch with Wayne's previous wife? They must be your cousins, their kids. If they had a messy divorce or some grudge to hold she may open her mouth.'

Carter smiles.

'That's a cracking idea,' before stalling, '….only how do we find her? Wayne's not going to give me that one. They may be miles away. Not like you can go back to Grandad's and ask for another number either.'

'But if they are his grandkids then he must have their number?'

'Doesn't have mine?'

'True.'

'Her name's Shelley fucking Smith. It's not really an easy one to find either. She may be remarried, who knows, what.'

'But Wayne's not going to live far from the kids, did he have toys or anything at home?'

'There were a few DVDs and stuff but the kids will be early teenagers by now, maybe older.'

'Chances are he sees them on a weekend at some point. We could track him next weekend.'

Rachel's diving into the subject as intensely as she does speeches about corporate litigation.

'Yeah and now he's seen me, he'll get out the car and smack me over the head with a baseball bat.'

'Ouch...maybe Paul needs to come with you. Two men are a bit more intimidating than one.'

'And that's still another week, and what if it's not next weekend?' returns Carter.

'Maybe I could check? Maybe we could find your grandad's number and call?'

'I don't know. It's starting to seem like a mission. Let's see what Rowntree comes up with.'

***

It's Monday morning, first-thing, when Rowntree calls Carter back. Says he wanted to get all the details rather than doing everything 'piecemeal'. A phrase he overuses.

Rowntree doesn't want to email his findings, it's easier over the phone. Kevin Hudson is still at the police and pushing paper down at Tally Ho. Rowntree's had a think and offers to assist Carter in setting up a meeting and introductions. Thinks it needs some diplomacy. Carter agrees. Bob suggests that before any meeting Carter get in touch with Earl Beckford or Andy Braithwaite or both. Beckford runs motivational courses for businesses, has his own website, Twitter account, blog, various phone numbers. Should be easy to get hold off. Braithwaite's down at the Metropolitan police, in his native south. Rowntree's given a direct line number. Carter thanks Rowntree and agrees to meet later in the week, once they are ready to discuss meeting Hudson.

Carter's not ready to talk to a motivational speaker, at least not on a

Monday. He thinks Andy Braithwaite might cut to the chase a little quicker.

Carter dials from a corner in Café Nero on Corporation Street during an extended lunch break. It's quiet and empty enough to have a private conversation. The small smattering of Kurdish men slumped on the sofas are mainlining espressos.

Andy Braithwaite's voice is unmistakably London and Carter bumbles out an introduction before Braithwaite cuts him off.

'Hi there, I know who you are, old Bob Rowntree said you were going to call.'

Good old Bob, Carter thinks to himself.

'You want to speak about the former police constable Anthony Cole?'

'Yes, please.'

Braithwaite's speech is well rehearsed. 'Well, my words aren't going to be nice. I've done this job for over thirty years, worked with bent cops and good cops, helped good people, put in some bad. Anthony Cole was one of the nastiest people I've come across. He's a leopard that will never change his spots. What do you want to know exactly?'

'Just a bit about him as a person, I guess any connections he may have, any leads that will point to why he left home, anything really.'

'I was always more ambitious than Cole. He was a beat officer and that's what he wanted to be. He didn't want to manage, do paperwork, spend too much time with superiors. As part of my training I spent some time with him. I was a younger officer at the time, although he wasn't massively experienced either....sorry, just got to take something on the other line.'

Braithwaite tells the other caller he will get back to them in ten. And then orders a BLT and a café latte.

'Anyway, where was I?... I was with this guy Beckford, still a mate of mine although he was the sharp one and got out. Making a load of cash now. Done alright for himself. Cole was on the beat with a few of these dodgy fellas, only one I really remember is Kevin Hudson because he's still there and had a reputation. Anyway, Beckford lasted about three days. They gave him so much abuse for being black. Shocking. We filed reports but nothing really got done. Not for a while. I stayed a little longer with them. They took backhands, dabbled in drugs, were regularly drunk, abused girls, squeezed people. Not good sorts. And Anthony Cole was violent too. There were plenty of complaints about him inside the Force.'

'What do you know about Hudson?'

'Hudson's still there but he had some kind of life-changing experience apparently. Cleaned up, became a rank and file officer. Anthony Cole got transferred down to Coventry and Leamington for a while and last I heard, he left the Force shortly afterwards....Hudson was a nasty fuck. More intelligent than your dad, but he took pride in hurting people. Was a nasty, racist man too. Used to walk round spitting on punters. Don't know that much more about him.'

'And, ever heard of a Steven Baker?'

'Earl and I ran a check on Cole and Hudson once. To be honest we wanted to shop them. We succeeded in getting Hudson suspended. Steven Baker was a known criminal. Mainly petty stuff but he was implicated in plenty of football violence and got done for manslaughter later on. Did something like ten years inside. Drink driving. Never met him, but he was a bit of a button I think for Tony Cole, if you know that expression. Used him to crack a few heads, make a few arrests. I've actually done a check on him for you.'

'Oh yeah,' replies Carter.

'Yeah, he got out in 2002, on his manslaughter charge. Few charges since, shoplifting, stealing cars, burglary. He's done a month here and there. But nothing major since early 2007. Which is odd. Usual petty crime stuff. There's an address if you want it.'

'Okay,' replies Carter, gratefully.

'Well, look up Baker in the Smethwick Yellow Pages. Number ending '3561'. There's your man. Nothing I told you, just your own research.'

'Clear,' says Carter, gratefully, almost forgetting to write down the number.

'Listen, I've got to go. It's a long time ago. Earl might not be able to tell you much more but he's become all yoga, peace and love and stuff. And you may find yourself doing a six-month meditation retreat rather than getting anywhere, but try him if you want.'

They say their goodbyes. Carter calls Rowntree and thanks him for the advice. They arrange to meet in the same pub on Friday night. This time with Paul.

***

Paul instantly finds Rowntree pleasant and welcoming, Rowntree talking fondly of Paul's mother, bringing up the few warming anecdotes he had about their encounters together. Rowntree is the sensitive, uncle figure neither of them ever had.

Rowntree and Paul listen patiently to the week's developments. They agree it's best not to rattle Wayne Cole's cage although doing some research around his ex-wife may be fruitful. Paul offers to take this on. He gets a few hours spare during the week. Rowntree think it's time to visit Hudson. He admits Hudson was the nut that the private detective could not get that close to. Having been in the Force he knew when and how to keep his mouth shut. A man forgetting about his past, a convenient amnesiac. Rowntree says he will occupy himself with setting up a meeting, admitting it might not be easy. Carter's going to try and find Steven Baker but tells Paul he is not prepared to go alone, given the man's reputation.

They agree to get in touch within a few days with their findings.

***

Paul's job was made relatively easy. Instead of visiting Wayne Cole, he tracked down the haulage company Wayne works for through the Yellow Pages. A bit of bullshitting and acting as a National Insurance officer got him Wayne's home number. Luckily for him, the generous Catherine Hickson answered and pretending to be a friend of Wayne's son, Thomas, Paul managed to get a phone number. Catherine was a little suspicious, considering they had only moved address three months earlier but she gave out the details on autopilot. She says Thomas is unlikely to be living there but that's the last number they have for the mother. It's five or six years old.

Only when putting down the phone did Paul realise how risky it was. What if Thomas was dead? What if Thomas never saw Wayne? Catherine may not know about the kids. Wayne may have abandoned them like Tony. However, it was really that easy. Fortune favours the brave, mused Paul to an impressed Carter.

Paul Googled the address which was a little further than he anticipated. Shelley's now living in Water Orton, an hour out of town. Carter managed to duck and dive a staff meeting, much to the rage of Gorman, and meet Paul in the late afternoon. En route the two discuss what's best to say. They agree they must have met Shelley when they were kids and hope at least she remembers them. There's very little they know about her apart from a date of birth, two kids—Thomas born 1988 and Louise born a year later. Much older than they initially thought. There's no way Wayne Cole would be visiting them. They were divorced to boot in 1991. Nearly twenty years ago. They are going to appear like two phantoms from another life. As they get closer, they become more and more convinced that it's going to be a mistake.

Pulling into number 32 Wickham Drive, a relatively charmless and unremarkable lower-middle class estate with tightly mowed lawns at the front, their doubts multiply. The curtains are undrawn and the TV flickers against the darkening sky.

'Dutch courage,' says Paul as they head up the drive.

A thin, miserable-looking bald man opens the door, dressed in a golfing polo and Saturday morning jeans. Paul and Carter ask to see Shelley and the bald man waits at the front door whilst he beckons Shelley from the tumble dryer.

Shelley's certainly not an attractive woman. She has the look of someone whose wild days are long over but a youth spent eating fried food isn't. From pictures they'd seen, she was slim with long strawberry blonde hair but her hair is now jet-black and heavily moussed into some aggressive spikes. She bears rather masculine features, squat nose and square jaw and a heavyset body. She doesn't smile.

'Sorry to bother you,' introduces Paul, who takes it upon himself to lead conversation.

'And we don't want to keep you long. Don't worry we're not Jehovah's,' he continues, trying to lighten the moment. No smiles are returned.

'You actually met us a long time ago. My name is Paul Jeavons and this is Dan Carter. He is Tony Cole's son.'

'What's this about?' enquires the bald man a bit snappily, as if his dinner is getting cold.

'I'm not sure, love, but they are Wayne's lot.'

'Well you should bloody clear off,' orders the bloke.

'We're not actually Wayne's lot,' returns Paul. 'Neither of us have seen him in twenty years, we've just got one or two questions to ask you and then we'll be on our way.'

'What's this about?' repeats the bald man.

'You'd better come in for a second,' says Shelley.

Soon they are installed in a spick and span living room where a large sketch of Nigel Mansell's 1992 winning Williams sits over the mantelpiece. Car and golfing magazines are piled everywhere as well as ornaments of frogs and mermaids. Above the fireplace are pictures of several kids. Carter fears that the bald man and frumpy woman may have reproduced at some point.

'Can I get you a drink?' says Shelley.

'For Christ sake,' interjects the bald man, unnecessarily inhospitable, 'can't we just tell these reprobates to piss off!'

'Tea would be great,' says Paul with a wide smile.

'Same,' adds Carter.

The bald man has Top Gear paused and perhaps the root of his anger was having a review of the new Nissan GT-R interrupted by two out of towners.

'Alright boys, I'm listening,' says Shelley.

'You want to go for it, mate?' suggests Paul to Carter.

Carter mentions the death of Heather and the pursuit of what happened. Carter finding his dad and Paul the truth about what happened to his own. Just their quest to put together a haphazard family jigsaw with too many missing pieces and no instructions.

Shelley begins to look sympathetic and a little worried. The bald man has relaxed a tad and puts Top Gear back on with the sound almost at mute.

'It's been a long time, boys,' starts Shelley. 'I was your age at the time. What exactly is it you want to know?'

'Anything really,' replies Carter, rather unhelpfully.

'Well anything you remember about either of them disappearing,' adds Paul.

'Well, Paul,' begins Shelley, who in contrast to her harsh facial features, has a soft and gentle voice. 'I never really knew your dad. I met him a few times at weddings and some parties. He had some issues with my ex-husband, owed him money a few times, owed everyone money. I remember when he went missing, like it was yesterday. He'd been round that week to Wayne's, he owed us quite a bit for furniture, cash we needed to go on holiday. Then he went missing and the money appeared. Don't get me wrong, I detest Wayne as much as anyone, but he had nothing to do with it. Wayne always said Tony sorted the debt. Everyone thought your dad was dead, that the bookies got hold of him.'

'Did you ever talk about it with Wayne, how did he react to it?' enquires Carter.

'To be honest, he was really inquisitive and surprised, very interested in knowing more. I remember him bringing it up with Tony but Tony never talked about it, always said 'good riddance'.'

'Sorry if this is a bit direct, but is there any way Tony could have been involved, if he hated Al so much?'

Shelley takes a deep breath as if she's deciding whether to let a secret out.

'I'm not sure whether this is true or not. It came from Wayne, he told me once when he was pissed. So maybe take it with a pinch of salt. But he's convinced that Al and,' Shelley points to Carter, 'your mom had an affair at some point. Like I said, it's a long time ago, Wayne was pissed and I'm not sure how much Tony knew.'

Carter and Paul return strange looks, rather unaware of how they feel about this trajectory.

'Would anybody else know for sure?' adds Carter.

'Your mom!' replies Shelley almost sarcastically.

'Let's not go there,' says Carter taking another sip from his British Open mug.

'I don't know,' continues Shelley, 'I'm not sure how much your dad would give a fuck. He was always bonking other women anyway and he left your mom years before Alan went missing.'

Paul and Carter realise they need to head to their own conclusions.

They continued to make small talk about Shelley's kids, son who's a security guard and daughter a trainee nurse, already with a young kid.

As they finish their tea and prepare to leave Carter prompts, 'What was my dad like?'

'Well, he made my ex-husband look nice,' replies Shelley, 'Don't think I need to add more.'

The boys leave. The bald man doesn't twitch.

***

The meetings with Rowntree and Shelley have given Paul a taste for getting involved. They are buying into the suspicion that Tony Cole may have played a role in Al's disappearance but they're not sure whether they're riding the crest of a conspiracy. Rather they feel it's the most live hope—most of the protagonists are either long gone, inside, dead or mute.

Discussing the options on the car ride home they agree that whatever, Tony Cole is the last, final piece of the puzzle. Carter wants to look him in the eye as an adult.

***

The intrigue has had a huge effect on Bob Rowntree, who has been addictively drawn into the case. His notes and essays for the City Council have slowed down and he can't get the affair out of his mind. Seeing two young, pleasant men being drawn together has made him feel rather paternal, a feeling he rarely experiences now his own son is so independent. He misses his friend Hartley dearly. Misses his advice. His experience. His knowledge of the case.

Rowntree doesn't know how to attack the subject of Kevin Hudson. He thinks about a direct phone call regarding the case but know that will get nowhere. He contemplates turning up at the police station and seeing Hudson face to face but knows it's not really protocol. In the end he decides to use the powers of his journalistic bravado and present it as part of a book on the West Midlands police in the 1980s. He plans on playing to Hudson's ego.

Hudson's initially a little sceptical and surly. But as soon as Rowntree suggests he wants some quotes regarding the development of police work since the early '80s, and perhaps a picture, Hudson is more obliging. Rowntree deploys words like 'skilled' 'experienced' 'exemplary', even 'heroic' comes out at one point. In contrast, Hudson comes across like a tedious bore, eventually agreeing to meet for a drink near the station, at the Selly Park Tavern on the Pershore Road. Rowntree decides that he's going to invite the boys. In a public place, it will be hard for Hudson to make too much of a scene.

***

It's busy in the Tavern on a Thursday. Rowntree's retired and Hudson pushes paper, works on local crime statistics, goes into schools, but is always done by five o'clock. Rowntree plans on getting twenty minutes or so with Hudson before the boys come. Make him feel comfortable, massage his ego, get him settled. Then introduce the boys as part of a particular crime feature. 'Unsolved cases'.

Hudson's a slight man, dressed in a short-sleeved blue and white checked shirt, grey slacks and heavy, industrial black shoes. Shoes he must wear every day. He still sports a moustache and mousey, grey hair, its colour owing to heavy tobacco intake or a bad dye. His face is wrinkled, slightly rubbery. He wears a thin silver wedding ring and a few tattoos are fading on his right forearm. Rowntree's amiable nature puts him at ease, although Hudson's no smiler nor one for pleasantries. He mutters in a thick, laborious Brum accent, talking informatively, although generically, about police work in the 1980s, how the streets were and the city was tougher. He moves on to forensics, computers, how young cops today have it easy. Rowntree listens attentively, has even brought a tape recorder along. They reminisce about some of the old characters and issues. Hudson attacks his chicken madras and pint of Caffreys like a man who rarely has a free meal bought for him. It's essentially two old men having a yarn about the glory days. Hudson asks how many other officers are being interviewed and when the book will be out. Rowntree says he was given a list of officers who have worked through from the 1980s and is going through them. Remembers enough names to sound convincing.

As Rowntree struggles to keep the conversation flowing, Carter and Paul head over. Hudson's got his back to them. Rowntree motions in a fashion to suggest they can come over. Carter and Paul are charged with pints of Guinness.

'There's an additional chapter in the book,' says Rowntree as Hudson mops up his curry sauce with a folded naan bread.

'Oh yeah,' replies Hudson rather dismissively.

'It's about unsolved cases, you know the effect that can have on the Force and families.'

'Sounds interesting,' says Hudson, in a tone that couldn't be less enthused.

'I'd like you to meet two guys who are collaborating with me,' continues Rowntree.

As Carter and Paul sit on either side of the table, Hudson wipes his mouth and moustache with a serviette.

'This is Daniel and Paul, they've got some first hand experience of unsolved cases.'

Hudson doesn't offer his hand but nods at them both in a dismissive manner.

'There's a case they are both interested in,' continues Rowntree, 'not sure if you remember it?'

Hudson's started to feel rather caged in and intimidated by the presence of the two young men.

'Do you remember a case about a man going missing on Hillsborough Saturday? Family man headed up to Barnsley, never came home? He was from round here, Selly Park.'

Hudson opts to glance Paul in the eye and shakes his head, 'No, don't remember it.'

'That's a shame,' continues Rowntree, as well-versed for the occasion as an actor on the boards at Stratford.

'As these guys remember it well. This is Paul Jeavons, his son, and this is Daniel Carter, his nephew.'

'Ring any bells?' prompts Rowntree, teasingly.

Carter and Paul are rather enjoying the scene.

Hudson's gone a shade of white, looking terribly uncomfortable.

'I wasn't involved with murder cases, so can't really help you.'

'Who said anything about a murder?' replies Rowntree.

'You fucking did!' barks Hudson.

'I think I said 'missing',' smiles Rowntree.

'You're twisting my fucking words.'

Hudson prepares to head outside for a smoke. Rowntree's cleverly ordered him a third pint.

'Well, if you don't remember the case, you must remember your old mate, Tony Cole? That's his boy sitting next to you.'

Hudson reaches deep into his pocket as a measure not to make eye contact with anyone. He pulls it out slowly.

'Is this some kind of set up?' he continues as he pulls out a fag and his lighter.

'No, I'm just helping these boys with an old case,' replies Rowntree, softly.

Hudson gives a look of man who's been shafted.

'I came here to help you with your fucking book, not talk about some guy I used to work with and some case I know nothing about.'

Hudson storms out for a fag break.

Rowntree, Paul and Dan remain seated. The boys comment on how disappointed they are at how meek Hudson is. Rowntree knows he's going to come back with a rehearsed speech.

Hudson eventually ambles back as his pint is delivered.

'You've got me here on unfair premises,' says Hudson, trying but failing to maximise his limited vocabulary. 'If it helps you fellas in any way, I can tell you what I know about Tony Cole but I know nothing about the case and never worked on it.'

Hudson successfully separates the case from Tony Cole the friend.

'I've not seen Tony since 1992 when he left the Force. We worked together for five or six years, you get to know a man quite well during that time, he was a good mate, good officer but when he left the Force then we lost contact,' says Hudson, 'I'm not one for keeping in touch.'

'So you have no knowledge of where he went after 1992?' interjects Paul.

'None. Whatsoever,' replies Hudson, bluntly.

'By all accounts you two got into some scrapes, suspended, difficulties with other officers, unconventional policing methods shall we call it,' adds Rowntree on the aggressive.

'Things were different back then.' Hudson's replies are getting shorter and more coarse.

'So, did you ditch Tony Cole to further your career?' replies Rowntree.

'No, he left the Force. You're right, I was suspended. But it was a misunderstanding. I got given another chance and took it. Policing was for me, it wasn't for Tony. Running a pub and bars was.'

Rowntree's back at his investigative best. 'How do you know he ran pubs and bars? If you've not seen him since 1992.'

Hudson's stammering. 'Well, that's why he left, what he wanted to do.'

'You ever seen him in his pub?' motions Carter for the first time.

'No.'

'That's funny because Steven Baker tells us you used to drink the place dry in the mid-1990s,' shoots Rowntree, hoping his lie will pay off.

Hudson folds his arms and smiles.

'Gentlemen, I've said what I wanted to say. This is not a fucking inquisition. I've not seen Tony Cole in donkey's years, may have had the odd beer with him here and there but I've not seen him in fifteen, twenty years. He slipped off. And if Steven Baker knows so much then go and fucking talk to him. Now, I'm going. You call me again, I'll have you done for harassment. Tosser.'

Hudson pulls his jacket off the chair, aggressively stares back at the table and heads out.

'That went well,' smiles Carter.

'What now?' adds Paul, grinning through his teeth.

'Well, we've put the frighteners on him. He knows something but he's got enough influence to keep us away. If he knows your dad, your dad will know now. Although I'm not convinced he does. He's a man trying to forget the past as well. He's not stupid enough to talk either, I knew that. But he's given us a few hints and clues. That murder line especially. It's probably time to see Steven Baker.'

'Will you come?' Carter asks Rowntree.

'Nothing I like more than spending time with a fellow Baggies fan.'

CHAPTER 15
OAKWELL

(April 1989)

Tony Cole's lifting dumbbells. *Big fucking sets*. Reps. *Fucking hard, Tony Cole*. Best Boxing, a veritable Cov sweat factory. Forty fucking kilos each arm. Forty. Forty-five when Baker shows his fucking face. *Fucking hard, Tony Cole. Hard as nails. Harder than these coloureds.*

Long weekend ahead. Weights. Wife. Whisky. Worry. *Morgan's not fucking this up. Steven Baker's not fucking this up. Dead man if he fucking does. Twenty-four hours. Enjoy your fucking breakfast, Al. Fighting the war. Dick in my fucking missus. Sleeping in my bed. Spreading your seed. Revenge, Al. Fucking cunt Al. Enjoy your breakfast.*

Baker finally shows up. In a fucking Vauxhall Astra. 1986. It's not his. Never is. Never owned a fucking car, Bakes. Never owned shit. Borrowed it from the garage. *Some poor fuck's car being driven by Bakes.* MOT. Overnight servicing. Baker took it to Balsall Heath. *Shagged some pikey. Fucking Bakes. Mess.*

'You're fucking late!' barks Tony, wiping his brow with a small, sweaty, faded British navy towel.

'Fuck off.'

'You better not be fucking high, you cunt.'

'Just had a few shandies, get off me fucking back.'

'Find out you're fucking high, I'll blow up that fucking shit hole you live in. Yam yam cunt.'

Baker's a mess. Unshaven. Eyes barely open. Looks like he's been slammed over the head with a dustbin lid. Repeatedly. Scar down his face. Fly undone. Stinks of booze. Stinks of piss. High.

'You seen Morgan?'

'Sorted.'

'Knows where they're going? Time? Fucking place? Getting it fucking done? Want a stealth job.'

'Sorted, Tony, fucking sorted. Been through it five times. Knows what he's doing. What they're fucking doing.'

'You given him the cash?'

'Gave him half. Took my four hundred. Sorted Tony. Rest on Monday. When the job's done. Then no more contact with these buggers. It's sorted. I know what I'm fucking doing.'

Should never have involved Baker. Lost his fucking glarnies. A mess. Baker's never been any good. Not for years. Too many blows to his head. Too much up his fucking nose. Baker's gotta keep his mouth shut. Hand over the fucking money. Don't lose the fucking money. Fucking yam yam. Baker's a mess. Would steal from the fucking disabled. From his fucking mom. Baker's going to do more time. Can't have associates like Baker. Not anymore.

'Don't fucking call me whatever you do. If there's a problem deal with it. Don't want any fucking calls going to my house. Anywhere. Anytime. Got it?'

'Sorted, big T, you've been through it. We're sound, sorted. Plan's a good 'un. Take it easy, mate.'

'See you fucking Tuesday. Same place. Eleven o'clock. When the job's done.'

'Sorted, Tony. Don't suppose you got a fiver? After some grub.'

***

'Blues Need A Miracle'. Swindon game called off. Blues still alive. Still alive for Saturday. *Fucking Pendry. 'Pendry still in the dark'. Trap door wide open'. Pendry's to fucking blame. Should have gone months ago. Fucking liability. Blithering idiot. One hundred and fucking fourteen years of history. One hundred and fourteen. Down the toilet. All gone on Saturday.* Al's barely got any petrol money. Meeting Martin up at Oakwell. Martin's got mates up there. Friends of family. Going up early. Friday night. Up in Sheffield. Martin's going to get wasted. Al's got work to finish. And Heather's birthday. *Thirty fucking one.*

***

Forty quid. Blue Ford Transit. Back on Monday. Cleaned and fuelled. Morgan's got his wheels. *Sweeney's a cheeky shit. Left it fucking mucky. Pig sty. Fucking Mick.* Morgan's tidied the van. Spic and span. Job needs to be done properly. *Morgan's a professional. Morgan's got the rope. Got the fucking shovel. Got torches. Got fucking gaffer tape. Got big fucking sheets. Body bag. Got bin bags. Got a fucking machete. Got some booze.*

277

Got a knife. Sharp as his wit. Got fucking bleach. Got towels. Got a fucking game plan. Got half the cash. Best in the business. Nake thinks it's one and a half. Nake's getting five hundred. Nake's a fucking battering ram.

***

Jackie's done the lunchtime shift. Old Windmill. Did the evening shift as well. Got the weekend off. Wants to go out tonight. Get lashed. Tony's anxious. Needs a drink, finds a fag. Tony's worked his muscles and checking himself out. Toned. Tony's admiring his tats. Proud of them. *Born and bred in Brum. If you wish for peace, prepare for war. BCFC. Mom.* Tony's strutting. Tony's had a shave. Trimmed the tash. Spot of Grecian 2000. *Fucking huge grey streak. Right down the middle.* Tony's looking older. Tony needs a drink. Has another fag. Jackie wants to go out. Jackie needs pleasing. Takeaway tonight. Eight cans. Drive in the country tomorrow. Pub lunch. Liver in Henley-in-Arden. Mind in Barnsley.

***

Kids over in Erdington at grandparents. There till Saturday. Dan's over tomorrow with Pat. Heather's had her hair cut. Bob-style. *Ages her.* Out with Al. Thirty-one candles. Italian. Bit of drink. Bit of romance. Heather needs perking up. Needs a good night. Irish visit still on her mind. Al says it was a misunderstanding, says he's paid his debt. Last time, won't come knocking again. Al's been out recently. Every night. Was good until then. Good when the kids were born. Always home. Doting. Bringing in the money. Money's dried up. Al's always out. Al's always drinking. No money going in the pot. Heather needs a night out. Worn out. Worried about more visitors. Money going missing. Taking care of the twins. Al's always out. Al had been good.

Al's visited the Micks. Grovelling. *Fucking Carney. Declan was easier.* Declan went. In the dead of the night. *Fat fuck. Declan would break your legs if you didn't pay. Carney's fellas will break your fucking legs if you do pay.* Al's fucked. Was off the game. *Two fucking years.* Behaving. No debts. No hassle. Just the bookies. Odd flutter. No big games. No late nights. Left the whores alone. Behaving. Odd blow job. No screwing. Nothing more. Bored. On a winning streak. One last bet. Drawn back in. Back scrounging. On a losing streak. *Gotta change. Got to get the dosh. Carney's going to break legs. Carney's going to knock on the door. Hev can't answer the door again. Carney's a hard, fat fuck.* Al's gotta get the cash. Al's paid five hundred. Rest on Tuesday. Finishing council job. Three hundred coming in. Two hundred left. *Sell that fucking video recorder. Microwave. Don't need it. Fucking luxury. Fucking plan. Fucking sorted. Do it Monday. Carney's getting his cash through Connor on Tuesday. Job done.* Al done some breaking and entering. *Another hundred.* Al's taken the piss. Al owes Carney. *Another hundred. Carney's a persistent fuck.* Connor's been calling. *Connor's going to come knocking. Gotta get off the game. Got to behave.* Al's in trouble. *One hundred and fucking fourteen years of history.*

***

Tony Cole's relaxing. *First can of the day. Pint of the black stuff. The afternoon angel. Black fucking velvet.* Reading *Today*. Got stuck on the crossword. Can't do crosswords. Jackie's going to finish the crossword. *Always fucking does.* Tony's angry. Frustrated. Tony's got his muscles though. *'Peak hunt youth in garden shed'. Dumb cunt. 'Presumed missing in the fucking Peak District. Found in garden shed. In Coventry.'* Alive. Asleep. *Dumb fuck. Al's not coming back alive. Al's not sleeping in the shed. Al's going missing. Al's not coming back.* Tony Cole's having a second drink. Tony Cole wants it to be Monday. *Al's not coming back.*

Al's going to have to pay for dinner. Take some from the tin. Al's nicked a tenner on the job. Left lying around. *What ya gonna do? Gotta be more careful.* Needs petrol money for Barnsley. Al's making an effort. Gone for a haircut. Free job. Decorated the salon. Free haircuts for life. Al's in there twice a month. Tonight's a fuck night. Special occasion. Only chance of getting laid these days. Short back and sides. Tapered at the back. Al's buffed his brogues. Al's wearing an old suit. No tie. Silver. Shiny sharp. Heather's in a black dress. *Bit plump. Not got rid of the kid fat. Heather's still got her tits. Those fucking plump breasts. Tiny nipples. Thin black tights. High heels. Heather's made an effort. Heather needs to make more of an effort.* Al's trying to forget the Micks. Al's had garlic bread. Lasagne. Chocolate fudge cake. Heather's had the soup. Macaroni cheese. Tiramisu. Two bottles of wine. Chianti. And one for the road. Hev's on Al's back. Again.

'If the Blues are going down anyway, what's the point of wasting money and time going up there?'

'It's about supporting the team. Thick and thin. We're not like the scum, there through thick and thin.'

'You're only going to be depressed and miserable afterwards.'

'Going to meet Martin up there. Staying up with some of his mates, I'm back down on Sunday. We'll have a few jars whatever happens. About being with your mates through thick and thin, isn't it?'

'Just try and get back in time to see the kids before Monday.'

Heather's merry. Al's speeded home. Had a can in the car. Heather lets him do what he wants. Al's got his eyes shut. Easy peasy. Shafting from behind. Hands cupped on Heather's large breasts. Small nipples. Tiny. Thinking about something else. Someone else. Pat's round tomorrow. Pat doesn't talk anymore. Pat doesn't smile anymore. *Pat's tight fucking arse and long legs. Six fucking years. Six years since Al had a piece of that cunt. Pat's fucking disloyal. Fucking Carl. Wet. Waste of fucking space. Pat could have come back. Pat's long fucking legs. Tight arse.* Hev falls asleep. Al lifts thirty quid from her purse.

***

Morgan's parked at the top of Kitchener Road. Nake's there. Nake's not slept. *Nake's a fucking retard.* Nake's had ten pints. Half a fucking sleep. Nake's got no discipline. Morgan told him to have an early night. Morgan's pumped. Job on. Adrenaline. Plan coming together. Another two and a half grand. Nake's getting five hundred. *Nake's a retard.* Morgan's prepared. *No fucking music. No tales.* Get the job done. Military precision. Mission to finish. *A job from Steven Baker. Taking orders from Steven Baker. Impossible. Fucking idiot. Degenerate. Another fucking Nake.* M6 to M1. Al always stops. Steven Baker says so. Always fucking stops. Piss. Fag. Coffee. Paper. Wager. Al always stops. Al is not going to Barnsley.

Heather's made breakfast. Poached eggs. *Fucking rare treat.* Bacon. Sausage. Toast. Beans. *Fucking works.* Big cup of tea. Al's nervous. One hundred and fourteen years. Down the pan. Motorway's going to be chocca. Get up their early. FA Cup semi-final. Forest want revenge. Forest up at Hillsborough. Against the Scousers. Got to leave soon. Motorway's busy.

Nake's tetchy already.

'What's the plan, Dave? When do we stop him? Am I home in time for me dinner?'

'Just listen to the King. Follow my orders. Obey. And get back to fucking sleep until you've sobered up. Going to be a long day.'

Morgan's got it sorted. *Plan's fucking sounds. Steven Baker had no plan. Steven Baker's a liability. Degenerate.* Steven Baker's given an address. Given a destination. One instruction. That's it. *Probably taken a grand. Fucking Steven Baker. Not going to live long. Nake's asleep. Nake's a big fucking cunt. Nake's the muscle. No fucking brain. The muscle. Hired help. Five hundred quid and fuck off Nake. Nake's not going to live long either. Nake's a fucking degenerate.*

Al's left. Kissed Heather. Pick up sports bag. Brut, *The Sun*, clean shirt, clean kegs, toothbrush, johnnies, smokes, stolen money, loafers for the evening, face towel. All for the Sheffield lassies. *Gotta behave, Al. On the straight and narrow. For the kids. Al's thinking about Pat. Tony's fucking gone and Pat's still fucking cold. One for the road, Pat. For old times' sake.*

Al's got the radio on. Al's thinking about the Micks. Money's got to come in on Tuesday. Tuning channels. Martin. Pub outside Oakwell. Outpost. Sheffield Road. One-thirty. Few jars. Bit of banter. Game. Sheffield. Lassies. One night stand. *Thatcher's cleaning up the streets. Cleaning up Number Ten. Fucking Tories. Petrol price up by ten pence. Fucking Tories. US banned English eggs. Salmonella. Fucking Tories. Fucking Yanks. UB40. Boycotting Birmingham. If can't play at St Andrew's. Fucking Pendry. One hundred and fourteen years of history. Should have gone months ago.*

One hundred and one miles. Couple of hours in the car. *For these fucking plebs.* Thomas. Peer. Frain. Atkins. Overson. Roberts. Langley. Childs. Tait. Robinson. Yates. *Not fit for the fucking shirt.*

***

Tony Cole's nervous about the Blues. Should be up at Oakwell. Hasn't seen the Blues in a month of Sundays. Here and there, away from St Andrews. Away from the old crowd. Away from Al. Tony Cole's not happy. Wants to be at Oakwell. Wants the job done. Doesn't want Al coming back. Tony Cole can watch The Blues again from Monday. *In the third fucking division.*

Al's not coming back. Al's not sleeping in a shed. Should have done the job. Not Steven Baker. Degenerate. Best not to leave a trace. Job and all of that. Keep it clean. No ties. No link. Third party. Job better get done. No fucking up. No sheds. Not going missing in Yorkshire.

***

Morgan's prepared. Long day on the road. Up to Yorkshire. Up to a service station. Back of the van. Down to Wales. Sheep field. Field of death. Underground fucking cemetery. Eleven months. Eleven months since Nesbitt went down there. Don't pay your debts. Don't come home. Two grand job. Easy fucking work. Did it alone. No fucking Nake. Just a fucking burial. Others had performed the surgery. Back of van. Down to Wales. Underground. Two grand. Easy work. Went to plan. No traces. Nothing. Just a field in Wales.

Ashby de la Zouch. Ilkeston. Nottingham. Felley. Blackwell. Al's not stopped. Al's had a fag in the car. Al's going fast. Speeding. Al's had a tin in the car. Morgan's on his tail. Nake wants music. Wants the radio.

Morgan doesn't. Concentration. *The King's in the zone*. Put a Blues scarf up in the front of the car. *Morgan's method. Method murdering.* Not following. Just heading to the game. Up to Oakwell. Watching The Blues. Make history. Al's made good distance. Al's stopped. Woodall Services. Time. The Place. Game On. Morgan's moment.

Al's stretching his legs. Al wants a beer. Al's out of beer. Nervous. Twelve o'clock. Bags of time. Nearly there. Outpost. Martin. Martin and the gang. Pendry. Relegation. Sheffield lassies. Al's refuelling. Al's having a smoke. Al's heading into the slot room. Fifteen minutes. Pennies. Loose change. *Nothing ventured, nothing gained.*

Morgan's parked next to Al. Morgan's stretching. Limbering up. Peace and quiet over. Minutes to kick-off. Nake knows the drill. Knows the game plan. Quick and easy. No trouble. No witnesses. No noise. Gone. Forest fans about. Fucking tens of them. Wembley dreams. Red scarves. Hillsborough. Three o'clock.

Al's won three quid. Fifteen minutes. Three quid. Beer money. Al's spinning a pound. Heading to the car. An hour from the Outpost. An hour from mayhem. Al's spotted the Transit. Blues scarf. Lanky fella. Striking cheekbones. Mean eyes. Smiths fan. Spiky hair.

'You going up to Oakwell, mate?' starts Morgan.

'Yeah, for me sins. Noticed you fellas on your way up. You and your mate,' responds Al, flicking his fag end about five yards.

'Road's fucking busy. All these Forest clowns going up to Hillsborough.'

'Not wrong.'

'Couldn't ask you a favour, mate? Need to shift some stuff in the back of the truck. Mate's taking a piss and phoning his missus and want to get it done.'

Al obliges. Al opens his car. Puts his wallet down. Fags on the side. Newspaper on the back seat. Al locks his car. Al heads to back of the truck. Al's whistling. *Keep right on.* Steps inside. Big fella is there. *Black guy. Size of a fuckin wardrobe.* Door slams shut. Al's smacked over the head. Al's bleeding. Al's passed out. Eight seconds to oblivion.

Morgan's found Al's keys. Slips on the gloves. Clears Al's car. Overnight bag. Wallet. Fags. The lot. Car empty. Job's a good 'un. Morgan's not going to Oakwell. Al's not going to Oakwell. Nobody's going to Oakwell.

Morgan's driving. Nake's in the back. *Nake's a fucking brute.* This is Nake's time. *Earn your five hundred, Nake.* Nake's gagged him. Nake's tied him up. Nake's kicked him in the head. Nake's got to keep him alive. Nake can't get carried away. Meat needs to stay fresh. Little bit longer. *Instructions. Follow the plan. Job's not finished yet.* Denbigh. Hundred and twenty miles. M1 north. Driving towards Barnsley, Al. Not going to Barnsley, Al. Nake jumps out. Rotherham. Nake takes a piss. Nake's back in the passenger seat. Nake's hysterical. Still be a darn sight better than watching the Blues today. Laughs. Hysterics.

Morgan's not eating. *The King dines when the job is done.* Warm day. Sun's out. Sunglasses. *Pound a pair, keep out the glare* says the radio advert. The King has a mission. The King's made twenty grand this year. Twenty grand. Ten days work. Fifteen days planning. Not got caught. Best in the business. The King's going to dispose of Nake. Last job with Nake. Nake's a liability. Nake's like Holden. Holden's in the slammer. *Thanks for your help. Stayed too long.* M1. A616. A628. A57. M56. A5117. A541.

A543. Focus on the boards. Drive off the daylight. Stop in Stockport. Services. Waste a few hours. Wait till dark.

Al's been clubbed over the head. Taken one from the Micks. *In a fucking truck. Been fucking blindfolded.* Pitch black. Tied together. *Fucking Carney. Fucking prick. Fat twat. Last chance. Two hundred quid. Took the piss. Shouldn't have got involved. Took the piss. Should have stayed out of trouble. Horses and kids. Took the fucking piss. Carney. Carney's threatened. Carney's never hit before. Carney's all mouth. Carney's had me. Fucking Micks. Fucking Carney. Fucking Al. Won't happen again. On the straight and narrow. Money on Monday. No sweat. Money on Monday. Out of your hair. Just need to explain.*

***

Pat's quieter. Pat's met Carl. Got some spare cash. Carl's not Tony. Carl's quiet. Carl's scared of his own shadow. Carl stays in. Cleans the car. Does the pools. Carl wants Pat to move in to his place in King's Norton. Pat's said no to marriage. *Once bitten, twice shy.* Listens to the shipping forecast. Two beers a night. Eggs and chips. Question of Sport. Newsnight. Up at six thirty. Bed at ten-thirty. Pat's fancied Al. Heather's sure. Tony left. Pat funny in front of Al. Al's funny in front of Pat. Hev's not let it go. Pat was lonely. Al's nice. Al's good-looking. Pat's always stolen fellas. Pat's reading, flicking pages. *Today. Bella. Home Improvements.* Pat's quiet. Pat doesn't go out anymore. Pat's having a crafty fag. Silk Cut. Cup of tea. Kids gone to play football. Dan and the twins. Peas in a pod. Two in blue, one in red. Off to play on the red clay. Back by five. Don't be long.

Kids have left Grandstand on. Pat's reading. Heather's ironing Al's shirts. Gassing with Pat. Pat's half listening. Des Lynam. 'FA Cup Semi-Final Wembley or Bust'. Forest, Kop End, Liverpool, Leppings Lane. Two most attractive teams in the country. Heather turns volume down.

Morgan's parked the van. Stockport. Little side-road shithole. Perfect. Charlie Adams—Burgers and Bovril. Morgan's not eating. Morgan sips from a flask of coffee. Morgan's going to eat when it's done. Meal fit for a King. Nake's hungry. Having a hot dog. Second hot dog. That's your lot, Nake. *Fucking liability. Last job Nake.* Door to the van stays shut. Van's parked away from the shit hole. In isolation. Morgan's left the radio on. Beardsley's hit the crossbar at Hillsborough. Crowd trouble at Hillsborough. Al's listening. Al's waiting for The Blues score. Al should have paid up.

***

Grandstand. Bob Wilson. Hillsborough. Fans climbing up onto the second tier. Fans crushed. Game abandoned. Ref Lewis calls match off. Deaths feared. Grandstand stays at Hillsborough. Heather's turned the volume up. Heather's concentrated. Ambulances on the pitch. Stretchers on the pitch. Fans helping fans. Fans shouting into camera. *Fucking police. Treated like animals.* Advertising hoardings for stretchers. Coverage live. Coverage raw. Dalglish gives speech. Over fifty feared dead. Two hundred injured. Heather's thinking about Al. Al's up in Barnsley. Al's okay. Al's in Sheffield tonight. Getting pissed. Sheffield's going to be a morgue.

***

Tony Cole's got the wireless on. Tuned into BRMB. MPs want to scrap Grand Prix. Blues 0-0. Half-time. Tony Cole's heard about the racket in Yorkshire. Tony Cole's hoping the plan's come together. *Al better not be at Oakwell.*

Kids have come back. Dan's covered in mud. Paul's cut his knee. Lee's covered the kitchen floor with mud. Dirty football rolling across carpet. Kids slumped in front of TV. Kids can't work out what's happened. Kids bored. Mate Rolly is round. Rolly's a chubber. Kids have cheap pop and roast chicken Walkers. Carry on playing Wembley in the yard. Heather's shampooing the carpet. Pat's still reading, got one eye on the TV. Pat's saying it's tragic.

Matches have finished. Blues have drawn 0-0. Blues are down. Heather thinks about Al. Al's best up in Sheffield. Drowning his sorrows. Drowning his mood. Back tomorrow. Fifty-three dead at Hillsborough. Emergency number for relatives. Hundreds injured. More feared dead. BBC1 News. Moira Stewart. Seventy-four dead. Possibly up to eighty-four. Stewart says worst disaster in British 'soccer' history. Fans blaming the police. Crushed. Gates not opened quick enough. No spectator flow. BBC still at Hillsborough. Warm skies. Empty stands. Full morgue.

***

Morgan's now listening to music. Got his tapes. Smiths. Joy Division. Depeche Mode. Not Nake's type of music. Nake can stay outside. Nake can finish his hot dog. Nake's not the King. Nake's talking to the hot dog man. *Nake better not be blabbing. Liability, Nake.* Following Hillsborough with the hot dog man. Morgan's not interested. Concentrating. Morgan's locked in the van. Morgan's keeping one eye on Al. Al is trying to roll. Al is gagged, taped, tied and beaten. Al is not rolling anymore. Al knows the Blues result. Blues are down. A hundred and fourteen years of history. Third tier. Next season. Al's finishing his last season.

17:30. Morgan's revving the engine. Nake's back in the car. Nake's smoked a rolly. *Smoke that out of the car. Nake's not having a drink. Not until the job's done. This is Nake's last job. Last with the King. Nake's a liability. Dumb fuck.* Nake's told to shut up. Another couple of hours. Heading over to Wales. No more stops. No more breaks. Can piss in your fucking jeans if you have to.

***

Tony Cole's supping. Third of the day. Lunch sitting in his gut. Nothing a good shit wouldn't sort out. Jackie's had a good day. Jackie's walked the dogs. Country air. Tony's liver's back in Coventry. Tony's mind is elsewhere.

***

Pat's staying over in the spare room. Al's decorated it nice. Pat's still quiet. Pat's having a G and T. Heather's gone to get the kids McDonald's. Four cheeseburgers. Two quarter pounders. Six fries. Three large milkshakes. Two strawberry. One vanilla. Heather and Pat sharing pizza. Bottle of Australian chardonnay. Pat's got Heather some presents. *Like a Prayer.* And a brooch. Big blue brooch. Listening to *Express Yourself. Love Song.* Heather and Pat are getting on. Singing along. Kids watching Lost Boys. Kids quiet. Kids in their room. Heather and Pat. Better when the men aren't around. *Al's going to be pissed. Better be behaving.*

Destination Denbigh. North Chalk Farm. Patch of a land. B4501. Morgan's uncle's plot. Spent summers there. After his mother died. Dad dropped him off. Six weeks in Wales. Grim. *Sour old git. Old Taffy wanker.* Can't get round the farm anymore. *Stubborn old cunt. Will never sell this land. Not until he fucking passes out.* Jack's not using his land. Jack's got a couple of lads in. Ripping him off. Not using the land. Morgan's pulled up. Back of the farm. House no longer in sight. Forgotten land. Jack was in. Jack had bedroom light on. Jack's probably passed out.

Nake's got to dig a hole. Halfway there. Parked on a dirt track. Nobody's coming past. Couldn't be more secluded. More safe. Hidden. The King did this alone last year. One hour. Job done. Two grand. Great job. Handshakes all round. *Thank you very much.* Getting dark. Low light. Torches needed soon. Nake's digging. Nake's a wardrobe. Big fucking lad. Biceps like thighs. Lights hit the back of the van. *Fucking local. Fucking local on the path.* Young woman. Kid in the back. Woman stops. Light on. *Everything okay. Everything fine. Just got a bit lost.* Woman sees Morgan. Doesn't see Nake. Good job. Close escape. Morgan moves the van. Drives off. Nake's hiding in his own fucking hole. *Fucking local. Fucking plan. Can't stay.* Morgan's panicked. Plan's got to change. Been spotted. *Fucking local.* Nake's re-dug the hole. Nake's left the fucking spade. Too late to turn back. *Fucking Nake. Last job.*

Al's still motionless in the back. Morgan's driving off. Pissed off. King needs a new plan. King's a professional. Didn't happen last year. Couldn't stay. Been spotted. She had a kid. Complicated. Needs to be foolproof. Nesbitt's alone in that field. No mates for Nesbitt. Al's got a stay of execution.

Morgan's not digging any more holes. Got no spade. Nake neither. Morgan's heading to the coast. Going to dump the body in the sea. *Al can float off. Head to Ireland. Hope you can swim where you're going. Your team went down, you're going with it.* Al's still motionless.

Hev's having a drink. With Pat. Gorgeous Pat. Martin's in Sheffield. Martin's getting laid. Kids are eating burgers. Kids are having fun. Al's in the back of the van. *Fucking Connor. Fucking Carney. Fucking Al. Should have behaved.*

Morgan's heading to the coast. Wants to get this finished. Find a bridge. Big bridge. Big drop. Weights. Bag him up. Drop him. *Enjoy the swim, Al.* A55 Colwyn Bay, Llandudno. Bit of rough sea. Perfect current. First bit completed. Bag burnt. Bag destroyed. Wallet burnt. Cash kept. Hundred quid. Thanks, Al. Morgan's claiming the money. Nake's kept the fags. Keys in the sea. Al's lost his possessions. Al's surviving. Al's surviving another ten miles. Past Llandudno. No further.

No bridge. Drive on. Morgan's checked the map. Menai bridge. Beaumaris. Over the Irish sea. Nobody around. Going to be perfect. Job needs to be finished. Finished before he drowns. Has to be dead. Baker's message. No chance this one's resurfacing. Morgan doesn't like the bridge. Morgan's not an amateur. Morgan doesn't like the current. Morgan drives on. Near Black Point. Current stronger. Blustery evening. Perfect. Morgan's the King. Morgan follows instructions. To the letter. Nake's last job. Nake's last mission. Van parked. Secluded lay-by. Al's motionless. Al's still breathing. Al wants to explain. Money on Tuesday. Al knows what's coming. Another blow round the head. Morgan watches on. Nake unties the gag. Al's still alive. Al's saying sorry. Sorry to Carney. You'll get the money back. On Monday. Learnt his lesson. No more pain. Al's going to shit himself. Al's losing his trousers. Al takes a blow. Al's had a hammer in his balls. Al's not fucking again. Morgan's not cutting his dick off. *Tony will never know. Morgan's not a fucking surgeon. Not for that money.*

Nake's got a card. Thinks about a Joker. Al's screaming. Morgan chooses Ace of Spades. Stapled to his chest. *That's from Tony Cole. Enjoy your swim.*

Tony fucking Cole. The silent fucking killer. The tash. Those eyes. Stuck his dick in Pat. Got her up the duff. Shouldn't have touched Pat. Tony's wife. Tony's missus. Tony's fighting the war. Being a hero. Pat didn't see him again. Pat's got pregnant. Tony wasn't sure. Tony was never sure. Tony disappeared. Al's taken a blow to the head. Al's down. Blues are down. Al's being slung off into the sea. Direction Ireland. Or Liverpool. *Al's in a fucking bin liner. Al better not turn up on a beach. Al's not going to turn up. Al's down. Goodbye, Al.*

***

Heather's called Pat. Al's not come back. It's Sunday night. *Fucking selfish.* He's done it again. Said he'd see the kids. Probably getting drunk. Shagging around. Know it's going on. Got some girl up in Sheffield. Back to his bad habits. Pat's calm. Pat's not concerned. Pat knows Al. Al's coming home. Be on his way. Al doesn't come home. Not on Sunday. Not on Monday.

'*All Seater Plan—No Standing Could Become Law*', '*The Fences Have To Go*', '*The lessons of Hillsborough*', '*Villa Park—The Model to Follow*'. Heather's found a scrap of paper. Heather's called Martin. Martin never saw Al. Al had never showed up at the pub. Not in Barnsley. Not in Sheffield. Didn't see him at the match. Martin got hammered. Remembers nothing. Martin says Al will come home. Heather's called the police. Heather's thinking about Hillsborough. Al wasn't there. Confirmed. Police busy. Been a bad weekend. Wait twenty-four hours. Al's probably fucking. Shagging some whore. Having a wager. He's been so good. Heather's watching Miami Vice, World In Action, World Snooker from Sheffield. *Fucking Sheffield. Hate Sheffield.*

'Families To Sue Police'. Al's not back on Tuesday. *'Coma fan joy to see hero'*, Al's not back on Wednesday. *'Disaster fan's gift of life'*, Al's car found on Thursday. Al's not in the car. Desmond Tutu's in Birmingham. St George's Day parade cancelled. Tutu's sorry. Al's car empty. Nobody remembers seeing Al. Al never made it to Barnsley. Al took a ride. Al went somewhere. Al went with someone. With some girl. For some game. Irish come knocking. Irish threatening. Heather's not seen Al. Heather's told to get the money. Irish are knocking at the door. Kids are scared. Al's had strange phone calls. Al's had threats. Al's owed money. Again. Al's not come home. Al's in *The Mail*. Al's on the news. Local news. Local man. Family man. Missing on way to football match. Car found in Yorkshire service station. Police appealing for help. The threats have stopped. Irish stopped knocking. Phone stopped ringing. Al's not called. Al's gone. Al's not coming back.

CHAPTER 16
WEST BROMWICH

(October-November 2009)

Steven Baker's not got the stomach for it anymore. Flicking through *The Daily Star*'s ten thousandth issue. Too much time inside ruined his tolerance. Money's an issue, always an issue. His reputation is shot. Drugs, drink, debt, violence. It's infiltrated almost everyone he's been in contact with. Handed second and third chances and spat them back in people's faces. Hilda Baker died when he was inside in 1999. His brother, Craig, has nothing to do with him. His mother's last act was to leave him her house in Dudley, so he had something to come home to. The house's all he's got. He's done his best to ruin it. Ten years of neglect. No money to do it up. During rare moments of sobriety, he's able to patchwork the plumbing, the flooring, the decaying walls. He's taken to sleeping on the couch, passed out drunk in front of the box. Tried putting the house up for sale, take the money and move on, only to find out the house is in Craig's name and can't be sold without his brother's consent. Craig's happy for Steven to rot inside.

West Brom home games provide some form of structure. He can't afford to go to away matches, unless he pinches a lift or sneaks onto a train. Some of the old football crowd have been loyal to him, but they've mostly had enough of the trouble and can't get away with what they used to. There's the odd scrap or bottle fight outside a pub but the ground's become like a library for Baker. Like school. A place where you're constantly lectured. The odd bit of work comes in, usually cash in hand. He still knows his cars and does the odd shift down the garage. There's the odd score in a pub but the dealers no longer trust him. The occasional burglary or shoplifting helps out but he's slower and not as hungry as he used to be. He's fifty-three years old and never enjoyed a conventional relationship. He's alive in spite of himself. Sometimes he yearns for the simple life inside but the thought of enduring sobriety is enough to keep him out of serious trouble.

***

Rachel's infinitely happy with her motivated, inquisitive boyfriend. One who's talking about his feelings and his findings. Involving her. Even if there's a fear that the findings will push him back into a shell. She's a little worried about the kind of people Carter's coming across and the lengths they may go to in order to protect a secret. Scenarios and permutations are discussed over croissants and coffee at breakfast. What if Hudson has warned Baker? What if Hudson's been in touch with Tony Cole? What if they are all in it together? What if they plan on coming after Carter or Paul?

Rowntree has joined for breakfast as they wait for Paul to pick them up on his way over to Dudley. Operation Baker and West Brom versus Watford. Rachel poses relentless questions to Rowntree, who's enjoying the sense of seniority. Rowntree believes Hudson has lost touch with Tony Cole, and in particular Steven Baker, in order to protect his own career. Rowntree's also conducted extensive research in the subsequent days on Hudson. His work record's impeccable and colleagues speak of dedicated professional, if not a little unfriendly and private. A bit of a jobsworth.

***

It's a crisp Midlands day. The long winter days have not quite arrived, the horrendous pre-Christmas traffic and days barely distinguishable from nights are around the corner. Arriving in Dudley just after one o'clock, they worry Baker will already be in the pub for his pre-match pint. A decision is made to give it half an hour in the car, then try Baker's front door. Rowntree has another reason for being in this part of town. He has his Baggies' season ticket to honour.

They find the two-up and two-down houses on Russell Street. Steven Baker's abode stands out like a decaying flower in an otherwise neatly trimmed bouquet. Grimy windows, junk in the small front yard, a battered front door. After twenty minutes of near silence in the car, while Rowntree completed *The Guardian* crossword in the front passenger seat and Carter shot stills through the rear window, some movement occurred in the house. Or at least a light briefly flickered on and off. Suddenly a figure emerges at the door in a hooded cagoule, blue and white striped scarf, black jeans and large unlaced boots. The figure is an enormous, hunched character, stubbled and carrying the air of someone who's had a late night. It's unmistakably Steven Baker. Carter ducks. There are only a few cars in the street so they don't want to distract his attention. Given his state, he's unlikely to notice them.

'What now?' says Paul questioningly.

'Let's observe his movements for a few hours. Meet him in a casual situation. He's not going to respond to authority or regular questioning,' replies Rowntree.

'Few hours?' answers Paul, worryingly.

'Yep, looks like you two are Baggies fans for the afternoon.'

Rowntree suggests they follow Baker at a distance, become familiar with his habits and routine. Little clues will help when they eventually approach him.

They stay at an even pace behind Baker who is charging into the distance. Rowntree presumes he's heading on a bus to the ground. Paul complains that he's not got a bus since he was at school. Only Rowntree has dressed for an afternoon sat in the cold and damp as they venture down Wolverhampton Street, onto busy High Street. They catch up with Baker at Michael Supermarket and linger outside whilst he heads in. Baker emerges with a pack of Rizlas and a can of Irn-Bru. He isn't the most observant of characters as Rowntree and the boys struggle to remain discreet. Baker then heads into KFC, departs with a chicken burger and fries, eating it on the move before chucking the packaging on the pavement. Baker double backs on himself and heads to the main bus station. He seems to be following a confusing route but on arrival at the stop for the 87, it's apparent he's meeting up with a friend. A tall fella with a leather cap, long greasy hair and a knee-length black leather coat is waiting. The two jump on the bus and head upstairs. There's a fair few Baggies fans already heading to the game as well as old folk with cumbersome shopping carts. Rowntree takes the last available seat downstairs while Paul and Carter stand and reflect on the diversion the afternoon's taken.

It's about an hour to kick-off and Baker heads up Halford's Lane and into the Supporters' Club beside the ground. His mate mysteriously never got off the bus. Despite the rain and the cold, the place is packed with fans spilling onto the street. Baker makes a beeline for the bar and nods at a few people he's familiar with. In no time he's necking a pint of bitter and engaging in banter. Rowntree's able to grant the boys entrance and with his blue and white scarf blends in. Carter and Paul feel they stand out like away supporters. Rowntree suggests they hang near the door, get a quick drink and watch from a distance. Baker's muscled to a position at the bar and despite the queues of people trying to get a drink around him seems undeterred and doesn't move. He's laughing aggressively with a couple of twenty-something skinheads and seems on friendly terms with a bearded biker type at the bar, whose leather jacket is masked with hundreds of

Baggies' pins and sew-on badges. Despite the attention and bravado, Steven Baker still reeks of loneliness.

Baker removes his hood to reveal a navy beanie. His mouth is vast, extenuated by a missing canine tooth and charred lips. 'Freedom' is tattooed in capital letters across his neck. His arms, even under an ill-fitting baggy jumper, appear enormous. He's a menacing shadow of intent. Villainous.

'So what do you make of our fella?' offers Rowntree, rhetorically. Carter's being pushed around by people, entering and exiting, rushing his pint as not to spill it over himself. He needs a piss and is cold.

'Told you he wasn't going to be friendly,' smiles Rowntree with a comfortableness that comes from experience.

'So, how do we keep track of him during and after the game?' questions Carter.

'Well, I'm guessing that he's got a season ticket, most likely in the Birmingham Road End. That's where mine is. In any case we'll follow him. We'll get you boys tickets in that part of the stand and follow him after the game. If we split up, just call me with your whereabouts.'

Rowntree's clearly set on sticking to his own match routine.

At just before half two, Steven Baker leaves the supporters club and lights a rolly before he exits. The trio wait three seconds and then exit. A group of Watford supporters mingling about are goaded by Baker. He walks with an almost comedic aggressive strut, heavy shoulders bouncing forward. As Rowntree predicted, Baker's ticket is for the Birmingham Road End.

Paul moans about the twenty odd quid that he'll never get back. Rowntree's seat is in the lower part of the stand, the boys are ordered to sit in the upper section where the greater atmosphere is generated. Their mission is to not lose track of Steven Baker.

Carter and Paul move into some empty seats about five rows behind Baker, moaning about having paid to watch 'Birmingham's third team'. Baker's animated, shouting, screaming, raising his two fingers to all and sundry. He seems to have found his regular group of supporters and the long-haired, leather-clad individual has reappeared. Baker's up and down. Boing, Boing. Olsson. 1-0 after five minutes. Dorrans penalty after eighteen. The game's over before it starts. The Baggies hit five.

It's hard work keeping hold of Baker after the game. The lads almost lose him as he rapidly darts through the crowds. They had agreed to meet Rowntree back outside Baker's house unless he drops off en route. Only, Baker's not going home. He's on the tramway, headed towards Birmingham. Carter and Paul begin to wonder how long the evening will last. Baker rides on through most of the obvious stops, eventually jumping off at Snow Hill.

Baker slows down as he exits the train and salutes an acquaintance. He then jumps the barrier, having not paid for his ticket. As he turns he sticks his fingers up at the poor, motionless middle-aged lady behind the glass window of the ticket booth.

Baker heads about five hundred yards up the road and into the Red Rose pub. A proper drinker's den. The pub's half full, a mix of underage drinkers and all day bingers. Pregnant women in high heels and low cut tops nurse vodka tonics. Paul and Carter sheepishly follow. There's a rerun of the North London derby on the large screen. Baker is on friendly terms with the squat, balding landlord who says something about trouble. Baker continues to sink his pint and chaser while methodically rolling cigarettes at the bar. An imposing forty-something bloke, wide as he is tall, shakes Baker's hand on the way out and says something about 'work coming'. Baker heads to the fruit machines, pounding the buttons with force. Carter and Paul avoid eye contact and can't wait for Rowntree to show up.

Baker's continuing to feed the machines. A rolly dangles from his mouth as he anticipates another loss. Defeat's always round the corner for Steven Baker. Another guy appears from behind the bar and slips him a fiver. It's like Baker knows everybody in the pub.

Eventually Rowntree appears, his glasses steamed up and cheeks frozen. As he defrosts, Carter heads to the bar and orders a round of ales. Paul's pointing at his watch. Baker heads out for a fag and as he passes Carter senses a sinister shiver. Rowntree seems to have suffered from the cold, suddenly cutting a somewhat frailer figure.

As Baker walks back into the bar, a smiling Rowntree shouts, 'Good result.'

'Southern puffs didn't fancy it up 'em,' snaps Baker, without making eye contact or turning his head.

'Don't I know you from somewhere?' launches Rowntree, who seems to have come back to his senses.

'Crossed a lot of folk in my time,' says Baker, who heads over to the round table. There's an air of menace about him, even more apparent close up. He makes stern eye contact, his large head rests on a thick, violent neck. Hard alcohol and stale tobacco emanate from his clothing. His heavy hands reveal more cheap, homemade tattoos, advertising crimes from yesteryear. A hangman silhouette is inked on the palm of his right hand.

'Can't picture where I know you from,' comments Rowntree. The two boys are fearfully quiet, hoping their presence goes unnoticed. Carter realises that this is a man he couldn't have faced meeting alone.

'Anyway, can I buy a fella Baggies fan a drink? Thought Dorrans was outstanding today,' continues Rowntree.

'Pint and an Irish,' replies Baker with no hint of gratitude.

Carter slips to the bar instantly, largely to avoid being left in the company of Baker.

Baker takes a seat next to Paul, opposite the window and facing Rowntree. As Carter heads back from the bar, Baker's waffling on about the match.

'Think I've got it,' says Rowntree suddenly.

'I remember you. You're Tony Cole's old mate. I worked with him in the Force, must have been twenty years ago.'

'Don't remember you,' returns Baker. 'Look at me, fella, don't remember shit about those years.'

'Tony Cole,' continues Rowntree, 'top man, whatever happened to him?'

'Bloke's a cunt,' hits back Baker.

'I remember you two being tight,' continues Rowntree, playing this beautifully.

'Bloke's a cunt,' repeats Baker, as if Rowntree hadn't heard him the first time. Baker's concentration is drifting. He's incapable of holding a conversation, distracted and repeats himself.

'What ever happened to Tony Cole? Was just thinking about him the other day,' insists Rowntree, as he glances at the boys for support. 'Tony Cole was an old mate of mine, fellas, funny running into an old friend of his.'

'He's no fucking mate of mine,' snaps Baker. 'Bloke's a tosser. Wasn't there when I needed him. Bloke was all about himself. Fucking greedy cunt.'

'Is he still around these parts?' continues Rowntree, isolating the boys from involvement.

'Fuck no,' continues Baker. 'Took the money and run, didn't he? Got others to do his dirty work all the time.'

'When did you last see him?' Rowntree continues as if unaware that his questions are not leading to concrete answers.

'Fuck knows, years ago, fella. Fuck cares. Not been around much in the last fifteen years, have I,' laughs Baker in an almost demented way. 'Where I've been you don't see many folk.'

'You got a fiver for the machine?' snaps Baker, losing the train of conversation.

'You see,' replies Rowntree. 'I'd love to get in touch with Tony Cole if you can tell me where he is?'

'What's it worth?' says Baker.

'What do you know?' cuts Rowntree.

'For the Queen I'll do anything,' replies Baker.

'Twenty quid if you tell me where he is,' drops Rowntree, realising that as bizarre as this conversation has become for him, it's perfectly normal for Steven Baker. He's unlikely to remember it by tomorrow.

Baker drops his short into his pint glass. Literally.

'Let's see your dosh, old geeze,' says Baker.

Rowntree pulls out twenty pounds. Baker pounces up on it.

'Tony Cole, Tony Cole. Well when you find him, tell him we've got unfinished business,' says Baker.

'Like what?' replies Rowntree.

'Covering his back,' drops Baker shortly.

'I thought for twenty quid, you'd tell me where he is,' says an impatient Rowntree.

'Not seen him in years. Try a pub in Coventry, try that cunt Hudson or his fat fuck of a brother. He wasn't there for me. Cunt. Always doing his dirty work.'

Baker finishes his pint and pulls another pre-rolled cigarette from behind his ear. As he attempts to light it, Baker belches heavily, patting Rowntree on the arm in a 'thanks for the money, old man' gesture.

'How much to tell us about what happened to Alan Jeavons?' launches Paul as Baker heads on his way out for another smoke.

'Who the fuck's asking?' says Baker.

'I'm his son.'

Without a moment's hesitation, Baker leans over the table and has Paul in an unorthodox headlock. Paul's staring up, directly into Baker's hateful, aggressive eyes. Carter and Rowntree are both left momentarily motionless, paralyzed by the sudden thrust of violence.

Baker continues, the unlit rolly still dangling in his mouth. 'Your old man had a lot of enemies.' Baker moves away, laughing.

'Fifty quid for anything you know,' launches Rowntree.

Baker remains motionless with a broad smile.

Rowntree offers two twenties and a ten. He's rapidly running out of cash.

'Who wants to go chasing a dead man?'

'How do you know he's dead?' replies Paul.

Baker finally lights the rolly.

'Everyone knew he couldn't swim. Didn't Mommy tell you?'

Baker continues to cackle like a pantomime villain. 'Thanks for the money, fellas. Most I ever made from that fucking pair. Bent Al and Tony fucking Cole.'

Baker then leans over to Paul and blowing smoke in his face, cuts: 'Don't know what the fuck happened to your dad. I wouldn't wipe my arse with his fucking death certificate. Good luck finding Tony Cole. Cunt.'

As Baker exits, gesturing with a small, patronising wave, Paul feeling like it's the last chance to ask, shoots back.

'How many of Tony's birds did Al shag?'

Baker breaks out into hysterics.

'Nothing he didn't shag. Probably sucked me off as well. Little fucking queer.'

'What about him and Pat?'

Baker looks Paul squarely in the eye and barks,

'Well, they only had a fucking bastard kid together.'

***

It's been three days since the colourful exchange with Steven Baker. Carter's barely opened his mouth. The eventual car ride home passed like a wake, nobody said much apart from agreeing to reconvene in the week. Rachel had travelled to a hen night in Gloucester and not returned until Sunday evening. Carter managed to stay in his own little world. At moments like this, he could stay amazingly focused on his work and pull in extra hours to finish the customarily busy pre Christmas period—mostly party invitations and restaurant discount flyers.

***

Birmingham's full of joy. A nobody from X Factor coming to switch on the Christmas lights. Cheryl Cole's *3 Words* reverberates everywhere. Gorman loves her. Newcastle lass and all of that. *'Five Star Albion'*, *'Strikers sting Hornets'*. Carter can't get Saturday out of his head.

There have been a few lost lunch breaks walking round the Bull Ring and The Mail Box. Carter feels numb. Lost and unable to form coherent feelings about the events of the last three days. He bears intense hatred for his mother. More than ever. For keeping so many secrets from him. His head is still awash with questions, rumours and half-truths. He's convinced that Tony Cole killed Al Jeavons. Al Jeavons, his potential father. Paul and Lee, his brothers, born seven months later. He's not sure whether Heather knew for sure or just suspected it. It explains why Tony abandoned the family although not why he abandoned Leanne.

In need of a sounding board, Carter arranges to meet Leanne after work. She's the only person, aside from Rachel, who he feels he can trust. Carter arrives at the Utopia pub on Church Street typically early. Leanne had to make arrangements for Leon to come home early and look after Amber. Carter insists it's urgent and is halfway through a bottle of Rioja before Leanne arrives.

Leanne's not used to getting the train into town. She arrives babbling on about Amber's upcoming fifth birthday and sporting a weird shaved undercut. Work experiment.

Carter begins to divulge his findings. Initially Leanne appears irritated or jealous that she's been left out. Carter eases her through it, explaining and then justifying Paul's involvement. Leanne struggles with the waffling, butting in with 'then what?' and 'what happened after that?'.

When Carter delivers the phrase drunkenly versed by Steven Baker, Leanne is uncharacteristically quiet and then incredulous.

'He must have been pissed,' she stutters.

'Maybe so, but it adds up, sis, it adds up.'

Leanne remains stunned, resting her head on her fists.

'The timing's perfect and everything with the war. Otherwise, I must have been conceived as soon as Tony came back. Miracle sperm or something.'

Leanne raises her eyebrows when Carter pronounces the name 'Tony'.

'Plus, everyone's always said I look like Paul and Lee. Mom and Pat never got on as soon as Al left, like some kind of secret was blown. Tony's never had anything to do with me...okay, that doesn't explain why he's neglected you too. It might also explain why Mom's always had so much more trouble loving me than you...'

A tear drops from Leanne's eye. Carter's trying hard not to well up himself.

'Even if this comes from the mouth of a pisshead, I think it makes sense.'

'How are you going to go about proving it?' asks a defensive Leanne.

'The only person who can is Mom. I'm sure Al's dead, we all know that,' continues Carter, 'I just think this is a conversation that will finish me and Mom for good.'

'Do you want me to ask?' offers Leanne.

'I don't want to come between you and her.'

'It's not like we're best mates either.'

Carter and his sister go through the permutations and decide to visit their mother together. After Amber's fifth birthday.

Leanne offers her brother a warm hug on the way out and says everything will be fine.

Carter's not so sure.

***

Carter broke down later that evening. Rachel believes it's good, he's getting closer to the truth. Carter is adamant he's going to challenge his mother and then find Tony Cole.

Carter slips into a third bottle of wine for the evening, half concentrating on The Dark Knight playing on repeat. Rachel's struggling to keep pace.

As Carter contemplates ordering a Chinese takeaway to absorb the booze, his phone rings with the Mission Impossible track he's assigned Paul.

'Disturbing you?' cuts Paul.

'No, just a bit drunk, mate,' replies Carter.

'Got some interesting news for you, if you can handle any more,' adds Paul.

Carter holds his breath.

'That Smith woman called me. Got my number from the business card I left. Anyway, she says her son Thomas and Wayne are in touch with your dad. He spends most of his time in Benidorm, runs a bar with his missus and son.'

Carter's a little tongue-tied.

'That's kind of her to offer the information.'

'Think she felt a bit sorry for us,' says Paul, 'and owes that lot no favours.'

'She's asked for discretion though.'

Carter's thinking through options in his head.

'What do we do?' he asks.

Paul seems poised. Back to his confident self.

'Well. I'm up for a trip to Spain if you are. She said she would get an address for us if she could.'

Carter's knocked back by developments.

'Let's go and find this bastard. First, though, I need to speak to my mom. Bury these things with her and set things straight.'

'Shall we bring Rowntree along?' asks Paul.

'No, don't think so,' replies Carter, authoritatively. 'It's a family thing now. We can thank him when it's sorted.'

'Did you ever try that number Wayne gave you?' fires back Paul.

'No,' confirms Carter.

'Well, I guarantee it's good for nothing.'

They agree to talk in a week. Paul asked Shelley to see if they are down in that part of the world in December. It being off season. She's not sure how successful her rummaging will be.

Carter tries the number. It leads to an old lady living in Barnet. *Wayne Cole. Lying sod.*

***

Carter distracts himself with a few nights out. Long trip to Liverpool. Blues at Anfield. 2-2. Autumn's 'Battle of the Bands' proves a damp squib. *The Dovetails* Travis-style indie sounds received lukewarm applause to a dispersing audience at the Custard Factory. Deepak's married, Mace is busy at work and Carter's playing private cop. Band practice has taken a back seat and it shows. Despite the activities, his mind has continually flickered to meetings and discoveries of the last few weeks. How the findings could shape his character and relationships with people. He's grateful for the time with Paul, a family friendship which could develop. Branches which could strengthen on a rotting tree. It's a bond which could in some way reunite family ties. Rowntree's been an interesting character, a great support. The trips meeting people have provided an air of excitement and intrigue. The past few months have developed his relationship with Rachel and potentially ruined that with his mother.

Leanne's organised the evening in Redditch. Typically on a Carl-free Wednesday. She doesn't mention to her mother that Carter will be joining her despite suspecting this element of surprise will backfire. Carter can't believe he's heading back over to his mother's so soon.

Pat's stunned at seeing her son although whether for her daughter's benefit, she puts on more airs and graces than the previous visit. The customary takeaway is ordered as the first fifteen or twenty minutes pass into idle gossip. Pat's upset about being cut out of Amber's birthday. Leanne's not particularly apologetic. But the two have enough things in common to artificially paper over the fundamental cracks in their relationship.

Carter's finding it hard to sit through hours of tedious conversation. He wants to say his piece and leave.

Surprisingly, though, it's Leanne who brings up the conversation.

Pat's slumped on the sofa drinking a large glass of white wine with her daughter, the remainder of the bottle nursed in a clear cool bag on the floor. Carter's sipping the one bottle of Beck's left in the fridge.

'Mom, I've come with Dan because we've got something to ask you. Just don't want you to get upset,' says Leanne.

Pat rolls her eyes.

'More family history?' she says mockingly, looking at her son with a mix of fear but also a rare glimpse of tenderness.

'Not sure how best to ask this,' poses Leanne nervously.

'But Dan and Paul have been taking care of Aunty Heather's things and being doing a bit of clearing and meeting people.'

'Go on,' insists Pat.

'Anyway....'

'Cat bit your tongue?' snaps Pat.

Leanne's dancing words around the subject, leaving Carter to fire the line.

'Is Al my father?'

Pat doesn't shoot a look of hatred nor aggression, which is what Carter expected, but her eyes seem to widen, like curtains drawing open. She says nothing for about twenty seconds.

'We won't be angry,' says Leanne, reaching for her mother's hand.

A tear runs down Pat's face. She rejects Leanne's gesture.

'It could be that you are,' says Pat, tearfully.

'How likely is it?' says Carter.

'Possible,' replies Pat.

'Thanks, Mom, I just wanted to know that,' says Carter in a manner which relaxes Pat.

Pat wets up. Perhaps the fact that her sister is dead and that Al is most likely gone makes the truth easier territory. Black mascara pours down her face. She looks like a rinsed out funeral. Or an old Goth.

'Mom, I promise we can go no further after tonight. I just want to know one more thing,' says Carter.

'Did Tony know?'

Pat asks Leanne to get her fags. Leanne asks them to hold the conversation until she is back.

Leanne rushes off in her fold-up slippers. Pat lights up.

'I'm not sure.'

Pat's puffing away like it's her last cigarette. Carter remains attentive, Leanne supportive.

'I had a little affair with Al during the war. Then it stopped. I'm not proud. But your dad was a hard man and after the war he met somebody else and left me. He hung around a while but somehow he found out….or believed he'd found out. From one day to the next he was gone. Never saw him again, only bleedin' letters from solicitors.'

'So he never asked if I was his kid?'

'No, I guess he came to his own conclusions. It is possible you're his kid but it would have been more remote. Nobody had any interest in doing a test.'

'Why did you never tell us earlier, Mom?' asks Carter.

'Because, I just wanted to protect you.'

'Is there anything else, Mom, anything at all to do with Al or Tony? This is the last chance….'

'No, that's it, really it,' replies Pat.

Pat's still sobbing. Carter starts to sense a heavy lump in his throat and Leanne wells up too. Carter decides not to ask any more questions or raise any suspicions. He truly believes his mom knows no more.

Carter leaves. He kisses his mother on the top of her head, says he will be in touch.

He exits a house which somehow feels less unwelcoming, carrying shoulders that feel distinctly lighter.

CHAPTER 17

BENIDORM

(December 2009)

Possessed by tedious and demoralizing nerves, and challenged by Paul's frequent attempts to postpone, organising the out of season trip to Alicante has proved a headache for Carter. Carmen had played her part in Paul's indecision. Two weeks ahead of their wedding she found it impossible to fathom why he was insistent on searching for an uncle in hiding instead of collecting suits, organising the order of service, and, most pressingly choosing between traditional or truffle pesto.

There was some cheer in amongst the collective procrastination. Provided by Shelley Smith, the buck-toothed bruiser disguised as a guardian angel. Shelley informed Paul that she had more than a hunch that Tony Cole was on the Costa Blanca performing some winter repairs to his bar, St. Andrew's. Google-Earthing the location, Carter and Paul discovered that the pub lies two blocks from the sea on Calle Doctor Pérez Llorca in Benidorm. Without a moment's hesitation, they booked two special offer rooms in Hotel Cimbel, a high-rise on the sea front. Beach view. St. Andrew's has its own website. A classic, abandoned mid-90s design with flashing lights, awkward Comic Sans font and one of those calculator-style hit visitor counters. 1,032. And rarely counting. A few comical spelling mistakes thrown in for good measure. Carter joked that if nothing else he might get a job redesigning the site.

Carter and Paul decided to afford themselves a long three-night weekend. Convinced they are on the hunt for a murderer. No idea how they are going to prove it. And how they will take Tony Cole to task. Even whether they will locate him. No idea how Tony Cole is going to react to their arrival. They have talked about tricking him. Talked about claiming Steven Baker admitted Tony was behind it. They also know that Wayne Cole has most likely spread the word. Tony must know they've visited Wayne. He won't be expecting the visit but it won't be the coldest call he's ever received.

***

Paul and Carter both intentionally drank in excess the day before the trip. A drop of courage became a creeping avalanche of a hangover. They're irritable, twitchy. Rachel drops them off at Birmingham Airport. It's practically first flight of the day. Despite being dressed for work, she has her passport and toothbrush packed in the event Paul and Carter show a moment of weakness and need her support. They're too concerned with their aching heads to worry about the trip. The drink served its purpose. Rachel departs and following a fried egg sandwich and a flat pint of lager a sense of purpose is restored.

The morning is spent flicking through Nuts and FHM magazines and choosing a token perfume to take back as a present until Paul insists on ordering a couple of Bloody Marys on a crammed flight peppered with morning drinkers. He prods Carter for news from his mother. Conscious of an eavesdropping and heavily made-up middle-aged lady on his left, Carter whispers through his visit to Redditch admitting they are most likely brothers. Paul's somewhat uncomfortable. They agree that whatever the truth, they will always be cousins. Rather, mates. You can't suddenly become brothers after twenty-seven years. After another visit from the stewardess and a third bloody Mary, Paul drops a tongue-in-cheek 'bro'. Humour the necessary medicine.

Carter mentions that Rowntree offered some wise words during a phone call a few days ago. The old hack had even offered to come along but Carter didn't want him to miss a Baggies home game or become embroiled further. More the former. His advice was to tread carefully and be wary of provoking Tony Cole.

Approaching Alicante, with a tepid morning sun reflecting off holiday high rises, they feel a sense of what is about to happen. What could happen. Dread.

***

Tony Cole's closed a large section of St Andrew's for a week or two and for a few days a week. This time of year's not big business and some vital improvements will help plug some of the losses over the last year. The place had been doing well until a few spanking new bars opened on the strip. St. Andrew's has always attracted the older clients and harder drinkers. Those who leave home to stay at home. It's a classic 'England abroad' pub with a long main teak bar, dated, heavy television screens emanating a grainy picture, a side room with a few scuzzy pool tables, a tiny dance floor rarely used apart from the odd pre-booked party or car-crash karaoke night. Tony Cole's present three or four days a week. Rarely behind the bar. He'll watch Sky Sports News, keep an eye on the staff, read *The Mirror*, devour a soggy egg sandwich, banter with punters. He's more often found on the golf courses, reducing his handicap, managing some of the property he and Jackie invested in following the sale of the pub in Coventry back in 1997. Tony's spent well. And invested at the right time. But things are getting stale and he's using a bit of money to shake things up.

His son, Trevor, is taking a year out, managing the bar and helping with the repairs. Trevor's hardly a chip off the old block. More his mother's son. He's tall, slim, relatively introspective and apart from football, Tony finds it hard to relate to the lad.

Tony's had a few things on his mind. Wayne mentioned the visit. It's made him angry. An anger penetrated with a lingering sadness. A stench in his otherwise vacuous soul. It's always there. It prods guilt and annoyance. One Tony usually suppresses with eight pints of Guinness and a couple of chasers. The drink reminds him that it was all worth it. Al Jeavons deserved to be clipped even if the price was paid by his daughter and a boy who may or may not be his. *Definitely Al's bastard kid.* It's come and gone over the past twenty years, but the sensation is lingering more regularly. As the weeks and months have passed since the boys' visit to Wayne, Tony's conviction that they would show up has flickered more frequently. Paranoia a consequence of a life on the run.

***

Carter and Paul linger opposite St Andrew's, enjoying a night on the town before thinking about Tony Cole. But the allure is there. They're always one drink away from egging each other to go in. The bar opposite, the Pink Flamingo, is a typical soulless, blingy Mediterranean hole with large glass windows, pink leather couches, oppressive lighting and over-generous on cheap cash-and-carry cocktails. The sort of place that in summer is rammed with easy girls and guys with loose hands. A few pints are sunk as Carter and Paul sit on garden chairs facing St Andrews in case they get an early glimpse of Cole.

They're not entirely sure what they are looking for. Over twenty years have passed. Most memories drawn from a few select photos. Eyes are peeled for a stocky fella, bruising arms, piercing eyes, potentially a thick moustache and going by the mid-1980s, thick but closely cropped hair which should now have fully greyed.

As the beer goes down, the conversation loosens. Paul is open about his stag night. Looked but didn't touch. Plenty of the lads got what they paid for. They move on and hit the strip. Confidence is gained with every sip of cold lager and boosted when Carter decides to order a series of sambuca shots from a chatty and toothy Costa Rican barmaid. Any carefully laid patient plans are soon becoming lost in the flow of cheap lager and the tender touch of the fading sun. As they toast and down their fourth shot, they know that the next stop is St Andrews. After a communal piss and a conversation neither will remember they cross over the deserted street.

On entry, St Andrews reeks of cheap cologne and wet paint. The rear part of the pub, essentially the seating area, is under renovation but the bar itself and a few sofas at the front are open for business. The bar top is graffitied with carvings of love and hate and telephone numbers promising a good time. Everything about the place is dated. It's like a set design for a 1980s *Only Fools And Horses* Christmas special. The faded mustard carpet is scarred with cigarette burns, the beer taps require a solid pair of biceps to handle and the range of alcohol does justice to the bar's reputation as a proper drinkers' den. There are no alcopops, barely any bottled drinks. Tapped lager and hard spirits. A coronation portrait of the Queen pays surveillance over the bar. The one they used to have in hospitals and schools. There's a few donated football scarves, a signed picture of Trevor Francis, and a couple of framed newspaper articles celebrating the Argentine surrender.

With so much of the place shut off and the place covered with dust, it's a surprise the bar is open. On entering, Carter and Paul wonder if they've somehow stumbled into a lock-in. A kind of private club for expats toasting the demise of their liver and their will to live. There are three punters in total. One perched at the bar, chewing tobacco and staring blankly at his crossword or Sudoku. Another two, mean-looking and ashen-faced, sit on the sofa by the front door. They're together but give the impression that they've not conversed in years. If ever.

After lingering outside for a few seconds, Carter and Paul decide to head in. There's nobody at the bar and there's barely a flicker from the clientele as they enter. Dire Straits' *Alchemy* is running through *Romeo and Juliet*. Shortly before they consider serving themselves or heading straight out, a beanpole of a young man enters from behind a curtain in the main bar. Sporting a lumberjack shirt, loose khaki bermudas and a pair of desert boots, he looks like the sort of character Carter may end up drinking with following a Battle of the Bands. He seems amiable and welcoming of younger company. Paul and Carter decide to stay seated at the bar. The lad apologises for being out of a few beers on tap, explains renovations taking place. He's accent is definitely Brum and on inspecting the Birmingham City scarf above the whisky shelf, Carter asks if he's a fan.

'A little bit, my old man's the Blue nut and it's his place. I try and go to a couple of games a year. I'm out here a lot of time now.'

The lad babbles on as he hurriedly slices lemon and lime and restocks the ice. Carter and Paul look at each other, fully aware that in front of them is a potential relative. After some small talk, the lad heads off to replenish the barrel.

'Fuck me, it's Tony Cole's kid,' says Paul. 'Looks nowt like him. Fucking hell, this could even be your half brother. Fuck.'

Carter remains wide-eyed and takes a swig from a rather flat pint.

'What shall we do?' continues Paul.

'Think we should keep a low profile tonight,' states Carter, starting to feel sober despite the mounting level of booze in his veins. 'Maybe keep talking to him and get some information, but let's not go too far.'

'Loud and clear boss. Sound,' replies Paul.

The lad returns.

'You show many live matches here?' offers Carter, 'any chance of catching a few of the games tomorrow?'

'It's non-stop,' returns the lad. 'I've got the evening gig tomorrow, my old man and a mate are minding the place in the day. They'll be glued to it.'

'How often you down here?' continues Paul.

'Oh about four months a year,' returns the lad. 'Just finished term at uni, come down whenever I'm off, earn some money, fuck some birds, all of that.'

'Where you studying?' returns Carter.

'Back home, doing a design course at Aston.'

'Your folks out here all year then, are they?' questions Paul.

'Basically. Pretty much, I keep an eye on the place back home. My sister's there as well doing her A-Levels, so keeping an eye on her too.'

Paul introduces himself. Carter too. The lad is called Trevor.

'Yeah, me old man is fond of Trevor. Named me fucking Trevor Francis, didn't he. After the fucking Blues player. Have had to live with that burden for twenty years.'

The lads chuckle.

Transpires Tony Cole's been down here about ten years. Jackie too. Kids lived in Benidorm for a while as well but back home getting an education now. Mother's insistence. Tony Cole's got his hand in a fried chicken joint, a pool club and a bit of property. Residence is about ten miles away, huge place according to Trevor. The banter slips into the night, Paul and Carter give little away and get on with Trevor. He's a bit raw, a bit naïve, trying too hard to impress but somehow genuine at the same time.

At half one they are the last two to leave, bidding goodnight and fully aware that in the morning they will have to take their task in hand.

***

Carter barely slept. Alcohol left him feeling dehydrated and sweaty. Had Trevor Francis on his mind. Could be his half-brother. Didn't feel any connection or resemblance. Slept in fear of meeting his potential father or the man who may have had a hand in the demise of his real father. A head full of conflict and fear. Carter woke up contemplating a jog along the beach but realised he left his trainers at home. Needs to walk. Considers attacking the box of fags on offer with the peanuts in the mini bar. Resists. Thinks about shaving his itchy head, hair longest its been in a while. At seven o'clock he texts Paul for breakfast. Paul replies immediately. He's had an equally uncomfortable night.

They pick at their croissants and jamón, realising the morning is a long countdown until St Andrew's opens. Tony Cole will be waiting. Carter has no idea what to say, how he will be, knows their lives could be very different in a few hours' time. Breakfast passes slowly and silently.

Paul and Carter agree to head for a walk on the beach. A last stroll. Paul says Carter should do the talking, carry on as if he is Tony Cole's son. At least for appearances. Says they should only mention Al later on, just present it as Carter trying to find his dad. Carter feels sick, stomach violent and head throbbing. Feels Paul is being a bit of a coward. He's not got the concentration to reply to Rachel's well-meaning text messages.

***

St Andrew's is open early. Tony Cole enjoys the Saturday midday shift, older crowd, newspaper readers, contemplating day's football. Hasn't got the stomach for the wild crowds, mopping up vomit or Eurotrash techno music. There's a chill penetrating the morning sky but it is pleasant enough. Tony Cole's short-sleeved and in stonewashed jeans. With the kitchen closed, Birdie's not required to prepare egg sandwiches and plates of chips. Tony Cole's sitting at a small plastic table outside the front of the bar. A few punters have come in and out for coffee and Bloody Marys but nothing too frequent to distract him from *The Mirror*. There's a few builders in the kitchen, a couple of bruisers from Oporto. Tony's even got one of them trained to serve drinks in exchange for a few pints on the job.

Taking a heavy drag on his Marlboro, Tony Cole observes two slightly-cut lads walking towards him. Both in baseball caps, check shirts, Bermudas and cheap espadrilles. He recognises them immediately. Sporting dark sunglasses, a golf visor and polo shirt, he extinguishes his fag as the lads draw closer. He saves them the graces of an introduction.

'Wayne said you might eventually show up,' he offers. The boys are taken aback.

Tony Cole rises, stretches out his hand and before they can refuse Carter and Paul return handshakes. Paul is defiant, staunch, and feels in control.

Carter's a nervous wreck, overcome by the situation, focusing his energies on not letting go.

'Thirsty?' offers Tony Cole. 'I'll grab a few pints and we can go out the back.' It's barely eleven o'clock.

Not a word is said as Tony offers the lads a couple of pints of Estrella and beckons them through a curtained walkway and into a kitchen, in the process of being re-plastered and fixed. Tony Cole says something in pigeon Spanish to the labourers, and explains to the lads the work being done. Costing him a packet apparently. Eventually they are led through a winding industrial stairwell to a square rooftop terrace, with a few large pot plants, a hammock and some dangerously exposed open cables.

'Keep this place for myself, not the bleedin' clients. View ain't bad, is it?' starts Tony Cole.

The view's fine. Obstructed by a few of the high rises on the strip but the open horizon is as vast as Carter's anxiety.

'No need to make it any more awkward than it is,' begins Tony Cole, almost seeming at ease with the visit, not the perturbed, violent reaction they were expecting.

'What can I do for you lads?'

'We just want to know why you left, everything basically, what happened, why you've not been in touch,' stutters and stammers Carter.

Tony Cole reaches for his fags. The Mediterranean diet's done him some good. A tan, a full head of hair, and he still look strong and menacing although a solid beer belly and heavy wrinkles under his eyes reveal some of the excesses. He's had some new tattoos on his arm. A large swallow and a rather bizarre Harley Davidson logo aside some faded tats of yesteryear and the Falklands.

'In plain English, me and your mom got divorced and I moved away,' says Tony Cole. Confidently, dismissively.

'Moved out down to Coventry and Warwick, remarried, had a few kids and starting investing down here. In a nutshell.'

Carter's barely touched his pint. He observes Tony Cole. Struggles to retain eye contact. Paul sits poised.

'But why did you leave me and Leanne?' continues Carter.

'Good question,' replies Tony, taking a further drag. 'Look, kid, you're not mine.' Tony's masterfully matter of fact. 'Your mom was fucking around with his dad,' as Tony points to Paul, 'when I was at the fucking war. I didn't find out straight away, had no reason to suspect anything until I found out what happened a few years later. Didn't want to see a woman like that again. From that moment on, knew you were Al's, he's the one who should have been taking care of you.'

'What about Leanne? ' returns Carter.

'Got to cut your nose off to spite your face sometimes,' throws out Tony Cole, almost spitting a cashew nut on the floor. 'I was no angel myself, despised your fucking slag of a mom for most of our marriage and spent most of my time fucking around, fucking this, fucking that. Leanne was the sacrifice in not seeing your mom again.'

'She didn't deserve that,' offers Carter.

'I sent some money for a long while, left some in an account, your mom didn't go short...'

'But she went without a dad...,' barks Carter.

'She didn't need me as a dad.'

'So you're saying I'm definitely Al's kid?'

'Yep, and I can tell you're not surprised.'

'We'd kind of got that far...,' adds Paul for the first time.

'So you fucked off to start this new life and left us to fend for ourselves but what about Al, what the fuck happened to him?' questions Carter, forcefully.

'Did they never find him?' says Cole, rhetorically, almost jokingly. 'No offence lads, but your old man had lots of enemies. None of your lot probably want to admit it but he was gunned down by the Irish. You and your fucking cunting conspiracy theories are just there coz they never found the body...'

'....do you know my mom died last month?' returns Paul.

'...no, sorry to hear that, lad. She was sound,' replies Tony, almost genuinely.

'She wasn't so sound after Dad went missing. It ruined her.'

'She should have accepted the facts.'

'Which facts?' continues Paul, slowly taking over.

'Mom said the Irish came knocking for days and weeks after, that the police found nothing on them, some folk are convinced you know more…'

'What you implying?' snaps Tony.

'That it was convenient for you that Dad was no longer around?'

'Why?'

'Because he fucked your wife.'

'Listen, listen, lads. Get these bleedin' thoughts out your head. I found out about Al and your Mom in '87, Al went missing in what, '89, do you really think if I was angry I wouldn't have done anything earlier? I was in the fucking police, I had a bleedin' good job, I'd found another woman anyway and was not wound up about some bastard kid. Your old man was a fucking liability, he was basically a slimy, womanising, gambling fucking cunt of a cheat. He had plenty of enemies. These guys were professionals. They've put away plenty of bodies that have not reappeared. Guy called Carney, he was the man, and he's gone too now.'

Paul and Carter stay silent for a moment. Tony Cole's very convincing. He's had twenty years to rehearse this speech.

'If that was the case, why did they carry on chasing the debt?' asks Paul.

'Don't be so fuckin' naïve, lads. They would have known that the police were sniffing, fucking obvious that they would have covered themselves. And even if they sniffed out Al they would have still given a message that they chased a debt even when they'd dealt with the problem.'

'We met Steven Baker a few weeks ago, he said you were behind it,' tries Paul.

'Fuck me, is he still alive?' beams Tony Cole. 'No doubt money was involved. If Steven Baker is all you got, then I pity you. Guy's washed up, not seen him in twenty old years, pissed off he never got a piece of this. Honestly, Steven Baker would tell your that your aunt's your uncle for a fucking fiver.' Tony Cole finds himself in a fit of hysterics.

'Do you not feel sad, how it all ended?' says Carter, 'like we've had to wait twenty years to find out what happened and still can't be sure.'

Tony Cole is momentarily silent, finding his words. 'My life's worked out fine. You lads have got your lives ahead of you, you've got to forget this wild goose chase, accept that Al's dead. His body may never be found but the whole world knows that chasing the horses caught up with him.'

'Until we find the body, we'll never be sure,' says Paul.

'Can't help you there, son,' replies Tony.

'Listen, lads, I'm happy to have this chat and clear the air but I'll say this nicely. Don't come back here again, don't go bothering people, and get on with your fucking lives. Al wasn't worth it.'

'The truth is important,' snaps Paul, 'and for my mom it was too.'

'I don't know about your mom, I'm sorry she had it so bad but the best thing you can do for her is accept the truth. I've got nothing more for you.'

Carter and Paul are exhausted. They are not going to get much more out of Tony Cole. Paul feels like punching him. Carter's drained. Tony Cole's played a convincing hand.

Tony Cole escorts them back to the bar, says he has an envelope for Leanne and asks after her. Carter stays guarded when Tony asks if she's married or has kids. Doesn't feel he deserves that information. Tony tries to prod the envelope under Carter's arm. Says it has got two grand for Leanne in it. Carter tells him to deliver it himself. Tony Cole doesn't insist.

On leaving the bar, Carter lifts off his baseball cap to allow the fresh breeze to provide some comfort. Tony Cole takes a final glance, to ensure they are on their way. A fatal last glance. The piercing light reveals the faintest streak of silver across Carter's crown. *Fucking skunk.*

***

Paul and Carter don't say a word on the short walk back to the hotel aside from agreeing they should get out of Benidorm and stay in Alicante for the rest of the trip. Away from Tony Cole's shadow, away from his words, away from this history.

***

Tony Cole heads back to his squat terrace. *Mirror* folded under his arm. Stretches his legs onto the white, plastic garden chair Carter was sitting on. Takes a long drag as he looks out to sea between the cracks in the apartment blocks. Contemplates that Steven Baker is still alive. Scratches his head for the name of the lanky Trotsky with the quiff. *Twenty fucking years. And it wasn't Al's.*

DEDICATION

A warm thanks to my parents Barbara and John Bourne for casting their critical eye over the text and for proofreading the book. To Marie for her creative ideas and challenging the plot. To Mark Murphy at *Surely!* for the cover design and keeping the creative process alive. To the various baristas in Birmingham and caffeine haunts in far-flung places—Lausanne, Mevagissey, Miami and Paris to name a few—where along with the archives at the old Birmingham library, the core of this book was produced. Finally, to Tom Bourne for his help creating some noise.

11670800R00196

Printed in Great Britain
by Amazon.co.uk, Ltd.,
Marston Gate.